PLANE
Tales

Kellina Craig-Henderson

ISBN 978-1-63630-993-4 (Paperback)
ISBN 978-1-63630-994-1 (Digital)

Covenant Books, Inc.
11661 Hwy 707
Murrells Inlet, SC 29576
www.covenantbooks.com

To my husband for being my
perennial travel companion.

To my parents for unwittingly inspiring
my earliest and continuing travel lust.

To my son who is always ready for a long plane ride.

This book was inspired by the experience
of travel to many places. Travel brings
blessings, wisdom and insights.

CONTENTS

A PILGRIM'S
TRAVEL TO ISRAEL

The US Airways flight en route to Tel Aviv leveled off around 10:00 p.m. They had boarded on time at Philadelphia International Airport at eight twenty-five that evening. Jacob looked at his watch and calculated the likely time of arrival given the eleven-hour flight and the time difference in Israel. It would be a while, and he found that to be strangely comforting. Even with the two hundred or more other passengers aboard the flight, he felt as if he were securely tucked in his own little cocoon.

The long flight provided him with time to think about the circumstances surrounding his departure as well as what he was expecting to find in Israel. As the jet was being physically propelled forward across the globe, he felt himself moving forward symbolically as well. And while the initial impetus for the trip lay in the consulting assignment he'd accepted two months ago, he believed there to be a greater and more powerful reason. He knew from past expe-

riences that opportunities such as this one were mul-
tilayered with unpredictable outcomes.

What he was less sure about was what he'd left
behind. Although he was clearly feeling something
far removed from happiness, it would not be accurate to say that he was depressed, nor regretful about
the decision to leave. At the airport, they'd parted
ways and said goodbye. Even though their parting
resembled the typical goodbyes they'd had as of late,
he knew that (and he was pretty sure she did, too)
this really was the end of whatever it was that they
had enjoyed together. When they said goodbye, they
embraced and kissed each other perfunctorily on the
lips. It was more habit than passionate not unlike
the well-worn affection of those married for multiple
decades rather than a dating couple who had been
together for just under two years.

Of course, recognizing the finality of what they
had didn't mean that a new door could not be opened
sometime down the road, but it did mean that neither of them would be forced to enact the very same
steps in this particular dance of intimacy.

Under different circumstances, he might have
laughed at himself. Wasn't it just like him to think that
way? Calling it quits but reserving the right to resur-
rect their relationship in some new and improved,
somehow better, form sometime later? She would
have had a hard time with it if it ever came to that.

Jacob met Leah when they connected through
the social networking site called classmates.com just
before the thirty-fifth reunion of their graduating

class from the Catholic elementary school that they'd both attended in the Red Hook neighborhood of Brooklyn, New York. They were the same age, and it was a small enough school that they'd actually known one another then. But, with thirty-five years under the bridge, neither of them had very strong recollections of the other. When they were in elementary school, they had socialized in different circles; she with the neighborhood popular kids, and he with the kids who commuted. They had both moved away long ago from the city where the elementary school was located; Jacob to nearby Pennsylvania, and Leah to New Jersey before a recent job transfer landed her in Philadelphia.

For all intents and purposes, their reintroduction initiated by classmates.com was like meeting for the very first time. They had similar interests, and they both worked in the communications industry; she as an associate editor for a large regional publication, and he as a photojournalist for a nonprofit organization. Because he also did freelance work when possible, he'd accepted the assignment that required him to travel to Israel where he would be for the next six months. This was the kind of opportunity that others like him either dreamed about because of its locale or quickly ran away for the very same reason.

For Jacob, it was the opportunity to capture riveting historical and memorable moments against the backdrop of a part of the world he had always hoped to see. At the same time, he knew that if things had been better with Leah, he would have found the six-month separation challenging at best. People who didn't just love, but who were also in love with their partners, would not have been as excited about the six-month-long assignment away.

Two months ago, Jacob had received a call from a former colleague about an opportunity to record events around an upcoming potentially volatile election in a relatively remote settlement of Israel. It was small scale local politics that were occurring on the grand stage of the Arab-Israeli intractable conflict. As such, although the election was relatively small, there was a genuine risk that the election would ultimately result in a bloody outcome for people whose lives would be directly impacted by its outcome.

To be fair, his decision to accept the assignment and to go was motivated at least in part by his financial situation. He could always use the extra money that the assignment would provide. At the same time, he also accepted the assignment (this was something he was only willing to admit in his private thoughts) because this job would permit a break from Leah and from their relationship. He would be gone for six months, and although they would keep in touch through email and texts while he was away, it would not be continuous contact. Their long-distance communication with one another would not include the pining typical of those in love or among those who ardently missed each other.

Things between them had become unpleasant as of late. There was more disagreement and angst than agreement and tranquility. This season of their lives together, when they found themselves arguing over unimportant matters and finding excuses for not being together, seemed to be occurring at precisely the same time when they expected their relationship to progress to a more serious stage. They were at that point at which a couple begins to contemplate its ontology and consider the possibility of another incarnation. For Jacob and Leah, what they had seemed to have run its course. It had plateaued and begun to spiral downward.

After last Christmas following the time spent at her family's home, something had happened to them. It was as if the holiday signaled the end to the shelf life of their love affair. For better or for worse, he knew that when he agreed to accompany her home, the holiday and all that it represented would come to define their relationship. There would be a "before the trip to her family for the holidays" and an "after the trip to her family for the holidays" vantage point from which they would view themselves and their shared identity as a couple. Unfortunately, that identity as a couple had deteriorated.

A series of announcements from the flight crew interrupted his train of thought.

"Good evening, ladies and gentleman. We would now like to begin our inflight service. We will start with beverages of your choice. For your pleasure, we offer complimentary beer, wine, and soft drinks. A range of fine spirits are also available and can be purchased. Please have your credit card ready. After this service, we'll begin service of dinner for the flight. In addition to the vegetarian option, there is chicken and pasta choice. Please see the menu options noted on the inflight card in the seat pocket in front of you. May we please ask everyone to remain seated during the inflight service as it will facilitate us getting around the cabin area."

Within moments, the flight attendants began serving beverages. Jacob gladly accepted the complimentary beer offered him. It was a brand he didn't recognize—Negev Porter Alon, apparently brewed in Israel. It was a bitter, dark heavy brew not at all what he was accustomed to, but he decided to drink it as much for its aroma; it gave off a strong roasted malt smell, suggesting its likely sleep-inducing effect.

Jacob thought of his decision to leave and his struggle to be free of Leah, and for a moment was reminded of the 1975 Paul Simon hit. Was it true that there were really fifty ways to leave your lover? He was short on imagination and saw very few options because he cared for Leah and could not imagine wantonly hurting her. True, accepting a job for months and miles away was a cowardly way out, but it was the only way he knew to actually leave. Both of them had emotionally checked out on one another some time ago, and now it was time to break clean. He only felt guilty about physically severing their relationship because he hadn't actually said anything to her about doing so. It was neither mature, nor particularly honest.

After the dinner service was served aboard the jet, and the passengers made their respective trips to the restrooms, the plane's lights were dimmed, and those aboard either watched movies or slept or read. Jacob opted for sleep and closed his eyes but was immediately jolted by the plane's first real experience with turbulence. It was sufficiently strong enough to warrant the captain's request to stay seated and to fasten seatbelts. There would be more turbulence throughout the next few hours of the flight, making this one of the least pleasant flying experiences that Jacob could recall having had.

An hour or so later, he managed to fall asleep. He wound up sleeping for most of the remaining flight time. When he finally woke up, the plane had begun its descent. Because it had been a relatively rocky flight, the passengers expressed an audible sigh of relief when the plane landed smoothly. After another twenty-five minutes or so, the pilot navigated the jet to its assigned spot on the tarmac.

Unlike the case at most American airports, this airport permitted, indeed required airplanes to land on the tarmac apart from the terminals. Once the mobile staircase was wheeled into place and the door on the side of the plane was opened, the weary passengers began exiting the plane. They shielded their eyes and blinked at the sun as they descended the steep stairs. They each walked across the tarmac within the prescribed area to reach the inside of Israel's Ben Gurion Airport.

Unlike the experiences Jacob had had at immigration checkpoints in other countries, he sailed through customs here. The ease in doing so was as much a matter of the fact of his US passport as it was a matter of the security and military sensibilities of the Israelis. There were armed militia at multiple points along his path. It was easy to feel comforted by the display of security, but it was just as easy to be unnerved by the risk that such defense implied.

After retrieving his luggage, Jacob stopped at an ATM and withdrew what he estimated to be about $500 worth of Israeli money. The Israeli currency was called shekels, and he hoped that he had correctly followed the prompts provided in English. He noticed a hefty service charge to withdraw the money. Hopefully, he would not have to do this frequently during his stay, he thought. He planned to use his credit card for most things.

He looked away and made his way to the outside of the airport where there was a long line of taxis as well as shuttle buses. The taxis were similar in color to the yellow cabs popular in many cities in the US, but many of the ones he saw here at the airport were slightly larger and easily seated five or six people. As he shuffled to the back of the taxi line, he noticed that the weather was more humid than he'd expected and not too different from what he'd left in Philadelphia.

He waited for about ten minutes and eventually settled into the back seat of a bright yellow taxi. It was to be a thirty-one-mile trip to the "apart-hotel" that his friend and colleague Peter had arranged for him. Yet, because traffic was horrible on the expressways, it took nearly an hour to get to the city of Herzliya.

When the taxi finally turned off the expressway and entered the busy thoroughfare, Jacob caught his first glimpse of this part of the world's Mediterranean coastline. Its beauty transfixed him. It was an afternoon sun and the sheen that rested on the water's surface was dazzling.

When the taxi came to its final stop, it pulled up to the address he'd given the driver—Ninety-Three Ramat Yam, Herzliya. It was above a restaurant that he immediately knew that he would dine in later. He was hungry, and something about the restaurant looked inviting. Jacob paid the driver and tipped him with several additional shekels.

He stood outside on the sidewalk for several moments, taking in the building's facade as well as the neighboring structures on the street. This was clearly a residential neighborhood. He was pleased about that.

After carrying his luggage up the stairs to the front entrance of the building, he swung the door open and stepped into the cool space that was the apart-hotel's lobby. The building housed nearly forty apartments, which were rented under terms similar to hotels. They were cleaned regularly, guests received towels, and there was twenty-four-hour concierge service provided.

Adjusting his eyes to the slightly darkened interior, he saw a young woman with blonde hair seated at a reception desk. As he approached her and got a better look at her, he saw that she was blonde by choice (her hair was brown at her roots), and she was older than she appeared to be from a distance. She either spoke little English or was simply not in a talkative mood. She waited for him to say something. Because she did not know who he was, she may well have been waiting to see which of the primary languages spoken in Israel he would use.

"Hello, I believe I have a reservation. I'm Jacob Pope. My friend, Peter Goldberger, made arrangements for me. He said I should check in at the front desk, and I would then receive instructions and a key for my lodging. I've made a long-term rental agreement."

Jacob noticed that he spoke differently than he normally did to her. If he had been at home in the States, he would have walked in and simply said his name and indicated he had a reservation. Here, he had explained everything, as if he was trying to make up for speaking English only by speaking more of it.

"Yes [she pronounced it more like 'Yaaas'], Mr. Pope. I am waiting for you and have your key. You are staying in 4H, and everything is prepared for you to arrive. May I see your passport, please?"

Jacob handed it to her and looked around the lobby, noting that there was nothing particularly distinct about it. It could have been anywhere. Israel, Philadelphia, or Brooklyn. Anywhere. He saw a sign along the far wall with an arrow indicating the direction of the pool. That's right! He remembered that there was a pool! Given the heat and humidity that characterized Herzliya at this time of year, he knew that he would enjoy a swim at some point. She handed his passport back to him.

"Thank you. I need for your signature on this card and agreement. I assume that you saw this already when you made arrangement to be here. Please sign here."

Jacob wondered how many other languages she spoke. The fact that she probably spoke at least three and possibly even four made the small mistakes in what she said in English completely acceptable. He looked closely at the woman more out of curiosity than real interest. He realized that it was quite possible that she wasn't even Israeli. *She could be from anywhere*, he thought. There was no telling where she was actually from or what languages she spoke.

After signing the form in the place that she indicated (it wasn't in English so he wasn't sure what it was, but it seemed reasonable that he would be required to sign something), she gave him the key and directed him to the elevator.

"Over there is the elevator. You will take to four, exit, and then you will go to the right. It will be the second door on right for you. If you have questions or want to say information, you may call the phone number zero."

"Thank you. I'm pretty tired from the flight, I'm sure I'll be fine. If I have any questions, I'll save them for the morning."

He picked up his luggage, turned, and headed for the elevator. He was anxious to relax and shower. As he entered the elevator, he glanced at the envelope with the key in it that the woman had given him. Peter had signed his name across the envelope's back flap—Peter. Jacob was reminded of him and their enduring friendship.

The two had met more than twenty years ago at a small conference outside Belgium in the tiny city of Bruges. At the time, they both worked for a large media firm that was based in the US, which had sent its employees to the overseas training workshop in order to acquire what was then state-of-the-art global TV and production media skills. It was at a time when life was not yet propelled and reported on the internet. To be sure, the net was alive then, but it was still in its infancy. Most major media outlets had not yet altered their strategy for gathering and acquiring information. That step would occur within just a few years after that conference. It was a good thing, too, as Jacob and Peter were both fond of saying, because had the evolution of the media industry occurred any sooner, the two might never have crossed paths in Bruges, and their friendship might not have ever happened.

Jacob took the elevator up to the fourth floor and found the numbered door that opened onto a small, nicely furnished split-level apartment. There was a tiny bathroom to the right side of the door and a small open kitchen just beyond that on the left. He dropped his bags and walked through the space across the floor, stopping at the sliding glass door that led to a small balcony that boasted a table and three chairs. He realized with some satisfaction that if he leaned just a bit over the outer wall of the balcony, he could glimpse a sliver of the sea. It sparkled in the afternoon sunlight.

He looked around at the rest of the view and then turned back to the balcony and the rest of the apartment he had yet to explore. Without even seeing all of it, he was content. *Yes*, he thought, *this was good.* It would provide a comfortable place from which to work. Pleased with his good fortune, he turned and went back in to the apartment.

Just then, his cell phone vibrated. It surprised him because he'd forgotten about it. He knew he had turned it off for the flight and vaguely remembered turning it back on and glancing at it sometime at the baggage carousel. Before leaving the States, he had arranged to have an international calling plan so that he could make calls and be reached without the prohibitive roaming charges. But who would be calling him now? It was just after 6:00 a.m. at home. Was Leah calling to say that she had sensed something different about the way that they had parted? He looked at the number. It was his daughter, Jess, one of the few remaining constants in his adult life.

"Dad! You picked up! You're there? You make it to the biblical land yet? How was the flight? What's the weather like? Is the hotel nice?" She asked multiple questions in succession without allowing him a chance to answer before plunging into the next one.

"Hey, love, I'm fine. What are you doing up so early? You worried about your old man?" he teased.

"I couldn't remember what time you said you expected to arrive, and I am sorry I didn't see you off. I'm happy I got you on the first try. Leah went to the airport with you, right?"

"Yeah, she did."

"Good! So why do you sound that way? Is everything all right? Did something happen between you two?"

His little girl, now an adult, was always so perceptive. She seemed to grasp the subtleties of emotional expression way too early in her development. He realized that people matured at different rates, but in her case, he often wondered what happened to the stuff that she was supposed to be learning and getting accustomed to as a little girl. It seemed that somehow she'd skipped some of those developmental stages and went right straight to "all-knowing, fully capable, grown-up woman." How did that happen? She didn't get it from him.

Jess was asking more questions about how things were with Leah. She'd heard something in his voice. Something that had been unintentional and imperceptible to him, but that had slipped out in the same way water could leak out of a kitchen container when it wasn't tightly secured. Not enough to actually make the surface wet, but just enough to hint of moisture. She had detected that something was amiss.

"Did you guys have an argument before you left Dad? What happened?"

"No, dear, we didn't argue. It's just that…well, I just don't do so well with goodbyes. Neither of us do. We said goodbye in a perfectly civil manner. There was no argument, hon. Hey, we were pleasant with one another. We hugged and kissed goodbye."

Although Jess wasn't entirely convinced that Jacob was telling the truth, she decided to let it go. She knew that if she continued to press him, he would become evasive and at some point, they would both regret that she had called. Besides, she had never completely warmed to Leah. What she had come to like most about her, and this did not seem to be based on any positive traits that Leah possessed, was that she loved her dad. For that, Jess was willing to endure their differences. Where Jess heard music, Leah heard noise, and when Leah ordered steak, Jess cringed. They occupied different sides of most ideological debates and were separated by decades. But what neither Jess nor Leah was willing to acknowledge, which likely accounted for some of Jess's reticence to embrace Leah, was the fact that Leah was White.

Jess thought of her dad as an attractive Black man who was an eligible bachelor. In the beginning, during the early days of his relationship with Leah, it bothered her that he had established an intimate relationship with a White woman. She knew it was wrong of her to feel differently about Leah simply because of the color of her skin, but she couldn't help it. There were too many Black women she knew both young and old who wanted to be in relationships with Black men, and every time she saw a Black man with a White woman, it bothered her.

When Jacob introduced the two of them, he hadn't given Leah any warning. He never said, "Oh, by the way, the woman that I have been seeing and who I want you to meet happens to be White." So, when Jess sat down at the table in the restaurant and saw her dad sitting there with a middle aged White woman, she was confused. It had been a polite though brief meeting. Jess told them that she had a date, declined to order anything more than a glass of wine, and left before the entrees arrived.

When she next spoke with Jacob, she got right to the point telling him how she felt.

"Dad, that woman you brought to meet me was White! You never said that the person you have been dating for the past six months was a White woman."

"I didn't think that I needed to, Jess. Was I supposed to make some sort of official announcement about what Leah looked like to you?"

"It's not about what she looks like. I couldn't care less how attractive or unattractive she is. It's about the fact that she is White and this world, this world is just so... Really, Dad, this country still treats people on the basis of their skin color and their race. C'mon, Dad, you know this! Look at Ferguson! What about Black lives matter? How can you walk down the street with a White woman on your arm knowing everything that you know? We are not there yet!"

It was ironic that Jacob had come of age in an era in which a clearly demarcated line existed that separated behaviors that were permissible and acceptable from those that were not. It was only now during Jess's adulthood when the color line had become blurred. Things were not like they were when he was young. At the same time, this more recent climate included a host of contradictions that made it impossible for Black (and Brown) Americans to believe that they were actually living in a post-racial America. It was true that you could turn on the television at any given time and glimpse a scene of interracial intimacy, and there were well-known celebrity interracial relationships, which people pointed to as evidence of the declining significance of race, but there continued to be too many instances in which innocent Black men (and sometimes women) were being brutalized and killed.

Jacob knew something was still terribly wrong with race relations in America. He also knew that by making the choice to be in a loving relationship with a White woman, he had opted to live outside the parameters of the contradictions. He only hoped that Jess would someday come to understand the complexity of it all.

Not long after Jess learned about Leah, she'd heard about a lecture at Drexel one evening. She had taken a few classes at the university previously and was familiar with the campus. The lecture was free, and the author of a book called *Black Men in Interracial Relationships: What's Love Got to Do with It?* would be speaking. Jess bought a copy of the book online and attended the lecture.

Three days later, Jess had tempered her opinions somewhat. It wasn't the speaker, nor her signed copy of the book, which she read in the span of two days. The author and book had challenged her to see that in a vacuum love knows no color. People fall in love with who they fall in love with, and for certain people (like her dad!), love really was colorblind.

Jess sighed audibly on the phone and decided to let it go. She loved her dad regardless of whether Leah was in the picture or out.

"Okay, dude, I know you must be exhausted after such a long flight. I'm going to let to you go. Six months is a heck of a long time to be away, Dad, so I'm going to be calling you weekly. Be on the lookout for my calls, okay? Love you."

"Love you, too, Jess. Will talk soon. Bye now."

He'd hung up with her feeling a little more tired but happy that she had thought to call and check in on him. He put the cellphone down and continued looking around the apartment. After opening the refrigerator and surveying the kitchen cabinets, he decided to head out to a local market. It was as much an opportunity to get acquainted with his environment and neighborhood as it was a chance to pick up some supplies; the refrigerator was empty, and the cabinets were only minimally stocked with an odd collection of baking supplies and unrecognizable canned goods. If he knew how to make a cream of mushroom soufflé, he probably had the ingredients on hand to do so, but he needed to venture out to the market if he wanted anything else.

After a quick check of the upstairs and the bedroom, he unpacked most of his clothes. They were wrinkled, but that was okay; he'd noticed an iron downstairs in the small closet that also housed a washing machine. Oddly enough, the washer apparently doubled as a dryer; something he realized that made sense in principle but would require some consultation. Not one who had ever been particularly interested in housework, Jacob was pleased that his temporary quarters were spacious enough to be comfortable without representing an excessive burden to keep reasonably tidy.

He unpacked the special suitcase that was part of his carry-on containing all of his professional photographic equipment including three different cameras with as many lenses. He laid out each of the cameras and lenses on the small desk in the bedroom. As was his style, he would decide on the appropriate camera lens combination for each day on that day. It was determined as much by his mood as by his expectations of the event and circumstances he would photograph.

He put his toiletries and razor in the bathroom off the bedroom, headed downstairs, and looked around the living space once more. He grabbed the door key, and for a moment considered bringing his cell phone, but then figured that since he'd just spoke to Jess and had a scheduled call with Peter later that evening, there was no one who would be trying to reach him. He left the phone on the table and realized it felt good doing so.

Once downstairs and outside the building, he decided to walk in the direction away from the sea, figuring there would be greater options for shopping in the more residential part of the neighborhood. It was hot, and he thought about returning to the building to ask the clerk for directions but decided not to.

Several blocks later, and now damp with perspiration, Jacob came across what appeared to be a store in a circular driveway that from its outside appearance reminded him of a "bodega." This was the name for the urban, convenience stores in US East Coast cities like New York that were once owned primarily by Spanish-speaking merchants from Mexico, Guatemala, and elsewhere. Although in the last two decades, many of these stores had been replaced by similarly appearing versions of themselves with owners who now hailed from countries within the Middle Eastern region of the world, the cities' native inhabitants still referred to them as bodegas.

As Jacob tucked his head in to enter the shallow doorway, he was greeted by the shopkeeper. He returned the greeting and stopped at the register. The slightly balding man wore glasses and appeared to be in his late thirties. He had a cell phone in his hand. Jacob could not tell whether he was in the middle of a call, preparing to make one, or just hanging up.

"Shalom."

"Hello. I just arrived for a stay here in Herzliya." He nodded and took a step away. He wanted to make it brief in case the man was actually speaking to someone on the phone. Apparently, he was not or didn't care about keeping whoever was on the line waiting.

"Where are you from? Are you here on holiday?"

"I'm from the US," Jacob replied. "I am here on an assignment, so I'll be working here."

Satisfied, the man nodded, smiled, and put the phone back to his ear. He resumed his conversation.

The inside of the store did little to dispel Jacob's initial impression because the store was both as small and as crowded as the typical bodega with its offerings stacked one on top of the other, and there did not appear to be any real discernable order or pattern for display. It took him about a half hour to actually find items he knew he needed and that he recognized. He bought food staples and cleaning supplies, along with several items he was unsure about.

In the end, he spent 485 Israeli shekels for everything, and when he left the store weighed down with four large bags, he calculated that he'd spent about $120. He'd have to get a better sense of the exchange rate and value of the shekel relative to the dollar. This would be essential given that he anticipated his assignment would require him to spend a great deal of time in remote neighborhoods where he knew that he'd be expected to negotiate the price of any and all items.

Returning to the apartment, he was winded. The fatigue from the flight and the energy expended in carrying the shopping bags took its toll on him. He put his purchases away and decided to skip the task of preparing dinner that evening and instead decided to try the restaurant on the street level of the building. He took a quick shower that was lukewarm. Although his tired muscles would have preferred a hot shower, the natural heat of Herzliya made that a far less attractive option. Fortunately, he noted as he toweled off, it was noticeably less humid here than it had been in Tel Aviv. The coast of the Mediterranean provided cooling sea breezes.

When he had dressed in clean clothes, he headed downstairs to the restaurant. At the entrance, he was pleased to see a variety of offerings posted on a menu in English.

After being seated and ordering, Jacob looked around. Although seated indoors, he had a seat at a table for two that was right next to the window, and from there he could stare at the sea's beauty. Grateful that he had thought to bring a small camera, the sun no longer appeared as high, and it had begun its descent. He looked forward to seeing the sunset. He made a conscious effort to take his time with the entire dining experience in order to ensure that he did not miss it.

His thoughts turned to his plans and what he knew of his schedule. Peter had emailed him a detailed description of the locations and times for when and where he was expected to be present to photograph and eventually write up newsworthy descriptions of the events surrounding the elections as they unfolded. He had strategically scheduled his arrival to Israel to be on Friday, so that he would have the weekend to adjust to his new surroundings, wrestle with jet lag, and visit some of the holy sites in Jerusalem. After all, he was in the Holy Land.

Jacob did not claim to be religious and was not quite sure where he stood with God. At seventeen, he had turned his back on Catholicism, the religion in which he'd been raised. Throughout college, he'd experimented with passing trends and took several detours from a path that his parents proscribed. These days, his faith was manifested primarily in private prayer. Rarely did he attend church, and rarer it seemed did he make decisions on the basis of his understanding of God's will. Had he been inclined to think more deeply about this, he might have attributed his periodic feelings of being adrift to his lack of communion with God in his life. In many ways, it seemed that he had lost his faith.

If he had, he certainly wasn't alone. He remembered a recent conversation he had with a guy he knew fairly well at the photo shop he relied upon for certain services. No matter what the day or who was in the shop, the man always initiated a conversation with Jacob. Usually, it began with a question about something he'd just finished reading or hearing about on NPR or CNN. He wasn't a consumer of the Fox network.

"Hey, you happen to hear the latest new survey saying Americans don't have any religion? Who didn't know that?" he had asked Jacob rhetorically.

Apparently, findings from a recent national poll that was just released showed that Americans are more distant from worshipping than ever before.

"Really, I hadn't heard that," said Jacob at the time, thinking about his own spiritual unmooring.

"Yep. Folks just don't seem to be buying into the sanctified, sanctimonious you know what anymore." The salesman chuckled.

Regardless of the veracity of these conclusions, Jacob always found the reporting of results like these to be somewhat distasteful. It seemed to be in a manner that was celebratory, as if the country's atheists, who he simply regarded as misguided fools, had scored some sort of victory.

But what of his own faith? Had he lost it or some part of it? Although this was not something about which he thought a great deal, the idea was not without footing in his psyche. He was aware that his moral compass had shifted over time however imperceptibly it may have appeared to others. In the last few months, he had made some decisions in his work life that challenged his sense of integrity. It had had to do with the accounting system he employed for the consulting work he did. He had not done anything illegal, but neither was it entirely honest. On more than one occasion, he found himself behaving in ways that conflicted with the image he had of himself as a person who could be trusted and who was above all honest.

It was at this time that Jacob began his private conversations with God in earnest. One time, Leah walked in on him while they were at her parent's home over the holiday. Her folks were "normal" enough, but they towed the line at allowing them to sleep together. Jacob had wanted so desperately to hear or feel something in response to his plaintive prayer that he did not hear her entering the room. He had been enraptured with prayer when she came in and startled him.

"Oh, so sorry, I didn't know you were, well, what were you doing, Jacob? Were you praying?" she asked incredulously.

"Yes, as a matter of fact, that is exactly what I was doing, Leah. You okay with that? Want to join me?"

He offered a hesitant laugh when he'd said that as much to lighten the weight of the situation as to give her a way to leave the room, which she did almost immediately.

If only she had been as similarly courteous to him. At dinner that evening, when everyone was seated at the table, poised to begin eating, Leah explained to everyone that although they didn't know they had a minister in their midst, they did.

"Why not let Jacob minister to us and the food now?" she asked the others gathered at the table.

Most of the guests including her mother seemed confused and unsure of whether she was serious or only joking. Her father in his seat at the head of the table shook his head at her remark and simply welcomed everyone to begin eating.

For the rest of the time at her family's home, Leah seemed to be unsettled and ill at ease. They were out of sync with one another. At the time, Jacob did not understand what it was that bothered her so much, but later he came to understand that it was the act of him praying that had unhinged her.

"I understand that you really do believe that there is someone up there pulling our strings and making us turn right or left. Okay, fine. But are you really serious? Do you actually think that if there was someone powerful enough to control the universe, he'd have the time or interest to look after Jacob Pope's stuff? I mean, I think you're great and all, but a higher power caring enough to turn away from making the sun set or the planet turn, to answer your request to land that new contract? Really? What makes you so great to deserve his attention? And why on earth would he do all of that for you?"

What Jacob found so disturbing about her questions was not so much the actual questions themselves, but that when the two of them first met after connecting on social media, she had professed to be a Christian! True, it had only come up in some offhanded way, the details of which he could not remember, but he did remember she referred to herself as a Christian. Clearly, she either didn't know what a Christian was or had knowingly lied.

"Leah, you said that you were a Christian. Are you telling me now that you are not?"

He most regretted that it felt as if he had somehow failed. That she was just seeing that he was a Christian after they had been dating for nearly two years meant that his own behavior failed to reflect this. And, perhaps more importantly, he regretted not having spent time answering the questions she hurled at him with answers that would have helped her with her own faith.

Although inexplicable to him given her self-pronounced status as a "Christian," it was possible to chart the steady deterioration of their relationship, at least in part, to his increasing tendency toward prayer and her apparent discomfort with this. This may very well have been the true reason for so many of their subsequent pain-filled arguments and angst. Oddly enough, it seemed that she believed his decision to pray to be akin to him giving up or failing to be proactive.

"When are you going to stop looking up to the sky for some miracle to grant you your wishes? What about your own ability, Jacob?"

"Leah, I am well aware of my ability and thank God for it every day. That's part of my prayers, thanking Him. I am not just asking for something but also praising God for everything He has given me, from my health to my relationship with you."

"But when we first got together, you were such a go-getter. You used to have the confidence it seemed to go after your dreams. Now it seems you just whisper them to the air in the dark."

Most recently, when he had asked her about her beliefs about God and past experiences in worship, she turned defensive and had become downright hostile. It was as if he had criticized her for being something that he was only beginning to think of her as being. She had bristled at his questions. Leah said she was a Christian, but she also said that she couldn't quite believe that God was anything more than some benevolent spirit of the past who caused some miracles she had read about. She did not believe, for example, that the universe was created by God, and because she associated those who vociferously claimed religion with dubious political machinations, she remained unconvinced in her belief of the reality of God.

Now alone, without her and in the Holy Land, he was looking for some direction and meaning in his own life. He realized that this was something he needed to do by himself. He would have to be the pilot; he could not be a passenger on another person's spiritual journey. He didn't exactly think of the trip and his plans to visit the Holy Land as the beginning of a spiritual awakening. Rather, he saw himself as already aboard a voyage that he hoped would ultimately strengthen his faith and bring him the peace that he knew in his heart was possible only through a faith in God.

When he landed the assignment in Israel, one of the first things he had decided to do was to visit those places known to have witnessed the presence of Christ. More than two thousand years ago, Christ walked throughout the land before being killed and providing an open door to eternity for all who believed in Him. Jacob knew this as much as he knew that the sun that he was watching had begun its descent. He saw the sun with his own two eyes, and he knew God's presence from his own heart and earthly experiences.

That evening at the restaurant, he ordered a light salad with salmon, and he ate it heartily when it arrived. The food was delicious, and he was keenly aware of how fresh the fish tasted. As he finished his glass of wine, the sun seemed to take this as a cue and began her descent in earnest. It was as beautiful as he had anticipated. He took several shots as it descended, glad that he'd remembered to bring his camera. He had captured the sun's retiring brilliance on his first night in the Holy Land. He paid the check, thanked the waitress, and returned to the apartment.

Upstairs, he took off his shoes and eased himself onto the sofa. He turned on the television and settled in for the evening, making himself comfortable. The sofa was conveniently located in front of the TV. He was beginning to feel the effects of jet lag, and although he dozed, he woke up at 2:00 a.m. He decided to shower again and turn properly into bed. This time, he took a hot shower, and after drying off, he settled into the bed. He looked forward to the tour he had arranged to take the following day with the enthusiasm of a tourist and the yearning of a disciple. He managed to sleep a couple of hours.

The next morning, he was up a little after 5:00 a.m. He prepared a light breakfast of toast, an orange and some black coffee. The tour guide arrived promptly at 8:00 a.m. Jacob was waiting for him and greeted him and introduced himself as Jacob Pope.

"Hello, I am Sabbo Mahlof at your service. Please call me Sabbo," said the guide.

He appeared to be in his late thirties, balding slightly, and reasonably fit and tall. Jacob caught the faint whiff of cigarette smoke from him, and he knew that Sabbo was a smoker, something he would eventually understand to be fairly common in Israel. Sabbo spoke to him with clear and slightly accented English explaining the plan for the day.

As Jacob climbed into the passenger side of the small sedan, he suddenly remembered that he had neglected to pack his wide-angle lens. After apologizing hastily to the guide, he ran back upstairs to the apartment. He couldn't understand how he'd forgotten it because it was a necessity he was sure he'd need given the sites they would be visiting.

As if to make him feel better, when Jacob returned, Sabbo attributed his forgetfulness to "the jet lag," telling him of a few examples he'd witnessed of clients who had been challenged from the young couple who has slept throughout the entire tour to the ultraprofessional businesswoman who had left her wallet, camera, and glasses at the hotel.

The two got into the vehicle and strapped themselves in.

"We will set off and head for Jerusalem, seeing all of the many important places you have come here to see, eh? I understand you are a photographer and would like to take some special photos. With that in mind, I have arranged to stop at the most breathtaking sites to see. After we visit Jerusalem, we will head off to see Galilee. I understand you expressed particular interest in visiting the region. It will be a full day!"

"I hope that you have scheduled lunch in there someplace, Sabbo," Jacob said. "Because I know I'm going to be hungry at some point. I'm a little off kilter given the jet lag, and I did not have much of an appetite for a big breakfast."

"No problem, Mr. Jacob, that is accounted for, and we will stop for a lovely lunch you will enjoy en route to Galilee."

They set off. The sedan was relatively new. They passed multiple memorials along the road whose significance Sabbo explained. Within about thirty minutes, they emerged in a hilly and mountainous region of Jerusalem. This terrain was noticeably different from the upscale landscape characteristic of Herzliya and the gritty urbanity of Tel Aviv. At various points, Sabbo pulled over, and Jacob photographed the sites that were most visually appealing.

While he described the importance of what they were seeing as they passed, Jacob wondered about Sabbo and most of the Israelis he knew. All of them seemed to have a strong sense of history and an even stronger sense of patriotism. When they exhibited a combination of knowledge and outspokenness that was accompanied by their distinctive sense of bravado, it could be off putting at times. Of course, it depended upon the individual and the circumstance, but more than once he'd assumed arrogance.

He was willing to give Sabbo a proverbial pass in this regard because it was his job as a tour guide that required him to be extremely knowledgeable and vocal. He felt differently about the other Israelis he personally knew in the US. His experiences growing up in New York in certain settings had led him to feel somewhat defensive about his Gentile status.

They stopped at several places along the way, and each time, Jacob took pictures from different vantage points. Eventually, they arrived at a special place, which Sabbo seemed most excited to share with Jacob. After parking and entering the large open area, they gravitated toward an elevated point along a wall where they looked out at the vista before them. Jacob immediately began taking photographs. Sabbo left him there and went to park the car in a temporary spot. They were at the Mount of Olives, a place dotted with grave markers indicating the places of more than 150,000 graves buried there. It was a significant place historically given that several key events of Jesus Christ's life took place there.

When Sabbo returned, he stood beside Jacob and explained the historical relevance of the site to most of Israel's current residents.

"Most Israelis today believe that when Jesus returns to gather His followers to heaven, He will appear at the Mount of Olives first." He turned around and pointed in the opposite direction. "Not far from here, you can see the shrine right there, which is called the Chapel of the Ascension. Christians believe it to be the location of the actual site where Jesus ascended to heaven. Israelis have defended the site against Muslims for many years. There has been a lot of blood that was shed at that site."

The shrine that they gazed upon actually appeared in the style of Muslim architecture and contained a mihrab (a niche in the wall of a mosque), which Sabbo explained indicated the direction to which Muslims should pray to Mecca. That feature resulted from a time during which Muslims ruled over the site at the time.

"The chapel with its Muslim features shows the past realities that Israel confronted from the surrounding region. There were deep separations among people that affected all aspects of daily living. But as you can see, the human spirit eventually finds a way to get on with the business of living."

He waved his arm outward across the expanse in front of them as if to demonstrate its breadth.

"That chapel is a site where Christians worshipped followed by Muslims followed by both Christians and Muslims."

"When you say Christians, you mean Israelis?" Jacob asked. He knew that he was a Christian but wondered what that word meant to contemporary Israelis.

"You know, the thing about history is that it has a way of smoothing the rough edges of the past so as to make it more acceptable, smoother for the present. No, I do not mean Israelis. I mean the people who followed Jesus and believe that He was resurrected from the dead. Surely, you know that story. This was a holy site for them, but Muslims in subsequent eras defeated them and took control. This place reflects the historical tensions."

Jacob was reminded of how he himself had fallen into the habit of differentiating between those people who truly seemed to know God and His son Jesus, and those, like most of the people he knew, who called themselves "Christians" but who rarely seemed to behave in ways bearing any resemblance to Christ. There were a lot of people he knew who professed to be Christians but failed to acknowledge the omnipotence of God, or who didn't really know what acceptance of Jesus as the savior of souls really meant.

Leah came to mind. When he asked her why she seemed to be put off by his decision to actually pray or to even refer to prayer, she became irritable and defensive.

One day, following a discussion about this, she had said, "I just wish that you had been upfront about being 'so religious' before I'd fallen in love with you."

He took umbrage with the remark, but at the same time, he couldn't help fixating on her profession of love. He admitted to himself that what had redeemed her, what had prevented him from leaving her then, was the fact of this pronouncement. She'd never told him she loved him before, and it pleased him to hear that she did, even if the profession itself was encased in a barb.

Sabbo was speaking. He was explaining that their next stop would be in Galilee, and it was a good distance away so they should stop for lunch.

"Would you prefer to dine with tourists or with the locals? I have made tentative arrangements at two very different locations, each with excellent cuisines. Please advise me of your preference and we will go there."

"I believe I would like the experience of eating with the locals," said Jacob.

"Very well, my friend, you shall be rewarded."

Some twenty-five minutes later, they arrived at a small building in an area with similar structures. Each small building boasted its own small parking area in front of its doors. It was hard to tell whether the other buildings were also restaurants.

They opened the large wooden door in the building that Sabbo had chosen and entered. Aside from one or two other patrons, the restaurant, if one chose to call it that, was nearly empty and had a reddish decor in a clean wide-open space. Jacob sat on a bench at a table across from Sabbo. Together, they discussed the menu and decided on which dishes to order. As the first of several dishes arrived, Jacob bowed his head to quietly say grace. Sabbo noticed but said nothing.

The meal began with a fantastic spread of different salads and small cold dishes and bread. This course was followed by a tender lamb stew. They ate contently exchanging few words, and eventually, other diners began to drift into the restaurant. There was too much food for the two of them to finish, so they nodded thanks to the cook who also served as the waiter, and they asked for the check. Jacob paid the bill for the two of them, aware that this expense like any other required in the course of his contracted tour was expected of him.

Sabbo explained the next leg of their journey as they headed back to the car.

"Now we head for Galilee. The ride is about one hour to one hour and a half. Along the way, there may be things that you wish to photograph, and I am at your service to stop. Please advise me."

They headed north to the town of Tiberius on a road that alternated between one and two lanes. Tiberius had a fairly mountainous terrain. As they drove along the road that twisted and turned, eventually they were stopped by at least two cars ahead of them. They could not see beyond the two cars. Both cars were headed in the same direction as they were, but they seemed to be stalled. Amazingly, it was impossible to see the hood of the car furthest in front because it, like everything else within ten meters, was engulfed in thick black clouds of smoke. Something was on fire.

"Stay put, I have an idea of what is happening," said Sabbo, as he quickly exited the car and ran ahead through the smoke to the driver of the first car.

Despite being told to stay put, Jacob followed him, camera in tow.

An older man with a young boy who was visibly uneasy spoke in Hebrew to Sabbo and the other driver as they gathered by the right side of the second vehicle. They spoke quickly and with several voices at once.

"I can't accept this! They continue this tactic. It must stop. It is wrong! Why must they do this to us? When will they stop this? I know that it is them trying to force us out. We will not be moved. We are not going anywhere!"

They were so agitated that it would have been hard for someone conversant in Hebrew to immediately understand them, let alone someone like Jacob with no knowledge of the language. Noticing that he was there, Sabbo turned to him and explained that the field bordering both sides of the road had been intentionally set ablaze.

"You will find this to be amazing I am sure, but this is actually a routine tactic of aggression that Palestinians engage in to harm Israelis. It creates many, many problems for the landowner whose property and crops are compromised, and it also creates problems for people who are not even related to the property owner. People like us!" he said, pointing to himself and waving at the others who stood beside their vehicles.

"We are only trying to use these open roads. And now we will all have to backtrack to find another road. We will lose time as we try to find another way to get to our destination."

Jacob was amazed and disheartened to witness this particular manifestation of the continuing problem of Arab-Israeli conflict. He knew that it existed, and that it explained the large scale acts of aggression that made headlines, but things like this, the burning of an individual landowner's property was not something he'd considered. Acts like this were too common to disseminate in news outlets that reported internationally.

Here it was, only his first full day in country, and Jacob had had a firsthand encounter with the conflict. And while he did not wish to get into a philosophical debate with Sabbo about it, he felt great sympathy for the landowners and the other drivers, who were all Israelis. For a time, their little group which gathered on the road said nothing as they stared at the flames.

Eventually, Sabbo identified an alternate route that would take them to their stop in the Galilee region. After about forty-five minutes of driving along a flat road that revealed little worth photographing, they eventually stopped at the visitor welcome center. The site they were visiting was known as the Yardenit site along the Jordan River. Jacob did not recognize the name or the historical significance of the site.

"So, what is this place? Looks like a lot of tourists are here." He saw people with different types of dress and yet also noticed that there were as many people in western clothes as there were those in long flowing robes. Some were from as far away as India or Pakistan, and some from sub-Saharan Africa.

"Here are people from around the world who come because this site is the place where John the Baptist baptized Jesus. Do you know this place from your Bible?" Sabbo asked Jacob.

"Yes, yes, as a matter of fact, I do. Each of the four gospels within the Bible describe this event," Jacob said, as he turned completely around for a full view of the holy place.

"The gospels talk about how, at first, John didn't want to baptize the son of God, and how Jesus told him to do so. They also describe how the heavens"— he leaned his head back and looked up to the sky and shielding his eyes for the sun—"opened up to reveal God's spirit in a voice acknowledging Jesus and his love for him. This is that place, huh? I feel incredibly humbled."

Sabbo said nothing; he'd gotten that reaction from previous clients.

For Jacob, this place, more than any other, resonated with his own sense of what it truly meant to be touched by God and to feel his spirit. It wasn't just the historical reality that blanketed the sandy shores and river, nor was it the deeply peaceful air that seemed to engulf the entire area including the banks of the river. No, there was more to it than that. It was hard to explain, but at that moment, he knew that he had made the right decision to leave Leah, to come to Israel, and to make this pilgrimage to the holiest of places.

As they walked along the path bordering the river, he stopped to watch several people of varying nationalities who were dressed in white robes and who were being baptized. He wanted desperately to hear of their faith and their willingness to provide a symbolic attestation of it. He walked slowly down the steps to get closer to them as if his physical proximity to these particular Christians would result in greater spiritual understanding and affinity for himself.

Jacob was entranced by the pilgrims who were being baptized in the water, so he did not notice the three young men who walked swiftly from the parking area to the balcony above the levee where the baptisms were underway. They appeared to be in their late twenties and seemed to be ill at ease as they spoke among themselves. Although Sabbo saw them, he was standing too far away to make out exactly what they were saying. As he turned his head to look once again at Jacob, the sun reflected on a glint of metal that caused him to do a double take. What was that in the hands of one of the three men?

It was a gun! In that moment, Sabbo pushed Jacob away nearly knocking him off his feet. The two recovered quickly and Sabbo explained, "We must get out of here! The man over there has a gun in his hands!"

They quickly moved back away from the area where the men were standing, just as one of the young men began shouting. He directed his remarks to no one in particular but seemed to want the attention of everyone within earshot. And everyone who heard the young man, including many of those being baptized below, stopped and listened. In doing so, within seconds, they'd left the idyllic plane of communion with the Holy Spirit and all the saints to return heavily to the earthly realities of existence in one of the most conflict-ridden regions of the world.

The man with the gun spoke first. Jacob noticed that there were no police or guards. He thought this strange given the prominence of the site.

"I have come here, and I have this gun in my hand because I wanted to make sure that I would have the opportunity to speak to you. I know that it is frightening to see a man appear in one of the holiest places on earth with a gun in his hand. I am sorry for that. But this is what I had to do in order to command your attention and to say what must be said to you."

Jacob listened carefully, and because he had his bag containing a small digital camera, he decided to discretely record what he could of the man's remarks.

The man spoke in heavily accented English, presumably to reach as many of those gathered at Yardenit as possible.

"We have come here today to express to you our willingness to live in peace with everyone and with our closest neighbors. We are not here to fight or hurt anyone, nor do we wish to disrupt your worship of your gods here. Instead, we make a plea to you as visitors from other countries to take back our story of repression and injustice to your governments. This is a land that our people have populated for thousands of years. It is impossible to simply wipe us away in the interest of Israeli Zionism. While we have struggled to retain the land that is ours and the rights we are entitled to, we have family and friends who cross the boundaries that separate us every day. During your time here in Israel and Palestine, please pay attention to what you see. Look at the people who live here, talk to them. Try to understand their situations and come up with your own opinions. Only after you have engaged the people of the land throughout this region and throughout all of Israel, Galilee, Bethlehem, and Palestine should you truly and fairly form an opinion. We came here in peace, and we will leave you in peace. Inshallah Allah."

Jacob wanted desperately to learn more about the young man's story. He turned to Sabbo.

"Who are those men? Where do you think they live? Is this something that happens often here?"

As the three men hastily turned to leave, Jacob started off after them, but Sabbo grabbed his elbow.

"Where are you going?" he asked him. "You cannot follow them. They are terrorists!" he said emphatically. From the look in his eyes, Jacob knew that Sabbo believed what he said to be true, but something about the message of peace that the young man had articulated suggested otherwise. He shook off Sabbo's hand.

"Sabbo, man, I'm sorry, but I do need to know a bit more about their stories and who they are." He ran quickly to catch up with the young men.

As a photojournalist, he knew that this was something worth documenting, and given the young man's plea for visitors to take information back to their home countries, he was optimistic about getting the men to talk with him. Sabbo reluctantly followed Jacob though kept several paces behind.

Jacob finally caught up with the men as they approached a vehicle in the parking lot directly across from a large bus with the name of a local tour company appearing colorfully in Romanized letters on the side. He called out to them, waving as he did so.

"Hello, I'm an American journalist and photographer. My name is Jacob Pope. I heard what you said back there, and I wonder if you would be willing to talk with me?" The men turned to him and stood where they were. Jacob approached them. When he was close enough to them, he handed them a business card. The men turned to one another and whispered briefly among themselves. They spoke in Arabic.

The man who had made the impassioned speech moments earlier appeared to be the leader among them.

"We will talk with you if only to get our word out. You are an American with the means to communicate our message. The police will be coming shortly, and they will either take us away or harass us so we must talk quickly." The other men nodded as he said this.

"First, we must have your assurance that you will represent us and what it is we have to say accurately. Do we have your assurance about this"—he looked at the card—"Mr. Pope?" He'd pronounced it as if it were two syllabus, "Po-pe."

"Yes, one hundred percent, you do. I assure you that I will represent what you say accurately."

The leader spoke. "I am here now with my brothers. One is my mother's son, and the other is a son from my mother's sister. I am the oldest among us. We are fighting for the right of Palestine to exist. We are activists. We believe that we can do so alongside Israel, but we cannot be deprived of our own rights. This is the point that makes us different from the people your friend here [he pointed to Sabbo] thinks of as terrorists. They too are our brothers, but they are not willing to live together with Israelis."

The second man, who he had indicated was his brother, spoke up then.

"What he says is true, and each one of us has personally witnessed Israeli aggression that has killed our own friends and our family members. That is what makes our effort so important. Even though we have experienced all of this, we still want to speak for peace.

The leader interrupted.

"Peace. Some of our own people say that we are naive, but we know that peace can be achieved, because nothing is impossible. It is critical for us to work toward a solution. We have a desperate need for any and all peaceful solutions."

Jacob was moved by their impassioned perspective. At the same time, it bothered him that he found it hard to be as optimistic as they were. Like most Americans who enjoyed the relative safety of life outside the world's contested hot spots, he heard only the news that made its way to American airways. Those news stories that provided details about Arab-Israeli conflicts tended not to end on a positive note. And more often than not, the conflict that was described was reported against a backdrop of continuing conflict. That made it nearly impossible for any outsider to identify the actual cause of any conflict.

"Do you think that it is possible for people on both sides who have lost so much to be able to simply shake hands and arrive at peace?" he asked the men.

Without waiting for an answer, Jacob told the men about the challenge of getting to the Yardenit site that day because of the unexpected but required detour resulting from the fields on fire along the way.

"Today, I learned that as a form of protest, Palestinians sometimes burn the fields of Israelis. That's not the kind of thing that gets reported in the news when there is coverage about conflicts occurring here. A fire that was deliberately set caused great damage in the area we had to pass to get here. Do you know the people who did this? Do the people who burned the fields see themselves as committing an action with far greater consequences than the economic upheaval to one farmer's crops?"

The third man in the group who up to now had said nothing spoke.

"Those fields were set on fire to send a message to tell Israelis that they must leave these areas in which the fields were located. The fire is not only meant to cause economic distress, but it is meant to disrupt the smooth everyday actions of the Israelis… it is meant to be a disruption of their peace of mind. Yes, it is to trouble their peace of mind."

The man smiled strangely as he said this, realizing its disconnect with his cousin's pronouncement of peace.

Remembering Sabbo, Jacob turned and noticed that he remained several feet removed from them and displayed a sullen expression. Jacob beckoned him over, and begrudgingly, he joined them.

It occurred to Jacob that not only were the young men who were Muslims far off from understanding the gospel and the message of salvation through Christ, but also Sabbo, an Israeli Jew, was as well. He sighed and thanked the men for talking with him. Then he asked them, "Do you believe in God?"

Each of the men, nodded yes, murmuring praises and other words to "Allah."

Jacob knew then that if there were anything useful that he could personally do, it would be to share his knowledge of the grace of Jesus Christ's salvation with them. Of course, in order for them to accept what he had decided to say to them, they would have to actively turn away from "Allah" and his particular brand of vengeance and turn instead to Christ. He knew that it was unlikely that they would do so, but he was certain that he had been led to that location and that day's events for that purpose.

"I know you said that we had limited time, and I am sure you have to leave from this area because when the police arrive, they will detain you. But could I have a little more of your time? Maybe over some coffee or tea? My guide [he pointed to Sabbo] can direct us to a place not far from here I am sure."

The men talked again among themselves, and then shrugging their shoulders as if to say, *"Why not?"* they agreed.

Jacob smiled as he turned to Sabbo. He needed for him to come up with directions to some place nearby where he would share the Gospel with the all of them.

PLANE ANXIETY

Penelope woke up suddenly in flight somewhere over the Atlantic to the voices and images that often entered her sleep. She was anxious to land and relished the thought of walking on ground in a familiar place. Squinting at the small screen two rows up that televised the jet's course heading northwest, she saw that the plane appeared to be on schedule. It would be touching down at LaGuardia Airport in less than three hours as planned.

What was unscheduled was her current state of fear and anxiety. Her heart was pounding as she felt the creeping tide of terror that sometimes gripped her usually snatching her from slumber. With any luck, she thought, she'd be able to extinguish the storm of anxiety that foreshadowed a full-blown panic attack. Ironically, what she was most afraid of was the all-too-familiar state of inexplicable fear. When it overtook her, it managed to rob her of the respite sleep promised for most, and it disrupted the immediate wakening moments that entered on the heels of sleep.

After glancing around the dimly lit cabin, Penelope decided to get up. She would use the bathroom to escape the cramped space that she was allotted for the window seat in row twenty-three. It was either that, or audibly expressing the anxiety that was quickly taking hold of her. If she did that, she'd wind up waking all the other passengers near her and, worst of all, humiliating herself. She really wanted to avoid causing a scene. Not just because all eyes would be on her and she'd look like she'd lost it. She imagined how the other passengers would recount their experience on the plane with the crazy Black woman traveling from Austria. They probably already thought she was angry given the ubiquitous stereotypes about Black women, and on top of that, she knew they'd also think of her as crazy.

She did her best to keep it cool because what she was experiencing would inevitably subside at some point. Although the attacks might feel as if they lasted forever, when they occurred, she was usually on the downside of fear's peak some fifteen to thirty minutes later.

Penelope also worried about causing any sort of scene because she knew that most of the American carriers, like the one she was traveling on, routinely employed air marshals on many of their international flights. Any outburst from her was likely to be interpreted as hostile and possibly even as an act of terrorism, at least initially. She did not wish to be the protagonist in yet another tragic tale reflecting anti-Black animus in traditional American spaces.

The stories of "driving while Black," "golfing while Black," and "dining while Black" were everywhere. No matter how well-educated or well-off any Black person happened to be, the countless senseless arrests, stops, and murders made most Black people in America particularly sensitive to situations in which innocent behavior could be misconstrued. As such, at that moment, Penelope was especially aware of the way that an uncontrollable panic attack could be misperceived in a setting in which she was one of few people of color where there was someone nearby whose goal was to bring down anyone perceived to be dangerous. This awareness coupled with the simmering fear and anxiety that had awakened her was enough to propel her out of her seat.

Getting out of her window seat and the row required a bit of maneuvering. She climbed over her seatmate—a middle-aged blonde woman, whose gratifying sleep she envied. She hated having to climb over the sleeping woman who looked so peaceful, but she had no other choice.

Although Penelope regularly flew coach and only rarely had ever flown first or business class, she had never quite adjusted to the fact that accommodations in the "economy" section provided very little space beyond the volume required of a human body slightly less than the size of the average American traveler. Even the plane's aisle was a challenge to navigate for those with ample-sized hips and rears—attributes of at least two of the flight attendants working this flight.

Once out of the row and into the aisle, she headed first toward the plane's restrooms located upfront near the cockpit, but then she thought better of it and turned toward the rear of the plane. Cautiously, she made her way back and headed in the direction of the bathrooms located there. She was dreading the impending panic and desperately needed to move. When the anxiety hit, it kicked in a "flight" response, and the instinct was to flee. But other than being able to get up from her seat, exit the row, and head down the plane's aisle, there was no real escape. No place to go.

Standing in the aisle, this cold hard fact hit her. What should she do? Although there was less room to roam, the bathrooms provided a private space where she might be able to stifle the anxiety. She headed to the rear of the plane.

Penelope was well versed in the psychology of this particular problem. After seeking professional counseling last year, she learned that this was not uniquely her problem. And, although she felt that she alone "owned it" when it hit her, the truth was that millions of other people suffered with similar types of symptoms. What led her to finally seek help was a particularly rough stint she'd had. The worst of it prevented her from sleeping at night for days at a time. She'd felt like a zombie when that happened.

When she tried to sleep, the panic demon (she'd come to think of it in this way) would sneak in and rifle through her thoughts. Within a moment, she was awake, wide awake. Her eyes would fly open, and after having jumped out of the bed, she'd find herself walking the floors mindlessly and fearfully racing through her apartment.

During those times, Penelope would often cry until she could cry no more. Her eyes, red and swollen, betrayed the night's tempest well into the next day. She felt smothered by the walls of her normally comfortable home. Only when the worst of the anxiety accompanying those episodes began to abate could she begin to think about the actual implications of charging across the hardwood floors in her third-floor apartment at 3:00 a.m. She was sure that the thudding sounds of her footsteps disrupted the sleep of her neighbor below. That might explain why she sensed that her normally friendly neighbor in the apartment directly below had seemed distant as of late.

At the height of these spells, she felt that she flirted with madness. She had succumbed to this dalliance, and she was terrified at the prospect of never being able to divorce herself from it. For what seemed like an infinite amount of time during the panic attack, she raged, roared, and feared everything that was anything and even nothing. What she feared most was the fear itself, and it consumed her, causing her each time to glimpse over into that other side.

She was pretty certain that she treaded the fine line between sanity and madness. Unpredictably, at any given postmidnight, predawn moment, she'd often find herself skirting the divide. It was an imaginary line after all, wasn't it? Just a way of talking about those who appeared "normal" and played according to the rules and lived ordinary lives. As for those who didn't, she felt that she was intimately acquainted with them, and she visited their world every time the panic hit and took hold of her.

Physically, she was left feeling drained and exhausted when the attacks occurred; though this unfortunately did not guarantee that sleep would be forthcoming even later. She usually wound up passing out close to the time just before her alarm sounded, and inevitably, she woke up exhausted. On the mornings after those eventful nights, it was daunting just getting out of bed.

So, it was not without grave trepidation that she laid down to rest each night. After a fitful night of panic, she was particularly attuned to the subtleties of sleep preparation. Should she take a hot bath? Was that glass of wine likely to be a problem? Ever since her first experience with panic, she tended to be conscientious, indeed paranoid, about the ritual she followed for sleep, but on nights immediately following a panic-filled one, she was obsessive about it.

Although the worst of it lasted for less than fifteen minutes, it seemed like forever, and each time she tried to fall back asleep, it was the fear of its return that jolted her back to consciousness. That was probably the most debilitating part of it. Like an unrepentant and merciless lover—it, he, or whatever—had managed to track her down and find its way back to her. It was as if it taunted her. Even the isolation and remoteness of the plane on which she now traveled was accessible to it.

At the plane's rear, Penelope found both bathrooms were in use. The little light located in the door handle on both doors glowed red indicating "occupied." She wondered how long the occupants had been inside. The anxiety was still with her, and she found myself fidgeting in the small space that doubled as the flight attendants' seating area and rear kitchen. She looked up and noticed that two of the flight attendants were heading toward her. The first of them to reach her, a woman in her midforties, looked at her inquisitively and before saying anything, Penelope volunteered, "I'm having a bit of an anxiety attack and need to ride it out here, if I may."

"Sure, that's fine if that helps you, by all means stay," said "Carla," according to her nametag. She inched around her and focused her attention on food preparations. When the other flight attendant, a male, made it to the rear, he looked curiously at her. Carla noticed and said immediately in a hushed tone, "She's having an anxiety attack and just needs to stretch here for a while."

That seemed to satisfy "Jack," who then offered to get her some water.

A few months ago, at the suggestion of a well-intentioned friend, Penelope explored the study of mindful meditation. One of its contemporary progenitors had apparently visited her friend's office and made a life-altering appeal to those gathered there. Her friend, who was several years older, married and divorced multiple times over, swore that it had changed her life.

With mindful meditation, the goal is to reach a place in one's mind that is stable and at peace. The key to this exercise is to discover that being calm or experiencing harmony is a natural aspect of the human mind. Her friend's instructor continuously reminded her that the practice of mindful meditation was actually an exercise to better develop and strengthen that calmness or mindful state.

Penelope's friend made an impression on her, and in the end, she had convinced her of its value. When she showed up for the initial exercise on the Beginner's Mind at the Zen Centre downtown, she was taken aback by the apparent diversity of those who'd already discovered the benefits of this form of mindful awareness. The lesson was open to beginners like her, as well as those who were more experienced at achieving the experiential awareness and peace she ultimately sought.

Several of them were young as in the case of the three White college students who were seated in the small area near the defunct fireplace in the front of the room. There were quite a few older regulars, too, who brought their own small rugs and other paraphernalia, which she soon became familiar with. Taken together, they were a diverse lot. What Penelope was least prepared for and what continued to intrigue her even after her third session was her teacher.

She was a tall Black woman, striking in appearance. It was easy to say she was beautiful, but that word didn't really capture Penelope's impression of her. She was attractive by anyone's standards, but there was something else about her that transcended the meaning of the word beautiful; a word used at random to describe the likes of Hollywood's current starlets and the richness of a portrait or still life found along the walls of world-class museums. Perhaps what contributed to the image she held of her teacher was the complete and consummate humility with which she greeted and interacted with all who showed up at the Centre.

It was an all-too-unfamiliar trait, and it also probably explained her instructor's reticence to be called anything but her first name—Jasmine. For Jasmine, anything other than that implied a sense of superiority that she was unwilling to claim.

At that moment, one of the bathroom doors opened and the passenger who'd occupied it, a middle-aged heavyset man with a beard, exited. Penelope braced herself against the opposite wall to allow him enough room to pass. Thanking the flight attendant but deciding to pass on the water he'd offered, she quickly headed for the vacant bathroom.

This particular part of the flight was always a less than pleasant experience. The other passengers it seemed invariably relinquished basic hygienic habits on international flights. Too bad, she decided. She'd just have to make do with it because this really was the only place she could get past the panic in private, away from strangers' eyes. Holding her breath and being certain to lock the door as it closed, she turned to the mirror above the sink in the tiny stall. The image that gazed back at her was not especially beautiful, but neither was it homely. This was a visage that reflected its bearer's mileage and distance.

True, she was suffering inside as the panic lurked just beneath the surface, but on the outside, she still looked like herself. A thirtysomething, attractive Black woman with a complexion and short haircut that ultimately posed challenges for strangers who attempted to discern her ancestry. Knowing that Black folks in America came in all colors of the rainbow, she took some measure of pride whenever she revealed that she was "Black." That happened exclusively with Whites. While they were the ones who seemed to be most curious about her precise lineage, Black people never seemed to ask and always knew that she was an African American.

But no one could possibly know from her appearance that she was as fragile and vulnerable as she really was. No one could know, and she would not tell. Ironically, if she were to share any of what she'd learned during this last week with anyone, it would only be the details of the panic that had taken hold on this flight. No, she was hesitant to disclose the reasons she'd traveled as well as the fact that she'd even been gone.

It was a complicated matter, and one about which she remained uncertain as to where right was reasonably distinguished from wrong. Her sense of right and wrong, usually irrefutable, resolute, and above all accurate may have failed her. By acknowledging this, she opened the door to the tidal wave of doubts and uncertainties that had collected there just outside memory's dam. With this realization, another wave of panic hit.

Penelope was now forced to acknowledge that her decision to make the trip had been driven by her own selfish desires. True, he had invited her, but she could have said no. The deciding factor was her desire to once again play tourist and to save money while doing it. This time, it was a trip to Salzburg, the storybook old town in Austria where Mozart was born. She had accepted his invitation after just a moment of doubt.

She had ostensibly agreed to visit in order to see Salzburg and to catch up with an old friend; someone she regarded as an old friend, nothing more. She did not view him romantically, nor did she feel in any way attracted to him. But if she had been truly honest with herself, she would have admitted that she had never really been attracted to him even during that brief period when they had dated some years back.

Unfortunately, her actions in the past belied her feelings and her general reluctance for a physical relationship with him. Yes, it was true that more than four years ago, she'd mustered up the resolve to tell him she had no interest in being anything more to him than a friend, a buddy. But that was only after a year's worth of intimate entanglement in yet another interracial relationship.

He did not seem to understand that "friendship only" meant no physical intimacy as there once had been. Penelope felt compelled to cut off any social interactions with him. As a result, they had not seen one another for quite some time.

Now even with that past safely tucked away, her recollections of her relationship with him were unsettling in light of what he'd chosen to disclose to her in Salzburg.

Like most people, Penelope didn't like to think of herself as a user, but more than once the thought had crossed her mind. When she first began spending time with him years back, the boredom and isolation of her life in that small dusty town east of Houston and west of the Mississippi had settled upon her. She was without meaningful social prospects, and his initial invitation to dinner came as a welcomed distraction. One dinner led to another, and then another and before she realized it she'd made it through six months with something to do on almost every weekend for almost all of that time! Thanks to him.

He had been divorced for nearly five years when she'd met him. His ex-wife raised their two small sons. The two were from the same Jewish community and had married young. They lived an adventurous life together that was reflected in their first son's birth occurring in the Australian outback. He spoke kindly about his ex-wife, but he also made clear that the marriage had run its course. Although he often talked about missing his sons, he had not contested his ex-wife's primary custody of them. Penelope wondered about that.

When she had first begun seeing him, they had spent a great deal of time together. So much time then that it would have been impossible for him to see his boys on the weekends. It was true that they did not live in the same town, but the distance that separated him from his children was less than two hours in either direction.

Penelope eventually came to believe that the pleasure he derived in talking about his sons surpassed his feelings in being physically present with them. She knew this to be the case now, and although she had suspected it back then, it hadn't really mattered to her at the time. As shameful as it was, she was concerned first with her own number one priority, namely herself. If she now felt some guilt about the self-centered attitude that characterized who she was at that time, it paled in comparison to the doubt that plagued her judgment of character.

Even then, something about her relationship with him didn't sit quite right with her. It was true that she'd never felt physically drawn to him in the way that he obviously felt about her. But that wasn't the only thing that had bothered her. There was something else, and if pressed, it would have been hard to pinpoint exactly what about him troubled her. She couldn't say at the time.

Now because of the passage of time and perhaps more importantly because of the grisly incident he'd described to her, she knew. She now knew what happened to the person she had been nearly five years ago when she knew him best.

They'd dated nearly a year. Eventually, she broke off any and all contact with him, though it was difficult because it required a complete change in routine given the limited venues that existed in the small town they both called home. But she'd managed. When she finally moved away to take on a new professional opportunity that was bigger and better than what that small town could provide, she hadn't looked back twice, nor had she bothered to contact him.

When their paths next crossed, it was well after she'd relocated across the country to Oregon. Somewhat reluctantly, she had reached out to him then because she needed information that only he had. He was a highly regarded scientist with obscure interests and expertise that only a handful of others in the country could boast of having. What a coup it was for her on a new job to have direct access to someone of his stature.

Although she initially hesitated contacting him, fearing what this would mean in terms of opening the door to him again, she did so anyway. He was delighted to hear from her and so began their periodic, long-distance correspondence often by email but just as frequently in longhand letters. The content of the letters was light and breezy, detailing the day's or week's activities. In one of those letters, he told her of his upcoming year-long sabbatical to

Salzburg. She'd followed up by wishing him well, and he'd responded by inviting her to visit.

Now nearly seven months after that invitation, she was returning from the eagerly awaited trip to Salzburg where they'd spent part of each day together for the last two weeks. If only she'd known more about the circumstances of his "sabbatical" beforehand. It had never occurred to her that it was anything more than a break from routine teaching obligations to pursue research that was provided to a deserving cohort within the world of academia. Toward the very end of her stay, he'd chosen to disclose the true nature of his sabbatical.

It was then that she had decided to leave immediately.

His sabbatical was actually a mandatory leave of absence. Apparently, he'd had little choice in the matter. Because of a series of events he was involved in, he had been forced to leave his life and the small town he called home. That he had landed in Salzburg with a post at the Universität Salzburg attested to his wide network of colleagues and research associates. It was doubtful that any of them knew anything about what led to his sudden desire to affiliate with one of Europe's oldest universities.

The details were sordid. Penelope was shocked. From that point on, what he told her had affected the nature of her interactions with him. How could it not? She couldn't bring herself to think of him in the same way. He had crossed a clear and critical line, and now represented what she knew to be a "perpetrator," a criminal; quite possibly even a murderer! This was new for her.

As far as she knew, Penelope had never willingly danced nor dined with the type of person any reasonable woman should fear. In the course of an hour that began with a plaintive plea of sympathy from her, he had become transformed before her eyes.

Someone was knocking. She splashed a few drops of water from the bathroom's miniature faucet on her cheeks, took a deep breath, and opened the door. She was feeling a little better. The panic had peaked, and the anxiety was gradually dissipating though leaving her feeling worn and tired.

She exited the bathroom. A disheveled woman in her twenties appeared to be patiently waiting to enter. Sliding past her, their arms briefly touching, Penelope decided to make her way back to her seat. As she passed the young woman, she smelled a faint whiff of her perfume. It was vaguely familiar and reminded her for a brief moment of a scent her mother once favored—lightly floral but with more presence than nature's intentions would knowingly allow. Heading up the aisle, she looked for row twenty-three, located it, and once again climbed over her still lightly snoring seatmate.

Before she'd gotten her seatbelt fastened, the flight attendant "Carla," who she'd first spoken to, leaned in and asked, "Is there anything I can bring you? Anything that would help you?"

Penelope thought a drink might help her to relax.

"Yes, thanks. Could I please have a glass of red wine?" Carla nodded yes and left to get it for her. Five minutes later, with the plastic glass filled with cheap red wine in hand, she settled back into her seat. Her thoughts turned back to his disturbing disclosure.

Within months after she'd stopped seeing him, he'd begun a relationship with a new faculty member. She had just arrived to town and joined the faculty of the university that semester. Because everybody knew everyone in the insular community whose live-lihood was driven by admission rates at the university hospital, he had met her within days of her arrival. He gushed as he described her to Penelope, his eyes bright with excitement.

"She was so special and refreshing. She was pos-itively captivating and yet at the same time so inno-cent. When she showed up, I thought that she was a student, but she was not! She was a very experienced and knowledgeable woman. Her energy was amaz-ing and she was interested in meeting everyone and learning everything about our boring little town."

Although he did not mention her age as he described her, Penelope was pretty certain that one of the things that he liked most about the new woman was her youth. He acknowledged that most of his male colleagues who encountered her were also smit-ten. Even under the circumstances and with all that had happened, he couldn't hide the fact of his pride because she had chosen him.

"She was like a breath of fresh air and everyone, I kid you not, everyone wanted to be with her. But she reached out to me."

She silently wondered whether that fact would sustain him in the midst of what he was going through. Because she too had arrived to that town and university only a few years earlier, she knew firsthand what it was like to be the "new kid on the block." The new woman whom every available bachelor wanted to check out. But what she didn't know was what it was like to be thought of as beautiful. Attractive, yes. Beautiful, no.

Penelope knew that most people would not describe her as beautiful. She was not foolish enough to think of herself in that way. And perhaps it was this damning evidence of the relative importance of beauty to him that she found to be just as revelatory as his alleged role in a crime. It surprised her, and she was profoundly disappointed. If she was forced to admit it, she'd have to acknowledge being just as disappointed about the fact that he was taken by this other woman's beauty as she was about the actual circumstances that led to his mandatory leave of absence. For some reason, however, ridiculous a reason it may have been, she thought he was a man who was riveted most by a woman's mind rather than her physical beauty.

He explained that he and his new girlfriend had had a standing Thursday night dinner date and by the second month, they had become intimate. This part of the story was more than a bit difficult for her to listen to. It was not because she was jealous or envious of the affair (indeed, it felt good to remind myself that she wasn't attracted to him), but she found listening to him talk about his intimacy with another woman to be off putting and something of an ordeal. Although it made little sense because he had opted to tell her all of this, she couldn't help feeling a bit sleazy, like she was some kind of a voyeur.

"One evening, we were making love, and I asked her to try something else, something new. It was a position that we had never tried together before, and I'd explained that it would intensify our intimacy. It would take us to another level of pleasure, she really believed this. I swear to you, you have to believe me."

Penelope wasn't sure that she could, and he had continued.

"We were so aroused. We were at the peak of excitement. It was not just me, but she was really into it, too. It's true that we both had had quite a bit of wine with dinner and afterwards, but we weren't drunk, uh huh, no way. Actually, the fact that she was excited to try this with me was just the way she was about everything. It was one of the things that I really loved about her. When I got inside of her, she seemed to really enjoy it, even with whatever pain she may have first experienced, you know because it was her first time for that position. The whole time she was into it."

Penelope's lack of belief must have shown on her face because he had continued.

"Seriously, you know anal sex is extremely popular around the world. It is just here in the States where so many uptight Americans see it as something perverse. It really is a source of grave pleasure for others around the globe."

He spoke of his own and the young woman's enjoyment idyllically, and it was only as his tale unfolded that the reason for his insistence in describing it this way became apparent.

He said that they were both satiated when they'd fallen asleep—he to a deep, dreamless slumber, and she the same, or so he assumed. In the morning, he described his inability to rouse her from sleep.

"I couldn't wake her up! I looked closely at her, and then I noticed that she was not breathing. I kept trying to get her to come around, and I even gave her mouth to mouth and then performed CPR on her, but I couldn't revive her! I panicked, I didn't know what to do. I must have thrown on some clothes and run from the apartment."

It was at this point in the retelling that Penelope assumed he would get to the point about how he'd run to a neighbor, or contacted the police. But that never happened. Instead, what came next stretched the limits of credulity. Knowing him as she did— his conscientiousness and penchant for details, it was hard to reconcile what he said he did with the person she thought him to be.

"I think that the entire experience of waking up with her like that, she was cold and unresponsive, it had apparently pushed me over the edge somehow. I think that I must have fallen into some sort of amnesiac fugue state. It's the only way to explain what happened to my memory and thinking at that time."

He insisted that he had no recollection whatsoever of what he'd done next or where he'd gone. Even now, almost a year after, the fact he was adamant about not remembering what had happened.

The plane dipped quickly, and Penelope caught her breath. She was immediately brought back to the present and found herself grasping the armrest she shared with her seatmate. There was more turbulence, and as the plane dipped several more times, the pilot announced that they would be experiencing the effects of a distant storm system for the next fifteen minutes or so.

"Please refrain from moving about the cabin at this time. I have turned on the fasten seat belts light. Flight attendants, please return to your seats."

Either the turbulence or the announcement woke up the woman seated next to her. She looked about and immediately reached for the shared armrest. Their hands touched briefly before she moved hers back somewhat, permitting Penelope to have more of its space.

As Penelope turned to gaze out of the window, she thought more about his exceptional failure to remember.

"It was so incredibly strange I tell you. All I can remember is somehow arriving at home shortly after my afternoon lectures, and when I got there, the police were waiting. Can you imagine my shock and horror after they told me why?"

That he had proceeded with his routine of conducting his classes while not remembering or bothering to remember that a woman's dead body remained in his bed after he had had rough sex with her seemed more than odd, but that was how he'd explained it to her.

"It was Elena, my Turkish cleaning lady, you remember her? She comes each week to clean the apartment. She discovered her!"

In addition to the normal dregs of dirty socks and shirts strewn about the apartment, the old woman had confronted another type of matter. Penelope imagined her reaction to seeing the dead woman's body, and then she thought how she must have struggled to communicate what she'd found given the limited English she spoke. She'd managed to call the police, and when he arrived home that evening, they were waiting for him.

Penelope wondered why they hadn't bothered to interrupt the class he was teaching, or detain him on campus. Aside from the questionable period in which he insisted he'd been in shock and couldn't remember, his steps were amazingly predictable. Because he was truly a creature of habit, had they wanted to, the police could easily have arrested him during the day. On the other hand, his absence from the apartment permitted them a full swatch of time to conduct the necessary preliminary investigations without his knowledge or approval.

He was charged with having raped, sodomized, and murdered the young woman.

"Can you believe that they accused me of raping and killing her? I was shocked, and to tell you the truth, I am still in a state of shock. It is unbelievable to me that they would think me capable of something so horrible. I mean, it is shocking!"

He asked her whether she, too, thought it crazy. She had been grateful that he had not paused to allow her time to actually respond. She wasn't convinced of his guilt, but neither was she so sure about his innocence.

He described his arrival to the police station as the most harrowing experience of his life.

"They took me to the police station where they formally interrogated me. It was unlike anything you have probably ever seen on television. I was humiliated. They put me in a holding cell where I spent the night. And if that wasn't enough, can you imagine how I felt when I had to call my ex-wife? And tell her why I was in jail? It was just so terribly horrible, never in my life…" He shook his head, and his sentence trailed off.

"Of course, I told them that I was completely willing to help them in any way possible in order to clear up a very obvious misunderstanding. But then, when I had finally gotten over my shock and I realized that they were seriously wanting to accuse me of murder, I contacted an attorney."

As he went on to recount his tale, Penelope had watched his face and eyes searching for any sign of deception. She'd stopped listening to him at that point. Somehow, she believed that if he were so gravely guilty, there would have to be some spill-over from his countenance. Did his left eye twitch? Was he speaking faster than usual? She knew it was naive, but she couldn't stop searching for some hint of dishonesty. Didn't they say that the eyes were the window to the soul? And if that was so, wouldn't she be able to tell if she were in the company of a liar or worse, a murderer?

Hadn't she herself been close to him at one time, very close? If she let her mind wander back dimly to the past, she could remember that he'd asked to take similar sexual liberties with her. Hadn't he done more than ask? The thought was far too painful to linger upon. She couldn't go there.

Because of her own dread about the past and the images that populated her mind, Penelope could barely hear what he'd said beyond the arrest and his actions leading up to it. She was fixated with the thought that she had overlooked some important detail in his character or personality that would have served as a premonition to all of this. What of his behavior while with her? Was she blind? How could she not have known this about him or recognized him for what he was?

But what was he? And what was she for having been intimate with him at one time? What did those long tucked away and increasingly painful memories ignited by his disclosure say about her?

The real challenge she now faced was in reconciling this new image of him as a murderer with the former image of him that did not resemble this. Admittedly, the way that she thought of him before all of this was somewhat blurred by the haze of admiration and wine, which characterized most of her time with him in the past. But even in the stark clarity of a morning after, she could not easily conjure up a wholly negative picture. She looked out of the plane's window and thought she saw a glimpse of something below the clouds that the jet's wake parted.

That he was out on bail for the crime of murder and had been asked to take a leave of absence from the university did not seem to accurately reflect the severity of the charge. His lawyer was presently engaged in preparing his defense, and his affluence and relative stature in the scientific community accounted for the privilege of being allowed to leave the country for the sabbatical. Indeed, because of a combination of factors including his status as a naturalized citizen with European roots, the fact that he was a highly decorated scientist, as well as a well-respected member of the university in that small town who was now being charged with rape and murder, his case had attained a certain degree of regional notoriety.

With some measure of difficulty, she realized that her reticence to look more closely at what had actually happened between the two of them years back stemmed from both fear and embarrassment. Penelope neither wanted, nor felt capable of looking close enough to see the similarities between what he was describing to her and the time that she'd spent with him. It would mean acknowledging her own familiarity with and status as "victim." But she would not and could not accept the label of victim of sexual assault.

She was embarrassed, and her embarrassment made it impossible for her to tell anyone. Admitting it to herself and coming to terms with her own experience was as far as she could go. It was where the act of peeling away the delicate, translucent skeins of memory ceased. It would go no further. She would tell no one.

Penelope also knew that her memories of past experiences with him that may have included the violations he was now being charged with were very likely related to the panic and its simmering anxiety that routinely visited. As she settled into this realization, she recognized that what had happened some years back, though covered with the protectiveness of the mind's fine dust of forgetfulness, instigated the waves of anxiety that descended upon her now.

She felt the plane begin its descent. Her thoughts turned to what the almost certain impending trial for him would entail. Because of her past (and now present) contact with him, it was likely that she would be subpoenaed. He said as much to her.

"You're probably going to be subpoenaed. I have listed you as a witness and given your contact information to my attorney. Will I be able to count on you to serve as a character witness for me?"

Penelope knew that if she agreed to this, she'd be asked to provide a deposition that would be followed by an actual appearance in court. Of course, he was hoping for her cooperation.

She was surprised by his request. It was as much of a surprise as the initial shock of learning of his arrest for rape and murder. Having put her on the spot at that moment, she was unable to agree to serve as a character witness for him, but neither was she able to deny him. At least not right then and there. The more she thought about it, the more her discomfort turned to anger. She realized now that his invitation to her had been calculating and above all strategic. He'd planned to convince her of his innocence and to extract a promise of support from her.

It was as if a light went on when she'd realized this. She'd looked him boldly in the eye and asked him if the only reason he'd invited her was to make sure she'd serve as a dutiful witness for him. He'd shifted his gaze and looked away from her.

"Don't be ridiculous! Of course, I didn't invite you for that reason. In fact, I hesitated to even tell you about any of this. If I had planned this, why do you think I would have waited until two days before your departure to tell you this? Don't you think that if that were the case I would have dropped all of this on you right away and then spent the next two weeks trying to convince you to do this for me?"

He had a point. Maybe she was being paranoid. But then when he turned to face her again, a facade of nonchalance seemed to cloak his countenance in much the same way that a guest's spilt coffee goes remarkably unnoticed. When that happens, both guest and host tactfully, if uncomfortably, practice the well-versed dance of apologies and hospitality. He was lying.

With that alone, she knew. She knew that the image he sought to project to her and others was as cultivated and affected as a painter's rendering of a beloved portrait. Not only was she assured of his complicity in the death of the young woman, but she was also fully aware that all the other things she'd accused him of in her mind's eye were as deliberate as they were irreconcilable. And while she did not scream the rage she felt building within, she resolutely and symbolically closed the door once held open for him.

Penelope didn't say any of this to him. Instead, she'd said that she'd have to think about it. She said she would have to decide whether she'd be able to help in his defense.

The day after their conversation was her last day in Austria, and not surprisingly, the air between the two had been tense. Late in the morning, she'd been able to arrange a ride with some of his neighbors who they had socialized with on a couple of occasions. She spent the better part of the day in the coffee shops in town, stopping in at a few museums and picking up some small souvenirs. While it may have seemed that she'd chosen to deny him the pleasure of her company on her last day there, it was more a matter of her not being able to be in his company. To put it lightly, she was sick of him.

As she prepared to leave the following morning for the airport, she said goodbye to him in the small lobby of the ample flat he rented in the town he now called home. She knew that as he watched her walk away into the cold Austrian morning air to the waiting car, he was wondering whether she would help him. She knew that he was calculating what he would do if she did not.

At that moment, Penelope felt the plane's engine shift gears and its wheels descend. Her heart weighed heavily. Outside the window, she saw the first hint of land and welcomed the sight. The flight was almost over, and she would soon be back on familiar ground. There she hoped to be better equipped to sort things out.

As the plane continued its descent, she felt the welcomed reprieve that reflected the weakening grip of the anxiety that had held her. She planned to actively engage in the mindful meditation techniques she'd learned when she finally got home. She would deliberately put off listening to her messages and checking email. She expected him to have contacted her by now, and she was not looking forward to hearing his voice. She needed time and distance from him.

Eventually, the plane landed. Her seatmate was now busy combing her hair and studying herself in a compact mirror. Penelope stole a few glimpses at her and realized that she was quite lovely even with the unkempt hair and spotty makeup. She wondered if she bore any resemblance to the woman who'd lost her life in his bed.

The pilot made another announcement.

"I'd like to take this time to welcome you to New York City. We know that when you fly, you have a choice, so we'd like to thank you for making the decision to fly with us. We appreciate your business and look forward to serving you again on your next flight."

Penelope looked out the window. She was several thousand miles away from Europe, from Austria, and from him. She shook her head to clear her mind. She knew that somehow she would get through this.

LIVE AND
LET LIVE IN
AMSTERDAM

She was disappointed at check in. What on the surface appeared to be a minor inconvenience somehow had the effect of multiplying its impact in unexpected and unpredictable ways. As she checked in for her return flight to the United States, Franny learned that she'd been assigned a window seat even though she'd specifically requested an aisle seat online. This was not just going to be an inconvenience. No, it was also going to be a real problem. She wanted, indeed she needed, the aisle seat because as a woman on the tall side of average, she needed the extra inches afforded by the aisle seat. And just as important, it also provided her the ability to get up from her seat and move about without the constraint of an unsympathetic seat mate.

The middle-aged woman at the ticket counter looked harrowed and none too willing to accommodate her. When Franny finally made it to the counter, the woman looked up at her.

"How can I help you?" she'd asked brusquely.

"I'm traveling to the US, my flight, 404, leaves at ten fifty-five. I tried checking in at the kiosk, but I didn't complete the process because it has me listed for a seat that is different from what I selected online previously. Can you please help me to select the right seat?"

"I'm very sorry, but you'll have to wait a moment. Our computers have gone down, and I am trying to reboot the system. You may choose to make yourself comfortable because I don't know how long it is going to take."

"Has something happened?" Franny asked, realizing immediately how absurd her question sounded. What she'd meant to ask was whether there was some sort of nefarious or otherwise intentional activity that accounted for the trouble with the computer system. But it hadn't quite come out that way. The airline agent probably thought her a tad dimwitted, which probably explained her relatively gentle response.

"It's hard to say at the moment. Right now, we are trying our best to get things running again. Of course, there will be an investigation later on, but for now, it's just manage as best we can." She then turned her attention back to the screen.

Franny put her purse down on top of her roller bag. The agent said she might as well make herself comfortable so that meant it could be a long wait.

She sighed. "Why is there always something like this to deal with?" Franny wondered.

Her thoughts turned back to her seat problem. She realized that as far as any one of the airline staff was concerned, whether she had a proper seat assignment paled in comparison to the importance of getting their system up and running again.

Nearly twenty minutes later, and following multiple conversations with several other ticket agents, the woman at the counter finally turned her attention back to Franny. Because she was now standing, Franny could see her name tag—it said "Greta." *She doesn't look anything like a Greta*, Franny thought. "Hmm…for that matter," she allowed her mind to wander, "what did she look like? Perhaps, an Antoinette? Or maybe a Julia?"

As she was considering this, she realized that Greta was saying something to her. She was apologizing. *How nice!* Franny thought. *And weirdly uncharacteristic*. Barring a plane crash or terrorist attack, these days, most airlines expected passengers to "tough it up" and "shake it off." No one, it seemed, had the patience to deal with a disgruntled or delayed passenger, and yet here was Greta apologizing. It was comforting in an odd sort of way.

"I am very sorry for the delay. As I explained, we are experiencing a technical problem with our system, and it appears to have made it impossible for us to get everyone checked in smoothly at this time."

Franny just now noticed her strong accent.

"Unfortunately," she continued, "in your case, I am not able to check you in at all. Your name appears as a *person of interest* within the global security system. Therefore, we are not able to check you in and allow you to board the flight until such time as airport security has evaluated you and determined that you do not pose a risk to the safety and security of our operation and the air travel of all other passengers. Do you understand? Would you please step aside?"

At that point, Greta waved her hand and gestured for Franny to step aside.

"What are you talking about? How can this be? I am, wait just a minute…do you know who I am? There, there…must be a misunderstanding! This is clearly a case of mistaken identity! I am an American and I am traveling home to the United States." She was close to tears at this point. But nothing in Greta's eyes or countenance conveyed understanding or sympathy.

What was this about? Was this because she was brown-skinned in a sea of white-skinned people? Rarely had Franny's mind ever considered this while in Amsterdam. Sure, it was explanation number one or at least two for the kinds of instances when she was treated quite poorly back home in the States. In fact, were anyone to ask about her comfort zone while stateside when compared to how she felt while overseas, she would have openly explained that her comfort overseas had a lot to do with her discomfort in being a woman of color at home in the States.

Franny began to panic and her anxiety escalated as soon as she registered the touch on her arm. It came from a stern-looking, armed, Dutch airport police officer. She turned her head, looking around desperately like captured prey, and for just a moment, she considered snatching her arm back and running away in the opposite direction as fast as she could go. But that fleeting thought did not take root. How far could she possibly get? Where would she go? They would catch her, of course.

Here was a problem she'd never imagined encountering in Europe. Of course, she'd heard about lists like the one her name was apparently on, but never in her wildest dreams had she ever imagined she would be on one of them. "What the hell!" she screamed out loud.

The police officer now spoke to her in perfectly accented English. Had he sensed the risk she might have posed during the millisecond that she considered fleeing? His grip on her arm was firm, and he spoke to her while making direct eye contact.

"Please come with me. Because your name was registered in the global security system as a person of interest, once you tried to check in, your ticket and boarding pass were flagged. I need that you should accompany us so that we may evaluate you. If we are able to tell that this is not correct and that this is not you but another person, we can let you go and you will be allowed to continue on your journey. However, you cannot go anywhere until we have completed our evaluation and analysis. Do you understand?"

Franny nodded her head indicating that she understood though she really didn't, and for the first time, she noticed that there were two other armed police officers who stood slightly to the side but who were obviously there to accompany the officer who was speaking to her, the one who had his hand on her arm. *Did these sorts of situations happen frequently?* she wondered. *And, did they typically escalate so that they warranted the presence and attention of three armed guards?*

Realizing that she had no choice if she ever hoped to get home, Franny reluctantly followed the police officers. As she walked along, she couldn't stop thinking about how she'd made a point of getting to the airport on time. Actually, she had arrived early! And now it seemed that it was all for nothing.

She was taken to a small room and interrogated by the three Dutch airport police officers. One of them, not the one who appeared to be the leader, enthusiastically rifled through her luggage. Was she imagining it or did he seem to take special satisfaction in doing this? As she watched, the whole time biting her tongue as he lifted each item, another officer asked a series of intrusive questions about whether she had had any intimate relationships with anyone in Amsterdam and whether she had used any illicit substances.

Franny answered no to both. From her perspective, it wasn't anyone else's business whether she'd slept with someone or indulged in one of Amsterdam's numerous "coffee shops." Both spheres were totally private, and she saw no reason why any of that would matter to the obvious glitch that accounted for her name being on Amsterdam's no-fly list.

Next, the three police officers had a brief conversation among themselves whispering in Dutch. After their conversation, they each turned to glare at her. Franny was then seated in a chair that faced the desk behind, which the three of them were seated. The interrogation continued.

"What have you been doing in Amsterdam?"

"Why did you come here and who have you been working with?"

Although they obviously knew how long she had stayed, they nevertheless asked her about this. They acknowledged that she was not under arrest and that she was not linked to anything unscrupulous or illegal, but the officer who seemed to have taken the lead among the others explained that it was important that they were assured that she was not associated with anyone who had broken the law or who had plans to do so.

"How long have you been in the Netherlands?"

"What was your role in the Gebrellasad Mohammad case?"

"What is your connection to the victim?"

"Do you have any relationship to any of the suspects?"

Franny was stunned at the direction the line of questioning had taken. So, this was about the hate crime, she realized.

The incident had happened within days of her arrival to Amsterdam. It was a horrible hate crime that involved an attack and a brutal murder. People who had previously given little thought to the actual quality of group relations in Amsterdam were not only concerned now, but it seemed that they could not stop talking about the matter. How horrible it was that it took something like this for people to wake up and realize that there were problems with the fabric of Amsterdam's diverse city. Every time she thought about the incident, it bothered her all over again.

A thirty-five-year-old Muslim man who happened to have been visiting relatives who lived in the city was brutally beaten and ultimately died from his wounds following a dispute and fight outside a popular bar in the city. The man was of Moroccan descent, and his assailants who were Dutch had been drinking heavily throughout the evening.

The few sober witnesses available were unable to pinpoint a cause for the fight, but all of them were in agreement that the man did nothing to instigate his attackers' ire. The case was unusual because of its brutality (they used pipes in addition to their fists) and because of the rarity of violent crime like that in Amsterdam.

Franny generally appreciated the typically low rate of violent crime in the city. During the six months she was there, she happily lowered her guard. It was a welcome relief from the normal state of affairs at home in New York City, which necessitated constant vigilance so that she was always looking over her shoulder, rarely ever going out alone at night and never really talking to strangers.

Learning that a brutal crime like this had happened in Amsterdam was considerably more unsettling than if it had happened at home in New York City. There, crimes like this happened more frequently than any law-abiding resident or visitor to the city wanted to think about.

"Look, I can explain," she said. "I am a researcher, and I study intergroup relationships in all of their complexity. I came to Amsterdam to collaborate with a colleague at the Universiteit van Amsterdam to work on a project. The first week I was here, the attack and murder of Mr. Mohammed occurred. As a sociologist, I was interested in understanding the factors that led the perpetrators to attack him as well as what led him to be in that location where the attack took place.

"So, to answer your question, I didn't personally know Mr. Mohammed or the men who attacked him. It is true that I tried to interview them, and I managed to speak briefly with the oldest of the two. Later on, I also spoke to a couple of journalists and members of the victim's family. That is the extent of my involvement," Franny explained.

Although it had taken them nearly an hour to figure out that she was who she said she was a thirty-plus something professionally employed, middle-class African American woman who had nothing to do with the commission of the hate crime, the officers must have been satisfied with her responses. They finally let her go. With about fifteen minutes to get to her gate before boarding began, Franny took off.

In the end, because of her status as a "person of interest" and because of the ordeal with the police, she was so happy to have satisfactorily answered all of their questions and be released that she'd said nothing about the undesirable seat assignment. She accepted the seat as her fate.

As she hurried to her gate, she thought about how she would make sure that she found some way to let the airline know that she was unhappy, though admittedly she was unsure about what it would accomplish. Were they likely to treat the next person appearing on the "persons of interest" fly list any nicer than they had treated her? Did she think the ticket agent would be more accommodating to the next person's request for a seat change? Were the police going to refrain from examining the lingerie of the next woman they detained? *Not likely*, she thought.

As she dashed through the airport, Franny happened to catch a quick glance of herself in a mirror she passed. She felt every bit as worn and weary as she appeared. She thought about the reactions to her physical appearance that she received from the Dutch. Although she was aware that she attracted attention from men and women alike who could often be caught sizing her up, she was most intrigued by the attention of the men.

None of the guidebooks she'd read had prepared her for their inviting looks often followed by a curious approach.

It was true. She clearly stood out. Her complexion was the color of coffee and as such, she stood out from the average native Dutch person. Her hair was thick and natural. It framed her face softly, and at times appeared wild and untamed. She noticed that it looked that way now as she flew through the airport to reach her gate.

It was her appearance that had attracted Lars to her and opened the door to their friendship. She had been standing on the ticket line for the Rijksmuseum, and the Dutchman had struck up a conversation with her.

"Allo, how are you?" he'd asked in heavily accented English. "What are you doing this evening? Where are you from?"

"I'm from the US, and I am waiting on line to see the Van Gough exhibit," she'd said. She was proud of herself for having pronounced the celebrated painter's name just as she'd heard natives do, with the guttural emphasis on the first letter of Gough. The man had said nothing, staring all the more intently at her. In response to the silence, she'd quickly followed up by telling him, "I am sorry, but I am not in a habit of giving out information about my plans to strangers."

And with that prompt, the man smiled and extended his hand to her introducing himself as

"Lars Ulia Kostep." He took her hand to his face and delicately kissed it. Franny was bowled over by his entreaty. She found this stranger to be both charming and handsome.

"I'm a social science researcher studying here with a colleague at the Universiteit van Amsterdam," she'd explained.

"Good to know you. As for myself, I am attending a close friend's engagement party later today, and I would love it if you would come with me. It is not far from here, and there is likely to be plenty of very good food and very nice people. I promise that you will enjoy the opportunity, and as a social teacher, yes, you should certainly find it to be of interest. You may even wish to do a study of it," Lars continued, obviously joking.

Although she found herself attracted to him, Franny's immediate instinct was to decline. This was not the kind of invitation she would have ever accepted at home in the US—an invitation from a complete stranger who approached her on the street! Yet here she was even thinking about it. Admittedly, she felt relatively safe and considerably more adventurous being abroad.

In the end, she'd accepted his invitation. That evening, for the first time in her life, she accompanied a virtual stranger to the home of another stranger. And so began her friendship with Lars. It was to be one of the defining experiences of her stay in Amsterdam.

That evening, after the party, when he had walked her to her flat, he'd kissed her. The new friendship began its course as a romantic relationship. Perhaps too prematurely, Franny and Lars began dating. It was exciting, but after about two weeks, the romance seemed to have fizzled, and with mutual agreement, the relationship evolved into a close and wonderful friendship.

Oddly enough, Franny felt closer to Lars when they were not romantically connected. He could always make her laugh no matter how she was feeling. She recalled one evening when they'd met for dinner at the small Indonesian restaurant around the corner from her flat.

"What do you want to eat?" the surly waitress had asked when they were seated. In a characteristically playful mood, Lars had asked, "What do you have?"

"What, can't you read? There's a menu right there in front of you. Are you expecting me to read the menu for you too?" the short-tempered waitress had asked him.

Whenever the waitress turned her back to him and spoke directly to Franny, Lars took it as his cue to mimic her. It was especially funny because not only did the waitress have a terribly poor disposition, but she also had a very large rear end, which somehow Lars conveyed as he mimicked her. Franny had had trouble holding back her laughter, which only seemed to further inspire Lars.

How satisfying it was to know that she'd accomplished her primary goal in coming to Amsterdam six months ago. She had successfully collected the data. Within six months, during which time she conducted fieldwork daily, she had amassed an impressive amount of data. She had both questionnaire, survey, and interview data from individuals who had agreed to participate. She had also managed to organize focus groups whose meetings she periodically attended during the six months she was there.

There was little doubt that when taken together, all of this information would be book-worthy. Franny planned to follow up with at least one of the publishers who had contacted her in the past year. Even on the off chance that an attractive book deal did not emerge, there were sure to be multiple journal articles, research presentations, and invited addresses. She was pleased with the way that things had fallen into place.

Now, even more than ever, she was convinced that the decision to collaborate with Sander and to visit his university in Amsterdam this past semester was a sound one. After all, she was an urban sociologist interested in cross-cultural differences and what better way to study this than to visit another country? Amsterdam, one of the most libertarian cities in the world, boasted considerable ethnic diversity, and as such served as a unique case study for human behavior and social relationships.

Her focus was on intergroup conflict with special attention to religious hate crimes. She'd come there to learn more about the deepening chasm in relations between the city's Dutch and Arab populations. She'd prepared accordingly and expected to interview people about their attitudes and the quality of their interactions with those from other ethnic groups, but what she didn't expect was to find herself engaged in this work in the immediate wake of a brutal hate crime that was committed within days of her arrival. This is what she planned to emphasize to the dean and any one of the members of the promotion committee who might choose to press her for details about her prolonged absence.

After hugging her briefly as he said goodbye, Sander had whispered the parting words "Een ezel schoppen" into Franny's ear. Knowing that her Dutch was unreliable at best, he'd quickly followed up with the translation in heavily accented English: "Kick some ass!" When she'd looked at him quizzically, he said, "You know, as I do that, they will give you a hard time because of the extension you took. You must be sure to show them just how important it was."

In nodding her head yes, she had feigned agreement. But at the same time, she believed that Sander, who was himself a tenured member of the Universiteit van Amsterdam faculty, was unnecessarily anxious about her status because the European academic system and its universities operated more rigidly. Of course, it was not his intent to make her worry about her job security and the upcoming promotion decision. But he'd succeeded in making her that much more anxious.

She told him as much, saying, "Sander, I will be fine, you are making me anxious. Our system is different, and I followed all of the steps in requesting and being granted the extension. So, no worries, okay?"

Although Franny firmly believed that tenure and a highly productive sabbatical protected her from the discomfort of an inquisition she might very well face upon return, she also recognized that promotion to full professor often involved a highly politicized decision-making process by a body of one's peers who didn't always see eye to eye.

Her colleagues at the university back home knew that she had come to The Netherlands to study human behavior in the unique context of the city of Amsterdam. Franny believed that there were similarities as well as differences in the quality of ethnic relations there with other affluent and diverse modern cities.

When people asked her about what she studied as an urban sociologist, she liked to describe human interactions in diverse urban environments. Recently, when a reporter asked her a question about her research, she'd said, "Like a trick mirror at the funhouse in a traveling carnival, reality seems to happen in unexpected and sometimes ghoulish ways. First, you observe something happening and then when you look a second later, it appears somehow different, slightly off with each subsequent rendering of the event. As a student of human behavior, I am especially interested in whether those renderings differ from one another, and whether they do so as a function of the unique experience and perspective of a person watching an event unfold."

It was not clear that the reporter actually understood that description, but more astute observers and thinkers usually did.

That a hate crime had occurred in Amsterdam was less surprising to Franny than to many of the people who called Amsterdam home. When others expressed shock and seemed to be blindsided by what had occurred, Franny explained that "the reality of human interaction did not automatically include the ability to get along." She remembered explaining as much to the older woman who occupied the flat above her own.

"Most people throughout the world, no matter their education or experience on the world stage, can personally recount an instance in which people raised fists [or worse] against others because of some perceived difference real or contrived. History is full of examples of people who fought their most geographically proximate and culturally similar neighbors, who waged war in distant lands, imprisoned and enslaved those who had assisted and even saved them, and in the darkest moments, raped and murdered those with different beliefs."

Franny didn't know what to make of her neighbor's reaction. She had said nothing in response to her "lecture." She had simply turned and walked away. Franny assumed that she had unintentionally offended her. After that exchange, her neighbor never again dropped by to chat.

Franny hoped to return to Amsterdam the following year, but she knew that a year away would seem like forever. Living there these past six months had been all that she'd hoped for and more; quite a bit more. Not only had her work progressed as a result of her professional collaboration with Sander, but she also freely acknowledged that her life was richer and fuller because of the experience of having been there for those six months. In a somewhat calculating manner, she reasoned that if things (and by this, she meant things beyond the scope of their current research arrangement) failed to progress, there would be other connections she would always have to the city she was now leaving.

There was Roxy, the "ex-pat" American who could be found on any given afternoon in any one of the hundreds of colorful "coffee shops," which peppered the city. Although she herself did not typically indulge in the various blends of cannabis available, she claimed to enjoy the company of her most creative muse while there. Roxy was a self-described "artiste" traveling toward what most regarded as a perpetual quest for something better, more ephemeral, and aesthetic. Her life had been marred by tragedy, and she shared this early within moments of introduction with just about anyone she met. "I struggle with the reality of the past," she'd tell a person off the bat. "I wasn't very lucky. I was married at one time, and something horrible befell my marriage. My husband was accused of having sex with adolescent boys who were under the age of fifteen, and there were police and criminal charges involved. They arrested him. One night, following his arraignment, when it was late and he was very alone, he hung himself in his prison cell."

Roxy said she never knew whether he had really done everything he was accused of, but at least once when she and Franny were alone, she admitted having doubts about his innocence.

Finally, Franny made it to her gate. She would even have time to spare. An announcement said that boarding was delayed and would begin in twenty minutes. Out of breath, she sat down heavily in one of the few remaining empty seats in a crowded row with a view of the large TV and the window looking out onto the tarmac. She sighed heavily and absentmindedly watched a breaking BBC news report, as she thought more about the "semester abroad" experience. It was ironic that she had come to think of it in this way given that when she actually was a college student (what seemed like a million years ago!), she'd never seriously considered traveling to a foreign country to study. If only she had, she thought wistfully.

From the moment Franny arrived at Amsterdam's Schiphol Airport some six months ago, she had been amazed by the people. They were so diverse! There were people of every shade and nationality. She'd heard at least five different languages in the thirty minutes it had taken her to reclaim her luggage, clear customs, and purchase her ticket for the airport train heading to Centraal Station where Sander had been awaiting her.

Franny knew that these were exactly the types of observations that a first-time foreign visitor to her native city of New York might have had, and although she was not at all naive in her awareness of the diversity of the world's populace, she nevertheless couldn't help noticing and consciously appreciating the many different types of people she saw within hours of arriving to Amsterdam. When she approached one young man in order to ask for directions, she was taken aback. She'd assumed (however incorrectly) that because he resembled any other "White" guy she knew at home, he would not only be approachable, but he would also be able to communicate with her in English, even if it was accented. Wrong! Not only wasn't he helpful, but he also apparently spoke little if any English. "Excuse me, can you please tell me if this is the right platform for the train to Centraal Station?" Franny had asked him. Brusquely, he'd said, "Ik spreek geen Engels. Er zijn kaarten om u aanwijzingen te vertellen."* With that, he'd rushed off in the opposite direction.

Later, on board the packed train heading into the city, though she feigned indifference, she couldn't help noticing three young, brown-complexioned men standing across from her. They were speak-

---

* I do not speak English. There are maps to tell you directions.

ing animatedly with raised voices. In some places of America, their presence alone would have been enough to engender fear among casual observers and nearby bystanders. The fact that they were engaged in a lively conversation would have only exacerbated the stereotypic, racial suspicions White people typically had about Black people in the US. But here, it was different—no one else really seemed to notice them. For her part, although she noticed them and periodically stole discreet glances at them, she could not understand what they were saying. They were speaking Dutch. Their roots to the Dutch colony known as Suriname in South America were betrayed by the reddish-brown complexions and their slightly different pronunciation of Dutch.

Back to the present, Franny glanced at the woman seated next to her in the waiting area who appeared to be knitting or maybe it was crocheting. She couldn't tell. She'd never taken the time to learn any of the advanced stitching techniques. She stretched her legs and leaned back in her seat. It was not the most comfortable of seats. She leaned back in the chair and allowed her mind to linger on those first days in Amsterdam.

On that first day leaving the airport, she gazed out the train window. The ride through the countryside from the airport to the city center had not been particularly remarkable. Aside from the unique way that the windmills on hills dotted the open spaces like billboards on some American highway, there really wasn't much to see during the ride into the "downtown" setting of this sophisticated city. Surely, this first glimpse of the city she planned to call home, however temporarily, belied its excitement within.

Despite the fact that she was a professor and researcher, she longed for excitement. Most people thought that professors were eggheads, nerds, and geeks. Not her. Like a dutiful tourist, she had begun reading the guidebooks very early on, and even before she received confirmation that her request for the leave of absence had been approved, she had made several lists of "must-see" and "must-do" activities. And at least one of those activities included visiting a "coffee shop."

In the time during which she began counting the days to her departure, she often found herself cataloging any and all things related to Amsterdam. She periodically made changes to her mental lists and then created new ones. The final list of places, which she had decided on, included such well-known sites as Koninklijk Paleis (the Royal Palace), Nieuwe Kerk (the "New" Church), Bloemenmarkt (the flower market), and of course, Rosse Buurt (the red-light district).

She had not been disappointed. At the very first party she'd accompanied Lars to, she'd met the host of the party—a young woman of mixed European and African ethnicity, who welcomed her warmly. She and the woman spoke at length in the flat's kitchen. "How is it that you know Lars?" she'd asked Franny.

There were about twenty people there when they arrived to the party, which she learned was meant to congratulate a couple on their engagement, though she never did meet the guests of honor.

"We met at the Rijksmuseum," Franny answered. At that moment, the thought occurred to her that the host may have had more than a passing interest in her newfound friendship with Lars.

"How nice," she'd responded. "But *how* did you meet? I understand you met at the museum, but did you bang into each other, did someone introduce you, how did you come to know one another? You said you just arrived in Amsterdam last week."

She was right! The host did have more than a passing interest, and when Franny thought about it, she realized that she too was distinguished from what native Dutch people looked like. Her hair, like Franny's, was curly and full, and although she was lighter than Franny, her complexion revealed its African influences. Franny thought her lovely, and although she planned to respond to the host, they were interrupted. It was Lars, he'd returned at just that moment to fetch her.

"Come now! What are you doing all of this time in here? You must come out of the kitchen. I want you to get a full sense of the party, and there are others I would like for you to meet."

She and the party's host had nodded to one another as if to acknowledge their shared understanding of the other's position. Franny as a "new interest" and the host as a "former one." She'd never said a word of the exchange to Lars.

Over time, as she got to know Lars better, she engaged in frequent and vociferous debates with him. To his credit, Lars freely acknowledged the inconsistencies in Dutch society.

"Yes, it is true on the one hand, we Dutch people are very proud of our touted progressiveness, our modernity, and tolerance," he'd said one evening.

"It is quite evident in our adherence to the 'live and let live' sentiment that we espouse so frequently. It is this which serves as the justification for how we can have so many different social groups with different identities who have historically always been ensured their own freedom. Of course, to some degree, it requires that these different social groups have a desire to maintain a separateness in our society. And the different social groups don't often interact with one another. That's how it is that we are all able to proceed freely of our own accord without interference from others."

While he'd said this so articulately, he also acknowledged, "Now, because of demographic changes that began when we (here, he meant the Dutch) invited immigrant laborers from Morocco and Turkey to work in our industries, there are well-defined non-Western social groups (here, he'd meant the Middle Eastern and Arab immigrants) who were never fully integrated into Dutch society. It is problematic. Anti-Arab and anti-Muslim feelings are evident in our tolerant society because of the expanding numbers of Arab immigrants and because everyone is sensitive to the September eleventh events in the US."

And so thanks to that live and let live mentality, few people actually interacted with one another across the well-defined boundaries that dictated their ethnic and economic status and positions. Franny and Lars agreed that the future situation in Amsterdam would be troubled by this unique constellation of variables.

When she found herself disagreeing with him, it tended to be over the national government's approach to dealing with the growing hostility between the country's native Dutch and immigrant populations. Lars advocated a "one size fits all" approach, but Franny knew from the failures of her own country that that approach rarely worked. She always argued for an alternative.

"This is not a reasonable solution. No! An approach like this will not result in any one side walking away satisfied. Not only won't anyone walk away satisfied, but the real question is just how alienated from the government, from society, and from one another they are going to feel!"

Franny knew that when there was conflict arising from two (or more) groups with seemingly incompatible agendas, it was helpful to have a third party to engage each group on their own terms. When the third party was fully aware of the distinctive cultural and historical context in which they existed, the mediation was more likely to be successful.

She didn't mind the debates that she had with Lars as much as someone else might have because she believed they contributed to her own mental agility. She had come to Amsterdam to conduct research and collect data on the topic of group conflict. Discussions about the increasing divide between Amsterdam's Dutch and Muslim populations fell squarely within the parameters of that research.

They were calling her flight. *Finally!* she thought. She gathered up her belongings as the woman seated next to her packed up her knitting instruments. A red ball of yarn fell off her lap and rolled across the floor. Franny caught it and handed it to the woman, who murmured "dankjewel" followed by a heavily accented "thanks."

As the flight attendants began announcing the boarding process and calling for people assigned to specific seats, Franny noticed the heightened energy that had settled upon the growing crowd of travelers waiting to board her flight. It was always like this. People began inching their way to the gate and jet way well before their seats had been called. When her seat was called, she handed her boarding pass to the flight attendant and began the walk down the jet way.

After finding her seat and securing the roller bag in the overhead compartment above her seat, she sat down next to the window. A tall man wearing wireless headphones stopped at her row, looked at the seat number, and then glanced at her. He removed his jacket and stashed a briefcase in the same overhead compartment she had used. He sat down, nodded after making eye contact briefly with her, and then he adjusted his seat and seat belt. She handed him the in-flight blanket that had been left in his chair. After thanking her for this, he adjusted his cellphone and closed his eyes. She turned her attention back to the window beside her seat and unconsciously watched the activity underway on the tarmac.

The details of the hate crime still haunted her. The victim was dead, and his attackers were imprisoned and awaiting trial. And the Moroccan community had been deeply wounded. While Franny knew it was impossible not to sympathize with the man's family who mourned his death, she also knew that the greatest casualty of the murder was the trust and goodwill that had existed among the city's Moroccan immigrants for their Dutch neighbors.

Hate crimes had a way of completely destroying what semblance of civility existed in a community. The effect of this sort of crime would be felt long after its occurrence and well beyond its geographic proximity. Herein lay the power of hate crimes. It wasn't just the Moroccan man and his family that had been harmed, but it was everyone else who was Moroccan that was irrefutably harmed.

She shook her head as she considered this. Fear follows hate crimes. Apart from the underlying antipathy any one incident exposed, it was the reverberating effect of fear and anxiety throughout society to unknown strangers that proved to be most caustic. Any Moroccan any place in the world who learned of this tragedy could, by virtue of their shared identity, put themselves in the victim's shoes and conceivably see themselves as a similar victim. Moreover, anyone anywhere upon hearing of this would be forced to confront and deal with the xenophobia that likely fueled the young Dutchmen's assault against the victim, Mr. Mohammed.

In addition to forcing widespread conversations about the quality of relations between Dutch and Arab residents of Amsterdam, this event also had the effect of enjoining national conversations about access and the availability of alcohol and other substances given that the victim's attackers were quite young and had been drinking heavily throughout the evening.

She remembered being out at night with Lars on several occasions and being surprised by how many young people she saw who were drinking in bars.

"Amsterdam is extremely liberal, maybe even a little insane," she'd remarked. "Those kids can't be more than twelve or thirteen and they are at the bar drinking!"

Lars had said, "No, they probably just look young. They have to be at least sixteen to drink beer and wine in a bar in Amsterdam. If they want to drink liquor and spirits, they will have to prove that they are eighteen."

Maybe the kids at the bar were of the legal age to buy drinks, but they sure looked a lot younger than Franny was used to seeing in the US.

As tragic as the incident was, she knew that its timing was eerily fortuitous. It provided a rich case study for in-depth analysis and inclusion in her research. She had needed to speak directly with the victim's family as well as his murderers. The conversations she had had were hard and painful though incredibly informative.

She was unsuccessful at first in her attempts to reach out to the family of the man who had been killed. Eventually, Lars helped her find them after the media had released enough information about the victim to identify the family members he had been visiting in Amsterdam. She'd contacted the victim's family repeatedly, and after leaving several messages, she finally made contact with a member of his family who was willing to talk with her.

"Hello, I am calling to say that I am very sorry about your family's recent loss. I am a researcher studying the matter of cultural relations in Amsterdam, and I think what has happened reflects problems in the society. Is there someone in the family who I can talk to about what has happened?"

Franny held her breath as she waited to hear the person on the other end's response, "I cannot talk to you about that, but maybe my uncle can. Hold on please."

It had sounded like a young woman or an older teenaged girl who'd initially answered the phone.

Franny held the line for what seemed like several minutes. The young woman eventually passed the phone to someone. A man's voice came on the line.

"Hello, I am Khalil Mohammed. Who is this that is calling about my brother?"

"Hello, sir, I am sorry for your loss." Franny identified herself by name and explained her reason for calling after expressing her regrets about his death.

"My name is Frances Winter. I am a researcher from the US, working together with a colleague at the Universiteit van Amsterdam. I was hoping to speak with you about the circumstances surrounding your brother's death."

"My brother's death? You mean his murder, right?"

"Yes, of course, sir. I know that he was murdered."

"Then what else do you know? Because the police don't seem to be sure of anything including the fact that those animals in jail killed my bother. Are you with the police?"

She assured him that she was not, and somehow the two remained on the line speaking for nearly two hours that first time. The conversation they had involved her sympathizing with the grief-stricken man, but it also included her questions about the victim's death.

"Why do you think that those men killed your brother?" Franny had eventually asked.

"There is good and evil in the world. My brother encountered evil that night and it killed him," said Khalil.

Later in the conversation, Franny had asked, "How are you and your family members managing to cope with this tragedy?"

"One day at a time."

She eventually got around to asking him, "Are there any changes in your perceptions of the Dutch people and the city of Amsterdam given everything that has occurred?"

As Franny expected, the question opened a watershed of emotion. Khalil railed against the anti-Muslim sentiment that he believed motivated his brother's killers.

When she hung up the phone with him that first time, she was emotionally drained. She'd learned far more about what had happened to Mr. Mohammed and the motives that gave rise to his attack than she had expected. It was far more than had been released by the police or discussed in the media.

She'd begun that first conversation with Khalil, the victim's brother, hoping to hear about his attributions for the assault. These were the standard kinds of questions she typically asked people, and they corresponded neatly to her questionnaire and survey instruments on which the bulk of her study's data was based. But unexpectedly, what she had also come away with was an entirely different understanding and awareness of a distinctly different set of motives for the crime that did not map neatly onto her survey instruments. The media and the public discourse surrounding Mr. Mohammed's assault and murder had emphasized the way that the Arabs (who were primarily Muslim) and the Dutch were increasingly at odds with one another. There were ongoing discussions in public forums about how communication between the two communities had devolved.

These conversations had an alarmist quality to them and more often than not they implied that increasing waves of immigration (of Arabs and those from Middle Eastern countries) was in part to blame. On more than a few occasions, there was even pointed reference to the 9/11 terrorist assaults in the US as some commentator, who in those cases tended to not only be opposed to immigration but was also downright hostile to Arabs, insinuated some connection between 9/11 and the impending conquest of Dutch civilization by Islam.

These conversations riled her, and she generally tuned them out or shut off the television or other news source when they aired.

"You are so vulnerable to news that disagrees with your principles," Lars had said to her. He was fond of teasing her about the ease with which she tuned out news she found disagreeable.

"How can you be a social scientist, who must be objective, when you do this?" he'd asked.

He implied that this quality made her a less than objective observer and researcher. He may have been right, but to her, it reflected her humanity, and this was a badge she happily wore.

Nevertheless, she had accepted the facts disclosed in the media and had assumed that it was extreme anti-Arab, anti-Muslim sentiment buoyed by alcohol that had driven the young Dutch men to assault and murder Mr. Mohammed. But what she learned from Khalil was quite different and implied a breach from the generally accepted narrative of

anti-Arab sentiment that had become all too familiar. Indeed, what she'd learned seriously called into
question the legitimacy of Dutch nationalistic pride
in its own tolerance.

Since World War II, Dutch society had been
viewed as a tolerant one. Yet, in the last decade or
so, the Netherlands was forced to modify that image
somewhat because of recurrent instances of ethnic
hostility that had been well-documented. There were
still many people who proudly boasted an image of
tolerance in other domains. Prostitution was legal,
marijuana was available in small quantities throughout Amsterdam's "coffee shops," and gay rights were
recognized by the government. People generally reasoned that things were certainly no worse off in the
Netherlands because of the one problem with ethnic
hostility; other countries weren't even that far along!

Although the public and Dutch majority were
willing to acknowledge that "Islamophobia" and
anti-Arab sentiment was responsible for the murder
of Mr. Mohammed, there was a subtle albeit unspoken sense in which Dutch culpability seemed to be
justified or at the very least explained by reference
to the rising numbers of Arab immigrants and their
unwillingness to relinquish certain highly visible
vestiges of their religious identity. So, while everyone agreed that it was a terrible crime that had been
committed, they did so with a nod to the problem of
immigration.

She resented this way of thinking because it
seemed to fix the blame for the murder on the very

group of people who had been victimized and not on the problem of Dutch animus for their Muslim neighbors. This, it seemed to Franny, was the most obvious offender. Yet it was only after talking at length with Khalil that she learned that there was another motive his brother's killers likely harbored that was also responsible for his death.

"My brother, I loved him very much. He went away to the UK when he was young because he couldn't deal with things here," Khalil said.

"What do you mean? What kinds of things?" Franny asked.

"He, he was not sure how much he wanted to get married, to be with the woman that he was supposed to be with. Our family had already agreed that he would marry a daughter of our parents' best friends."

"So, he did not agree with the arranged marriage and was opposed to it?"

"Well, yes and no. He was opposed to the arranged marriage, but he also was not certain that he even wanted to marry, to be with a woman, if you understand my point. And that would have destroyed my mother and father," Khalil explained.

Franny inferred from Khalil's remarks that his brother had long struggled with his sexuality, and that he had not had an easy time growing up in their family. He had moved to London when he was just twenty-two, and with that, the matter of his sexual identity and behavior was sufficiently cloaked from the family. He came to visit once a year, always alone, and during each visit, he patiently endured his mother's frequent requests for grandchildren.

On the night he was murdered, he'd left the house to get out for a bit on his own. He did not drink alcohol and so he likely wound up at the bar where he was attacked because he found something about the place especially appealing. Whether it was the food menu displayed outside on the sidewalk or a glance at the clientele inside, Mr. Mohammed made the decision to enter the bar.

Khalil did not contest the police report, nor was he willing to publicly articulate the motives that he suspected accounted in part for the perpetrators' assault. Over time, he'd shared this discreetly and reluctantly with Franny, and she in turn felt burdened by the disclosure. Consequently, she wrestled with what she would do with this information.

If Mr. Mohammed was attacked and killed because of anti-gay bigotry, the Dutch reputation for tolerance was even more compromised. This was extremely problematic for a society that routinely prided itself on ensuring rights for sexual minorities. Indeed, for many people in Dutch society, it was the national stance relative to gay and lesbian concerns that truly demonstrated their tolerance. The fact that there existed ambivalence and downright hostility toward ethnic groups was an entirely different matter altogether and did little to detract from their self-endearing image of tolerance.

After talking with Khalil, she reached out to the perpetrators. Of the three, only one was older than eighteen, and so she was only allowed to contact him. He was incarcerated and awaiting trial, but he agreed to talk with her on the condition that his attorney was permitted to read anything that she wrote or disclosed to the public beyond research reports.

Franny conducted the interview with the young man called "Emerens" in person in the area reserved for visitations with prisoners.

"Hello, thank you for agreeing to speak with me. I am a researcher from the US working with a colleague at the Universiteit van Amsterdam," she began.

Franny was initially struck by the young man's appearance. He was very tall, which she noticed as he was escorted into the room with the prison guard. Once seated at the small, round table designated as their assigned interview space, he looked directly at her. He was blond and had sparkling blue eyes. Franny thought "Nazi" then deliberately extinguished the thought from her mind. Emerens was formidably built though unexpectedly soft-spoken. He appeared intelligent as well as remorseful.

"Could you please describe for me the circumstances leading up to the assault?" Franny asked.

"Yes, sure, well, I don't remember a whole lot about that evening," he'd said.

"I had been drinking a lot that night. I mean a lot. I can say that I was at a bar, but can I be one hundred percent certain it was the bar that they are accusing me of being at? No, I cannot, I am sorry but I cannot."

"It is true I was in a fight that night. I know I was, but I would not have murdered anyone, and I am not responsible for that Arab's death. You must understand that they are trying to accuse me of something I did not do," Emerens implored.

Franny understood from the first few moments of her conversation with this young man that he was not willing to take responsibility for consciously assaulting and murdering Mr. Mohammed. Although he claimed to remember that at some point that evening, one of his friends said that some Arab guy had insulted him, he insisted that he did not remember anything more than fighting to avenge his friend.

"I do remember that my friend 'Puck' went out to smoke a cigarette that night. When he came back, he said he had some trouble outside. He said someone had insulted him."

"Really, what did they say to him?" Franny asked.

"I, I can't remember exactly, but it must have been pretty bad because we were all upset and willing to fight for him," said Emerens.

He couldn't remember what the insult was, but apparently, it was enough to have gotten him and his friends sufficiently roused to go looking for the person.

"I know I got punched, and I had to defend myself so I punched back," he'd said.

Franny heard nothing in the young man's description of events that led up to Mr. Mohammed's death that included any reference to him as a gay man. Nor had she heard anything about the use of a pipe in the fight. Was this because he was lying? She had no way of knowing for sure, but she suspected that it was. There were provisions in a number of western European countries' legal systems that could add stiffer penalties when crimes were motivated by bias. She was pretty certain that the penalties associated with the assault and murder of Mr. Mohammed would likely be enhanced if it were proven that biased sentiment had given rise to it.

Franny was inclined to believe that Mr. Mohammed had made an easy mark because he stood out from most of the other patrons in the bar who happened to be Dutch. And he may well have said something to one of the young men that could have been construed quite negatively by a person who was either racist or homophobic. The truth concerning the actual course of events would probably remain a mystery. The other two offenders would be tried as youth, and Emerens was not motivated to claim bias for his or their behavior.

In the end, she opted to include nearly all the information she'd obtained in her research report and data file, even that which did not jibe with the public narratives about the incident. She anonymized the information so there was no disclosure of the actual names of any of the people involved, but of course she knew that anyone with the right insights and analytic tools could track down the names of the victim and perpetrators in this incident.

She yawned and stretched as much as she could in the confined space of her window seat. There were only two other people with whom she had shared all the details of the case including the names of the victim and his perpetrators. She had shared these details with Sander and Lars only, because they were the only people she trusted to maintain her confidence. Sander would because he was her collaborator on the larger project that was associated with this case, and Lars, well, Lars was a special friend who she knew cared a great deal about her.

Her mind shifted as she thought about the fact that Lars, perhaps more than anyone else, would be waiting for her return. Although their decision to be friends rather than intimates was mutual, at times it seemed they both struggled with it. It hit her most when they were out together in the company of other friends. She'd catch a glimpse of him as others saw him, and she would find herself bewildered by the decision to be just friends. He was most attractive to her at those times. She supposed that it was this unique quality of his that had struck her that first day he'd approached her as she waited to purchase her ticket to the Rijksmuseum. And it also probably explained what accounted for the enduring interests of the woman who had hosted the party he'd taken her to that very first day.

The captain had just announced preparations for takeoff, and the jet began backing away from the jet way. She glanced at her watch. It would be about eight hours before she was home. She intended to use the time to catch up on some much needed sleep. Almost every person she'd met and befriended while living in Amsterdam was at the party the night before. There was music, lots to drink, and plenty of food. She drank quite a few glasses of champagne, though she could not say what she was really celebrating. She was after all sad to be leaving. Sometime around midnight, before it got too late, Sander had turned the music down and made a toast. Everyone raised their glasses to her. She felt quite special and in that moment vowed to return. She would be back. She pulled the window shade down and adjusted a pillow behind her head. She closed her eyes and willed herself to sleep.

TOKYO'S LONG-DISTANCE AMERICAN MARRIAGE

They arrived to Japan aboard United Airlines flight 803 from Washington DC's Dulles Airport. It was three of them. Kiera Jameson traveled with her young son and husband. Although they each bore the burden of the long journey differently, they were all exhausted. After clearing customs and retrieving their many bags, they passed one final check-in window presumably for immigration since it was there that they relinquished the form that they were asked to complete in flight. Between the fatigue and the language barrier (few of the airport personnel spoke English), it was hard to know what they were being asked.

Eventually, outside the airport, they boarded a large comfortable air-conditioned bus for Tokyo. She was prepared for the more than hour-long ride, having done the trip several months earlier during a brief visit before committing to accept the assignment. Nevertheless, she was not looking forward to this last grueling leg of the now sixteen-hour journey.

An hour later, when at last they arrived at their stop in the Akasaka area of the Minato ward of Tokyo, they each seemed to have been blessed with a second wind. They needed it for the short but uphill walk to the four-bedroom Western style apartment they would call home.

They settled in.

It was a new life. Indeed, a very different life from the one they'd left behind at home. Perhaps more importantly, it was different from the one they had envisioned, though recognition of this would only come later, much later.

Stateside, they took for granted the familiar creature comforts that were routine and in excess. Things like satellite English-speaking TV, sweet satisfying cereals, and traveling by personal vehicle to most places were typical at home in DC but a bit harder to come by in Tokyo. It was at first most challenging for her son who had a hard time understanding that the differences between his new life and home were a result of the new country and cultural context in which he had landed. Eventually, with school, sports activities (he'd acquired a liking for and expertise in judo), and playdates with new friends, he had adjusted with remarkable ease. This was reflected in his offhand comments about the casual observations he made almost daily.

She recalled the time while watching a traffic stop by security guards from the back seat of their car, he had commented on the guards' respectful behavior. The guards had stopped traffic while an oversized truck backed into the busy street, and when the truck righted itself and continued down the road, the security guards collectively turned to the cars they'd detained and bowed. It was at this point that her son, a small boy who had just turned six at that point, remarked with grave solemnity, "They are very respectful in Japan."

"Yes, honey, they are. It's a noticeable difference from the way things are at home in the US."

Satisfied with having made that observation, his attention drifted elsewhere. As the guards completed their action and waved traffic along, she thought more about what he'd said. Keira wondered if he even had a frame of reference against which to compare the Japanese. Did he even remember the absence of that kind of respect in America?

No, she thought. *That couldn't be possible.* He was probably making an observation based solely on his experience in Japan, and for that reason, it did not represent an indictment of his American compatriots. Nevertheless, she smiled as much because of the maternal pride she felt in thinking about her son's insights as for the fact that she genuinely appreciated this aspect of Japanese society.

It was true. Respect was a quality that seemed embedded within the very fabric of the society. It was manifested most frequently in the politeness with which most Japanese engaged others. As a foreigner, that is, a gaijin, who was immediately recognized as such, she was treated kindly. It was with more kindness than she likely deserved given that she sometimes found herself bordering on rudeness because she was exasperated by some unlucky Japanese person's inability to understand her. The communication broke down at these times when they could not interpret her strange pronunciation of Japanese words peppered with liberal amounts of English that was in turn accompanied by pantomimed gestures. She typically lost her patience at those times because she was certain that she was pronouncing the word correctly, and the smiling Japanese person with whom she was interacting hadn't a clue about what it was that she was actually trying to say.

With time, Keira realized that because she was not Japanese, most Japanese that she encountered did not expect her to speak Japanese. When she did, even when she actually managed to pronounce the words correctly, it seemed that their anticipation of her not speaking Japanese made it impossible for them to actually comprehend what is was that she was saying. Perhaps that was what riled her the most at times.

She considered it remarkable that despite all of this, including the times when she did mispronounce and miscommunicate as well as all the social transgressions that she had unwittingly committed, she had always been treated politely and respectfully.

She had a close friend who was living in Beijing at the time, and it seemed that only she could fully understand the complexity of being a "gaijin" in Tokyo and relocating to Asia. Her friend was there to open the China-based office of a large US conglomerate. Although she had been in Beijing for nearly a year, she still frequently found herself reeling with culture shock. The cultural differences were profound, and unlike Japan, there was no comparable cultural norm of respect in Chinese society.

The two had spoken by Skype recently. Keira had initiated the call and started off by describing her own challenges in living in Japan.

"It is not just the challenge of living outside of my comfort zone that makes the differences between Japan and the US so clear," said Keira.

"Oddly enough, it is also the really positive attributes of Japan, like the deference and respect in almost every customer service exchange. These are daily reminders of my distance from home. Here, I am more than five thousand miles from my familiar and more than twelve hours separate me from almost everyone that I know and love."

Her friend understood and said, "I know, I know exactly what you are saying, though Beijing is definitely different from Japan. Sometimes, I think about how it is that my 'right now' is almost exactly opposite from the time at home. When they are getting out of bed in the morning in NY, here I am finishing up dinner, washing dishes, and getting ready to go to bed."

It took a lot of getting used to for Keira. Whenever she had to make a business call to the US, she'd set her alarm clock for 4:00 a.m. in order to bolster her chances of communicating with anyone while they were still at work in their offices and not rushing out of the door. There were also those unpredictable meetings her employer scheduled that she was obligated to participate in which happened to crop up from time to time. She hated those times when a work-related meeting or teleconference had been scheduled without regard to the time difference. It was not unheard of for her to join a teleconference or videoconference (what she dreaded most) at 1:00 a.m.

She reminded herself that these were simply the logistics required of making a life here in Japan, so far away from the States. After a year of doing this, it had become routine. If you wanted to live abroad and continue to work for a US-based company or for the US government, this was the cost. It was the same for all the other Americans she knew who worked in Japan and were employed either as US federal employees or as employees of private American corporations. The person who made the decision to live abroad had made the decision to live slightly out of the comfort zone that was typical for the average American. Getting up at midnight to prepare for a business call was a part of that territory.

What had not become routine and would likely be something with which she continued to wrestle were the entirely different scents and smells that she regularly encountered on city streets, in crowded subway cars, and upon entering any one of taxi cabs she regularly took in Tokyo. It wasn't that they were always malodorous. No, sometimes the scents that wafted from the various *yakitoris* and *izakayas* she passed daily tempted any dietary inhibitions she may have harbored against eating such foods as fish eggs or fried chicken cartilage. Scents like these hinted of something delicious that yielded a strong anticipation for satisfying and succulent tastes. Whether she sampled the food or not, she enjoyed these scents while still acknowledging her unfamiliarity with them.

On the other hand, many of the other smells that permeated her life in Tokyo were of the kind that were naturally associated with human beings. They were not necessarily unpleasant, but they were different. Kiera knew that this might have sounded odd to someone else and perhaps even slightly racist, but she had come to believe that the Japanese smelled differently. On a packed subway car, with little ventilation, she often felt burdened by the collective smell of so many other people in the car. It was a smell that contained hints of perfume, cologne, hair oil, deodorant, cigarette smoke, and faint body odors. At times, when it was especially cold or rainy and the heat on the train was turned up and all the passengers were clad in winter coats and rain jackets, she was most sensitive to the different smells. The smell itself did not register familiarity with anything she had ever smelled before moving to Japan.

It was an interesting experience for Keira living in Japan. Oddly enough, despite all the things that were new or unfamiliar to her, she found great comfort in being in Japan where she was clearly and very visibly an outsider. She stood out wherever she ventured and yet she never sensed that others' reactions to her were because of her racial status. This was very unlike the experience of being a minority person in the US where informal standards still dictated treatment as "less than" what was typical for majority White Americans.

The Japanese responded to her first as an outsider, a gaijin, and second as an American. This was strangely comforting. In Japan, she happily put aside the racial baggage; the source of great fatigue. She typically carried this "baggage" with her in the US. It was an emotional and intangible baggage associated with race that weighed her down at home. She had very little of that to deal with in Japan, except for those times when she interacted with other American expats. It was then that familiar roles emphasizing white privilege were reenacted.

It had happened recently at an event she attended at the Tokyo American Club. She'd arrived early for the chamber of commerce networking function, and after signing in, she'd made her way to the table covered with flyers and other information brochures. The American woman manning the table was friendly enough, but when the conversation turned to what brought her there, Keira sensed the same curiosity she got from White Americans at home.

It happened at times when she'd arrive to some high-brow function and was greeted by a clerk or other hired hand at the door. It seemed their disbelief about her belonging there compelled them to work extra hard at verifying that she had a right to be there. Sometimes, that meant checking and then rechecking guest lists. When they were finally convinced that she was in fact invited and her name was on the list as proof, they would inevitably look curiously at her as if they were studying her. While this went on, Keira was scanning the room, taking note of the absence of any other faces that looked like hers in the crowd.

Sighing heavily, she walked away from the window she'd been staring out of. Surveying the scene beneath her bedroom window from the vantage point of her apartment on the thirtieth floor, she'd long since lost interest in the construction site below. Her thoughts had wandered.

There was always laundry to be done it seemed. She headed to the washing machine and dryer, which were discretely tucked in a large closet in the long hallway. She smelled the laundry as she removed the clothes from the dryer and dumped them on her bed in the master bedroom. This was a smell with which she was familiar and liked; it hinted vaguely of the lavender fabric softener she liked using.

Her gaze returned to the window as she began sorting and folding the clothes. This time, she focused on the view outside her window, made possible because of the building's height. It really was spectacular.

She remembered the second load that needed to be transferred to the dryer. After putting the wet clothes in and starting the dryer, she heard the front door open and close. Someone had entered the apartment.

"Mommy, are you here?" her son called out, no doubt surprised to find her there so early in the afternoon.

"Yes, love, I am back here finishing up a little laundry. How was your day at school?" she asked.

"Fine." She heard him running through apartment.

Joshua, her son, was accompanied by their "helper," Ms. Lydia. Keira had hired her when they'd first arrived. She sometimes referred to her as their *helper* and at other times as a *nanny*, which seemed to be the most common term employed by others within the American expat community.

The young woman in her midthirties who had become one of Joshua's closest confidants had two children of her own. The little boy was the exact age as her son. Lydia took care of various tasks around the apartment and was on hand to wait out the arrival of the school bus in rainy cold weather. Kiera thought of her as an invaluable addition to their life in Japan. Although the wage she paid her for the actual hours worked was slightly more than standard, it was in itself a far cry from what a domestic employee could demand for similar efforts in the States. And in the States, there would have been the added element of anxiety characterizing her decision to hire help and permit them full access to her most beloved possessions including her child. She was reminded of this whenever she returned to the US given the media reports of child abuse and theft that were ubiquitous. Because the domestic staff in Japan were vetted by the US Embassy and expat community she tended not to worry as much about these issues.

In Japan, a majority of the women like Lydia who served as helpers hailed from the Philippines. Like Lydia, they had children and families of their own back home. It pained Keira to think about all the moments, days, weeks, and months that Lydia did not have with her own children because she was working in Japan tending to Joshua. Keira had shared as much with her Japanese friend Naoko, expecting her to sympathize. But rather than sympathize, she had said in a detached manner, as if it were of little consequence, "They are different...it doesn't bother them as much."

"What do you mean? Of course, she misses her children!" Keira had said.

"Well, it's how life is for them, and they are happy enough to be in Japan. It makes up for that," said Naoko.

Although Keira completely disagreed with this remark, knowing full well how much Lydia and the other women pined for their children, she said nothing. The whole exchange bothered her. That Naoko had assumed that Filipino women were somehow different, and that she hadn't contested that assumption. For Keira, it was yet again another way in which she had held back.

She held back often living in Japan. It happened for the bigger conversations that sprang up about the more difficult issues as much as it did for the smaller perfunctory ones where a simple "no, I prefer such and such" would have sufficed. What would at home have been a simple matter of response or expression of opinion was much more involved and complex in Japan.

This was not only because of the language barrier given her elementary level of Japanese, but it was also because of the different way that the Japanese thought about themselves in relation to others and the world around them. That difference affected their speech and how they communicated in daily conversation. What an American would say as a direct pronouncement would be hedged with an implicit reference by a Japanese speaker. This she realized was the real key to learning the language. It required sensitivity to subtle differences in perception and how one oriented oneself relative to others. She noticed it most frequently in conversations with her assistant, an older Japanese woman.

For example, one day, upon learning that her assistant had scheduled her to meet with someone, she thought, *We just met with them last week to discuss this. Why is he now asking for an appointment to come to our offices, and why do I have to meet with yet another person? Haven't we already agreed to proceed with the plans?*

But knowing now how the Japanese preferred to proceed with business negotiations, she said only, "So, we are meeting with him again," more as a pronouncement than a question.

Her assistant, pleased with Keira's accultura-
tion, responded, "Yes, it should be a brief meeting."

In the beginning within the first three months
of studying Japanese, she routinely stumbled on
the first steps of sentence formation. Remembering
to keep the verb at the end of the sentence was a
challenge. In English, something as straightforward
as "My family and I went to the museum" became
"To the museum, my family went" when translated
to Japanese. Not only was the sentence structure different, but also the "I," that is the first-person voice
so prevalent in American English, was always lurking
in the background, behind the scenes in Japanese.

When one closely observed Japanese social
interactions, this form of speech was consistent with
the deference shown to others and politeness, which
characterized most exchanges. The concern for others and recognition of oneself relative to others was
always a defining part of Japanese interaction and
speech with non-strangers.

This was not to say that the Japanese did not
lose their tempers or fail at precipitous moments to
extend the gentility promised by their reputations.
She could attest to this on that occasion when she
found herself completely flummoxed by the expressway toll entry systems. She'd mistakenly driven into
the lane reserved for those enrolled in the automated
toll payment system and finding herself unable to
proceed or to pay for entry (there was no human
being working the booth), she found herself respon-

sible for holding up what looked like a mile-long length of cars behind her vehicle.

The irate drivers had honked their horns ruthlessly until a toll attendant made the walk to her lane, took her money, chastised her though she didn't know exactly what it was he'd said, and made it possible for her and the other drivers to drive through the toll way. The Japanese were not too nice then. No, even they had their limits she thought with a smile possible only in retrospect.

Joshua ran through the doorway of her bedroom and then jumped playfully on her bed, knocking most of the clothes she had folded to the floor.

"Joshua, look what you have done! Haven't I told you that this is not a playground?"

"Sorry. Andrew had a new game for his Nintendo, and he let me play it on the bus. Can you buy me that game too?"

"No, maybe. What is it called?"

As irritated as she was about having to refold the clothes, she knew that she would probably buy it for him provided it was for children his age and that it didn't have any objectionable content. She bought most things for him that he asked for these days. She knew that she spoiled him, but much of it as of late seemed to stem from a sense of guilt she struggled with. She had come to think of the guilt as the dues she paid for the challenge of the move that had not included a job for her husband. It was a psychic penalty exacted upon her, which she would continue paying until he either made the move to join them in Japan or they returned to the States. For the time being, she ponied up the tax.

Living in Japan meant changes that were not only a result of the new setting and culture, but it also meant changes for her marriage to Felix, Joshua's father. As the mother of the clan, as well as the initiator of their move abroad, Keira felt weighted by the responsibility of the move.

When the opportunity came up and she received the offer of employment to work in Tokyo, she was ecstatic. She'd called Felix immediately, her enthusiasm unrestrained, she'd babbled about how and when they'd go and all the promising aspects of the move. She was ten minutes into the call before she'd realized that he hadn't said a word. Not a peep. His silence spoke volumes about what would come to be his position on the move and the professional opportunity it afforded her.

For her part, she couldn't get past the fact that when she had first learned of the opportunity she had discussed it with him. In fact, the conversation about it—about whether she should apply and whether he would be willing to move if she got it—remained eerily clear in her memory. She remembered where they were at the time, what they were doing, and the cheerful tone that characterized his conversation.

Yet, when she learned that she'd actually gotten the job, he was far from enthusiastic and initially unsupportive. He eventually came around to giving tacit approval of the move, but it was never with any real enthusiasm. What troubled her the most about this was not so much his lack of enthusiasm, but her realization that he'd never seriously believed her to be a viable contender for the job. He'd said, "Sure, yes, I could do Tokyo, go ahead apply," with little belief that it would ever become a reality. It saddened her to realize this.

Now more than a year and half into this life around the globe, Felix had never officially made the move. He had come initially for the first week when they'd moved here over the Christmas holidays, but he'd returned to his job Stateside the first week after the New Year's holiday. The plan at that time was to continue an aggressive job search for him, though this search was admittedly compromised by the long-distance nature in which it was conducted.

On his behalf, she had sent out nearly eighty resumes to companies that she'd researched or heard about through colleagues. This amounted to nearly four times as many as he'd sent out, and in many of those cases, she'd sent a cover letter ostensibly from him accompanying his resume. After six months of searching that had begun four months before the move, she'd also reached out to a fair number of Japan-based search firms and headhunters.

It would be nearly another six months into the move to Japan when they both decided that they would stop the urgency that had characterized the job search for him. If something came up, it would be great. But they had begun to prepare themselves for the worst. And gradually, the worst had come upon them.

It had happened unexpectedly. The entire series of events had taken its toll, and gradually, as time passed, Keira's feelings about him had gradually altered. She tried not to think less of him, but she couldn't seem to help it. It was difficult to admit even to herself that she no longer held him in the esteem that she once did. She had wandered down a somber path of questioning. It had brought her to the penultimate question she now confronted—had she married the wrong person?

She was a high achiever. There was no denying that. It was that motivation which had led her to steadfastly pursue additional education some five years beyond college that eventually resulted in her obtaining three graduate degrees the last of which was a doctorate. She understood that he was not similarly motivated. Of course, she knew that part of it even before they had married. She knew that he had only a college degree. But because his salary had always been on the high side (he worked with computers), she hadn't thought much about it. It hadn't ever really mattered before.

He was a kind and decent man, and men like that were in short supply. She knew too many of them who were anything but kind or decent. She also knew far too many women who were highly educated but who lacked marriage prospects or male companionship. Back when they were dating, she considered herself among the fortunate few. There had been some compromises she'd made along the way in deciding to marry him. But those tended to be pretty minor in the grand scheme of things. So what if he'd never learned to properly hold a knife to cut his food? What did it matter if he used the word "ain't" periodically in conversation? All in all, she had considered herself to be pretty lucky, and without a look back, she had jumped the matrimonial broom. They had married within three years after meeting.

So, it was with some guilt that Kiera now found herself dwelling upon his shortcomings after so much time had passed. Given that he tended to gravitate toward the middle of the proverbial road for just about everything, she knew that it meant that he would always be the "trailing spouse." She would continue to work toward the next opportunity.

In the past, over the many years they were together, she'd presented papers and given talks at international meetings, collected data she later published, and started the next big project. Together, they had happily used each of these occasions to explore a new corner of the world together. At those times, he enthusiastically leaped outside his comfort zone for the mysterious possibilities that globetrotting promised. Yet, he could not, and she thought of it more like he would not commit to a permanent or at least semipermanent move abroad.

After six months of living in Japan, Felix had made the trip to visit her and Joshua three times already. In the spring, they both faced the fact that the move and imagined life abroad would not work as they'd planned or as she had hoped. He was not willing to leave his job in the States and come without one. He argued, and she had reluctantly agreed that he was too old and too far along life's professional curve to start anew some three or four years later when they would return to the US. And so it was that he lived in one of the bedrooms in his mother's home about ten miles from their home, which they had succeeded in renting out.

In the beginning, because they thought that a job in Japan would be forthcoming for him, it was an easy decision to temporarily camp out at his mother's. Neither of them anticipated that his stay there would be for as long as it had been.

The marriage was taxed by the stress of the distance as well as the inequity in experiences characterizing their lives apart. While Keira's world and life in Japan was rich with new experience, Felix's was not. She was immersed in a new lifestyle working in an exciting new space with different people and challenging responsibilities. And because of the esteem with which Japan held the US organization she represented, she found that unlike working at home in the US, she was personally held in high regard. If she wanted a meeting with someone, she had only to ask her assistant to make a call and more often than not, the meeting was forthcoming. She had a generous expense account, could come and go as she pleased, and make her own hours. Her housing was provided, and she lived in a luxurious four-bedroom apartment. Ironically, despite the fact that Felix had not permanently moved to Japan, she was provided housing for a four-bedroom home because they were a family of three rather than two or one. The apartment's wraparound balcony on the thirtieth floor overlooked Tokyo's spectacular and immense skyline.

Most of the other American expats she knew in Tokyo enjoyed a relatively high standard of living. They were rewarded handsomely as much for the long hours they worked and the expertise they possessed as they were for the "hardship" of living in Japan. Yet it could be argued that was a misnomer. "Hardship" didn't really describe their luxury housing and private schools, which their English-speaking children attended.

Felix only experienced the perks of her lifestyle in Japan vicariously when she described her experiences to him on the phone and in video calls, or on those occasions when he happened to visit.

He was resentful about all of this, though it was clear he tried not to show it. Because their time together and as a family was so limited (when he visited he typically came for five days or less), they both economized arguments or complaints. Indeed, the three of them were together for such short snatches of time, they breathed a celebratory air and acted as if they were on holiday. They celebrated often and relinquished a number of the restraints that were generally operative in what they thought of as their "regular" lives. They drank champagne in the afternoon, dined out frequently, and allowed their son to stay up past his bedtime; sometimes even on school nights.

Keira had come to expect each of these indulgences every time she began marking off the days on the calendar in anticipation of their time together. It was the new normal for how they interacted with one another. It wasn't better than what they had, and she was hopeful that what the future held would surpass their current start of affairs. Nevertheless, their current life together where they spent most of it apart was what they had now. For Keira, when they were together, it seemed in some ways superficial. It was as if there were a veneer that covered and protected the vulnerable raw spots that existed within the marriage.

Felix did not see it this way, and this difference in perspective was curious. On one occasion, she'd asked him about this.

"Don't you think it's kind of crazy how we are doing this?" she'd continued, "Our marriage is on the brink of something horrible. This cannot be good for it. What are we going to do?"

Calmly and without raising his voice, he'd said, "That's not true. This is a marriage, and I know you can't see things sometimes without all of the emotion, but there are ups and downs in every marriage. It's not always great every day. We have some low points that we are going through now. It's like the valleys of life."

It was clear that he saw their separation and life apart—she and Joshua on the other side of the globe in Japan, and he in Washington DC, as one of them. Despite her concerns about having married the wrong person, she realized that he was actually quite wise at times. He was able to consider and view their marriage through the telescope required of such a perspective. As evidence of this, he saw things more fully than she did when it came to their marriage. She tended to peer and fixate on just one or two details at a time.

They had spent more of the last two years apart than together, and he had missed out on a number of the developmental milestones that Joshua had experienced. In other families, this might have had significant negative repercussions down the road, but she reasoned that for them it wouldn't be so bad. From the beginning, Kiera knew that the child favored her more than him. It was not egotism that accounted for this belief, it was just stark reality. Felix had never really accepted the primacy with which she greeted and cared for their only child even when he was a newborn. Although it seemed that at times Felix was incapable of sharing her with his son, more often than not, he seemed incapable of sharing himself with him. At a very fundamental level (indeed, she supposed it may well have been biological), he could not and would not really share himself with Joshua.

In the beginning, she would ask him to take him swimming or to the park or to toss a ball or fly a kite. Felix would agree to do so but almost always reluctantly. At some later point in time, just when an argument was poised to occur, he would point to that occasion as an example of the sacrificial time investment (he saw it as this) he'd made toward the care of their only son.

That Felix saw these activities with Joshua as somehow hoisted upon him and stretching the bonds of his good will troubled her deeply. He was a good man but a wholly ineffective father, at least at this stage of his young son's life. Once she accepted this, she'd set about the psychological task of trying to make sense of Felix's relationship with his own dad; a man nearly forty years his senior who was a constant fixture around the house and in front of the television.

She'd first met him on the same day that she met her husband at his sister's housewarming. At that time, he was in his midseventies and avidly read two to three newspapers each day along with any number of popular cultural and sports-related magazines. He read voraciously while watching the news, sports, and classic movies. He was a friendly and upbeat conversationalist, who always seemed to manage to steer a conversation to a time since past. Indeed, after she had gotten to know him, she was struck by how frequently he wandered along memory lane. It seemed a tad too often and always seemed to be at the expense of time spent in the present.

Felix's dad passed away the year before their move to Japan. She often wondered what he would have thought about all of this. She knew he would have had many questions. First and foremost, he would have asked about their well-being and safety. Kiera would have happily reported that one of the things she most loved about living in Japan was that life was safer. It was easier. Indeed, the stress of the distance from home and difference from the familiar paled in comparison to what life was like here.

Crime in general was much less a problem and far less likely to disrupt the tranquility of ordinary living in Japan in comparison to the US. She hadn't thought twice some weeks ago when the stranger she had asked for directions had physically gotten in her car. He'd made himself comfortable in the passenger seat and proceeded to guide her and her sleeping son to the recreational park she was trying to find.

That day, it was a sunny Saturday afternoon, and they had driven some forty-five minutes out of Tokyo to a park they were looking forward to exploring. But once in the area, she could not find the park, and the GPS seemed to fail. Her son eventually fell asleep, and after meandering through narrow neighborhood streets for half of an hour, she had pulled over and parked the car. Distressed, she'd gotten out of the car and approached a Japanese man who appeared to be dressed for some kind of athletic activity. His English was quite limited, but once she showed him the paper she'd printed with the address to the park, he had immediately nodded his head knowingly and attempted to retrieve directions from his mobile phone's GPS. He struggled to describe how to get there and gestured to her car suggesting he direct her by driving there.

She didn't skip a beat, and without any hesitation, she directed him to the car, opened the door, and suggested he sit in the passenger front seat. Once they were both in with their seat belts fastened, she started the car, and they set off. He regularly said "right" or "left" when he meant the opposite, and after several wrongs turns, they eventually made it to the park. Along the way, her son had awakened and noticing the unfamiliar Japanese man in the car had asked only, "How did he get in here?" After telling him that he was helping them to find the park, he yawned and seemed satisfied, and then turned his attention to the scenes they passed outside the car window. After parking the car, the man accompanied them to the park's entrance. Once there, she and the man engaged in a short ritual of bows while she thanked him profusely. When he eventually walked away, she turned to enter the park, feeling pleasantly satisfied with yet another experience of Japanese "omotenashi" or hospitality.

All the expats she knew appreciated these qualities of Japanese society. She had conversations about this with Lydia, her helper who from time to time commented on the pervasiveness of petty crime in Manila, the city where her family and home were located in the Philippines. She said that people stole things there including women's purses and more valuable items. One rarely walked alone at night on the street and tended to avoid doing so. Lydia appreciated the improved safety of life in Tokyo, and on evenings, when she finished working late at Keira's apartment and prepared to return home to the dormitory where she lived with other domestic helpers, she declined the extra money to take a taxi that was offered her. Instead, she always preferred to walk, saying, "No, madam, its fine and safe. I can walk."

As she finished refolding the clothes he'd knocked off the bed when he first came in, Joshua peeked his head back in the room. She turned and looked at him. He was a handsome little boy and seemed to have inherited the best of her features as well as those of Felix. She looked at his little face and once again regretted that he had to wear eyeglasses in order to correct the nearsightedness he'd also inherited from her.

"Mommy, can I have a snack? I'm hungry."

"Yes, dear, what would you like?"

"I can get it myself."

"Okay, but remember, one single serving only. Dinner will be within the hour."

He quickly turned and padded off to the kitchen to examine the cabinet shelves. He'd recently begun moving the step stool, opening it and positioning it in front of the cabinet to better survey the availability of snacks. She did not mind this and encouraged his independence. She insisted only that he limit the snack to a small portion and return the stool to its place.

Keira's thoughts returned to Felix and the relationship he had had with his father. To hear him tell it, his dad was fully engaged. But whenever he described the time that he or either of his two sisters spent with him, his most frequent and vivid descriptions involved watching television or outings to watch movies. Though he especially enjoyed watching televised sports, he had never engaged in sports with his own children. Nor was he known for working around the house or carrying out general house-hold maintenance tasks. These tasks were left either to his wife, a hired hand, or Felix—the oldest and only boy in the house.

As adults, neither Felix nor his sisters interacted much with their father. As the older man aged, he became increasingly unwilling to leave the house for anything other than to purchase newspapers. Felix's only time with his father included watching an occasional football game together. Beyond that, he did not seem to engage his father on any real substantive level. Like his own son Joshua, he too was quite clearly his mother's son.

It occurred to her that destiny might well be positioned to repeat itself. She shuddered at this thought. She was responsible for making it physically impossible for Felix to interact with Joshua given their move. Now because they were living apart, there were so many miles that separated them. Yet, at the same time, because she knew that Felix did not interact much with Joshua even when they were in same house, she calmed herself. There was a silver lining to their present reality.

Had Joshua been especially attached to Felix, it would have made their separation much more difficult and painful. Ironically, the emotional distance between the two seemed to have had a sort of inoculative effect on the impact of their physical separation. The little boy did not pine for his dad. Whether it was a stage or the fact of his youth, he did not seem to miss him all that much.

She finished putting the folded clothes away and glanced again out of the window. She looked at the clouds and for a moment wondered what the sky looked like at home at the moment.

Spring was coming. They would experience some of what she thought of as the best of their experiences in Japan. She and Joshua both preferred the warm weather of spring and summer in Japan. The famous cherry blossoms, or "Sakura" as they were called in Japanese, were only part of what made springtime in Tokyo special. For her, it was also the sun that rose above the tops of the tall buildings bordering her view that provided her with an uncommonly upbeat spirit in the morning. The sun rose earlier here than she was used to in the States. When it came up, it blazoned, announcing its arrival with a shade of orange just shy of the hue of her favorite sherbet. It beckoned her, and when it did, she turned full face into it acknowledging its splendor. It didn't matter that it was 5:00 a.m., she took delight in it.

She recalled how the arrival of day and its first hints of light brought with it peace she pined for during some of her most difficult nights. It was at these times when sleep was most elusive that she found herself impatiently waiting for the dawn. How gratified she was when spring finally reared its head and signaled the approach of day as early as four thirty. She'd rise then and though weary, gratefully begin the day. Fortunately, those nights were fewer and further between.

Keira was grateful for the change that was reflected in having more frequent sleep-filled nights. Without even realizing it, she had begun to resemble any one of the other American expats adjusting her own rhythms to that of her adopted country. Like her, they were lured by the decision to travel abroad and like her, they lived daily outside the zone of familiarity—a zone that bred certain creature comforts.

Keira was friendly enough with a number of the other expat Americans she met, but she had yet to develop particularly close bonds with any of them. Instead, her closest intimates in Japan were not American. They included native Japanese, as well as Korean, South African, and Jamaican expatriates.

That this was her reality living in Japan dawned on her recently when she was faced with an urgent need to return Stateside for a daylong meeting and wrestled with the challenge of child care. This was compounded by a school holiday that happened to take place while she would be away. Keira could count on Lydia, their helper, to look after her son during her absence of course, but she also wanted Joshua to spend time, perhaps an overnight with trusted friends. She had turned to the Japanese family they had befriended through school.

Theirs was a family that bore little resemblance to her own, and yet there was something that had clicked between them. She and the mom of the family, her name was Kioko, had become friends. Admittedly, the common link was the boys' friendship—Joshua enjoyed playing with the middle child who was called Kei, but with time, they'd become friends independent of the boys.

It was the start of a rewarding friendship. Because Kioko was Japanese and extremely polite, she never asked pointed questions. Yet, Keira managed to draw her out, and Kioko found herself sharing various details about her life, details about her marriage, her life, and her past. For her part, Keira opened up though it tended to be in small servings. It had all happened in less than a year, and when it came time to figure how to ensure her son's care, she knew she felt comfortable enough turning to Kioko. In the end, it had turned out to be a wonderful experience for Joshua and for Kioko's family. They were gracious hosts who were honored to look after him during that time.

Both she and her son had made rich and valuable connections with many different people during their stay in Japan. They were far away and out of their comfort zone but immensely better off than they were before moving across the world. When the time came to return to the States, she knew that she would miss many of the things that had come to define her life in Japan. Things like its politeness, its safety, and cleanliness. Of course, there would be things about the overall experience of living in Japan that they would both forget, but there would be many rich memories they would inevitably share over the years. It had begun with a fourteen-hour plane ride. When their journey ended, it would be with another long plane ride.

THE DELAYED FLIGHT TO ST. PETERSBURG

The plane was delayed in its takeoff from New York City's John F. Kennedy airport to Amsterdam's Schiphol airport, and Louis was worried about whether he'd make the connecting flight to St. Petersburg. Flight delays were an all-too-common occurrence it seemed. When it was international travel, the potential inconveniences caused by a delayed takeoff were multiplied. Louis quickly calculated what this flight delay was likely to cost him in terms of missed connections, extra waiting time, and the myriad of missed opportunities in St. Petersburg.

It was this last reason perhaps more than the others which made him really hope that he would not miss the connection. A delay would mean forfeiting the preconference activities he had paid extra to do. He wasn't even sure what all that entailed because when he'd registered it appeared as either "To be announced (TBA)" or "forthcoming" in the conference materials.

Nevertheless, he didn't want to miss out. He decided that if necessary, he would make a mad dash by running off the airplane and doing his best to head immediately to the connecting gate. He had seen enough other desperate travelers in the past to know that it might require a somewhat less than decorous departure through the aisle of the plane upon landing.

Louis was the kind of person who fully recognized the value of being prepared, so he scolded himself because he hadn't thought to find out whether there were multiple flights each day from Amsterdam to the Russian city of St. Petersburg. That he hadn't done so reflected the swiftness in how quickly he had made up his mind, reserved seats and purchased tickets to travel.

Although he had hoped to make the trip for quite some time, it was only within the last few weeks that he'd researched flights, made the hotel reservation, and paid the conference registration fee. When he thought about it, he was reminded once again of the reasons why he had left so quickly. He wondered what she was doing now at this actual moment.

"Why was the flight delayed?" he'd asked an airline counter representative. He knew he would never know the true reason because the policy for most airlines seemed to dictate sharing as little information with customers as possible. He wondered what other options existed. What would he do if he were to miss the scheduled connecting flight? He had never been to Schiphol airport before and didn't know if there was anything to do there nor how far out from Amsterdam's city center it was.

Missed flights and unscheduled windows of time hardly suited him. He was very much a planner who took pleasure in managing his time and, begrudgingly, he acknowledged, those around him as well. This potential glitch in scheduling that was caused by the flight delay at JFK was out of his control and as such was even more unsettling. He started to consider what alternative scenarios might exist.

One alternative could involve canceling the trip and staying put in New York. He was confident that he could make the case for a full refund of his ticket price with the airline if the delay caused him to miss the connecting flight. That was an extreme course of action and one that did not sit particularly well with him. He couldn't help feeling the sense of powerlessness that had settled on him at that moment like thick fog on wet grass.

Louis was relieved when they finally allowed the passengers to begin to board only an hour and ten minutes past the scheduled time. It would now be possible for him to make the connection. He was grateful because this meant that he would not have to cancel the trip. Going forward made it less easy to go backwards. It was done. He had left and anything between them that came after this would be marked as such.

He boarded the flight, found his seat, and settled in. The eight-hour flight, though long, was uneventful, which he wryly acknowledged meant that it was a good flight. Uneventful in this era meant the absence of all sorts of mishaps and life-ending events like terrorism, lightning and military strikes, pilot suicide, as well as instrument failure. He slept for at least half of the flight and was happy to have awakened just as the plane began its descent.

From his window seat, Louis saw large expanses of green surrounded by broad swaths of blue and gray. As the plane neared its landing, the view from the plane became more focused, and he could make out the houses, open land, windmills, and waterways. Amsterdam was an engineering marvel and existed on land reclaimed from water.

The aerial view hinted at the land's relation to the water, but it did not reveal just how tenuous that relationship could be when the floods arrived. Louis knew something about the historical challenges the country had endured as a result of unexpected and extreme rainfall. He realized that the view from above disclosed nothing of the land's secrets.

The landing, which was typically the part of the flight that caused him the greatest anxiety, was smooth. The pilots apologized for the initial delay and made certain to point out that they had managed to make up the lost time. Following several announcements by the flight attendants, the jet touched gently down on the runway.

When the plane landed and the passengers gathered their belongings in preparation to disembark, Louis realized that he would make his connection for the flight to Russia with an hour to spare. Eventually, after getting off the plane and seeing the monitor inside the terminal, he saw that his connecting flight to Russia would also be delayed in taking off.

With time to kill, he walked leisurely to the connecting gate and stopped in a couple of shops along the way. He bought a small tin of the European cookies, or "biscuits" as they were called here, which he enjoyed whenever he visited Europe. He hadn't exchanged any US dollars for the Dutch currency, so he used his credit card for the biscuits and then again later when he picked up a small sandwich to take aboard the three-hour flight.

Louis eventually arrived at St. Petersburg's Pulkovo Airport around 3:00 p.m. on Tuesday afternoon. *Not bad*, he thought. They'd either deliberately padded the flight time or the pilots aboard both flights operated their planes in overdrive to make up for the delayed departures.

After clearing customs and picking up his baggage, he'd checked only one very large suitcase, he headed out to the waiting crowd. He scanned the noisy mass of people, noting the controlled chaos that was everywhere in the reception area. The voices were louder than he was accustomed to hearing, and there was a kind of frenetic energy that seemed to envelop those who were presumably waiting for loved ones.

As he walked through the crowded arrivals hall, he finally came upon a small blond woman bearing a sign with the letters "ICOPE" prominently displayed on it. He recognized it immediately as the acronym for the conference he was attending—the First International Conference on Psychology Education (ICOPE). He walked up to the young woman, introduced himself, and noted his affiliation with the conference.

"Hello, I'm very happy to see your sign. My name is Louis Henderson. I'm attending the ICOPE meeting."

"Very [she pronounced it 'veeery'] nice to meet you, Mr. Henderson, and I am Irina. I am assistant to Dr. Polovocjeck. This is Rudolfo." She pointed to the young man standing beside her who was beaming. Louis wondered if he was always so happy or whether it was his proximity to the lovely Irina. He couldn't blame him, she was a beauty.

"We are very delighted that you come to Russia. Zdrastvuyte!"

"Thank you," said Louis. He knew she had used the Russian word *zdrastvuyte* to extend an especially sincere welcome to him. After the long journey and flight, he was grateful to have made contact with the conference representatives.

"Please wait here with us. There were other people scheduled to arrive soon, and we will all go together to the hotel."

"Okay, I will use the restroom and come right back here," Louis said. He headed off in search of the bathroom.

When he returned, a middle-aged Black couple had joined the ICOPE group. They stood out because there were few brown-complexioned people in the airport. Louis recalled that there were very few Black Americans aboard his flight from Philadelphia or Amsterdam where he had laid over. He wondered if they were as aware of their distinctiveness as he was.

The next person to arrive was an older European woman. Louis could not place her accent. *Was she Israeli or perhaps German?* Louis wondered. It was hard to tell.

Irina made preliminary introductions.

"Hello, dear guests. We are so happy to have you here in our beautiful country Russia to work with the ICOPE meeting. Does everyone have their bags? Yes? Okay, then we can go. We will head to our shuttle bus. My associate Rudolfo is our driver, and he will help us put all of your bags in the bus and you will be seated, and we will travel to the conference site. You will be very comfortable and relax, and you will arrive there within forty-five minutes. So now everyone, please follow me." With that, she turned and briskly headed toward the exit at the opposite end of the hall.

Louis hurried to catch up with her as she maneuvered through the throngs of people. He banged into a few people with his luggage, but after the first time of apologizing only to find that no one ever seemed to acknowledge the bump, he stopped apologizing. He walked as quickly as he could without banging into any one of the many other travelers in the waiting hall.

Within minutes, the small group of travelers arrived to the parking lot. They had followed Irina who now stood beside a small truck. It actually looked like a passenger van but somewhat miniaturized. Louis wondered how they would fit. There were bags and at least six people. He was glad he was not Rudolfo who had the unenviable task of skillfully packing everyone's luggage in the vehicle.

The sun was bright, and its rays felt warm. Louis was happy to note the absence of the extreme humidity he'd left in the United States. At just that moment, there was something about the way the sun hit the parking lot, which caused him to pause momentarily. As he shielded his eyes to its light, for just that moment, he felt an inexplicable sense of confidence that this would be an entirely pleasant holiday. This was despite the fact that he was attending a work-related conference and that he had basically run from the problems he had home. He felt an unmistakable surge of optimism. The more comfortable climate that greeted him in Russia seemed to be reason enough to be convinced of this.

Rudolfo succeeded, and as soon as everyone's things were loaded and stowed in the tiny truck, they sped off. Construction was underway at the airport. The expressway they turned onto was open to four lanes, but because of the construction, it had been reduced to two, and as a result, there was traffic. Louis saw trucks, buses, and a variety of passenger vehicles, and with some surprise, he recognized a Ford Taurus. It was not a car he was particularly fond of in the US, though he had read somewhere recently that it was ranked among the top ten affordable vehicles sold. He wondered what it cost in Russia.

Just up the road, he also watched as a police vehicle pulled someone over. At least he thought it was a police car. Maybe it was the KGB, he joked to himself. Small and white with blue Cyrillic lettering, the vehicle had sirens on top of it. It seemed most likely that it was a police vehicle. What had led to him pulling the other car over? Had he been driving too quickly? Was he driving at a speed above the speed limit? What was the speed limit anyway?

The deluge of questions that came to mind was something familiar to almost all avid travelers. When one crisscrossed the globe and landed in a foreign country for business, pleasure, or mere exploration, it was inevitable that one faced inexplicable and unfamiliar situations. Sometimes, the answers to these mysteries lay within the text of a guidebook or an internet site. Other times, they were more elusive, requiring interpersonal engagement with native inhabitants of the foreign country at which point one could observe, ask, or infer. And at other times, the answer could be discerned from conversations with fellow travelers who shared a similar background or perspective in the world theater. For Louis, it would occur when he connected with a fellow American.

After they had driven for about a half an hour, they pulled into the Oktiabrskaya Hotel. It was a massive structure with an imposing facade. Recently renovated (this was not apparent from the hotel's exterior), the hotel boasted a number of Western amenities including a conference center as well as a barbershop and nail salon. The small group of travelers filed in and formed a line at the hotel registration desk located in the lobby. This process took some time.

Eventually, almost an hour after having arrived to the hotel, he had checked in and registered for the conference. As a part of his registration packet, he signed up for two tours that the conference organizers had arranged for the attendees. He was suddenly fatigued and felt the weight of his journey.

On cue, almost as if he sensed Louis's fatigue, a hotel employee who was either a traditional bellman (he did not have on a uniform) or some other paid employee, escorted Louis to his room after the brief elevator ride to the sixth floor and carried his luggage. At the door, the bellman-like person struggled to get the card key to open the door. When he eventually succeeded in opening the door, he entered gesturing with great flourish and waved for Louis to enter.

After ensuring that Louis was satisfied, he waited politely. Louis fumbled with the Russian currency before handing the man three hundred ruble, which he calculated to be slightly more than the equivalent of three US dollars. The man accepted it, grunted something incomprehensible. Was it a universal acknowledgment of thanks or was it disappointment with the amount? Louis didn't know for sure, but it didn't seem to matter much at that point because the man had already left.

The small room was stark and this, perhaps more than anything since arriving to St. Petersburg, reminded him of the stories and firsthand accounts he'd heard of the shortages that Russians routinely experienced during the worst of their country's separation from the West. There was one twin bed positioned in the center of the room, and a window on the wall opposite from the bed.

For just a moment, he remembered the email he'd sent last month to request a change to the reservation that had initially been made for two. At home in the United States, the change would have had implications for the amount of his bill; whether he was charged the double or single occupancy rate. Here, at this moment, his status as a single traveler was apparent in the lone twin bed, which represented the primary furniture in the room.

Louis caught himself thinking about the circumstances that had transpired. As was always the case during these disquieting moments, he felt weighed down by the emotion of his thoughts. He knew that he needed to think of something else.

Yet, it was never easy for him to do that. Instead of moving on to another thought about something else, it was as if he were being pulled by the current of an ocean's wave too large to jump. It felt as if he had succumbed to its overpowering force.

Louis walked across the small room and opened the window curtains. He adjusted the heavy shade in order to draw more light into the room. He would find himself adjusting the blinds and curtains multiple times at various times of the day during his short stay because his visit happened to coincide with the season of the midnight sun in Russia's northernmost metropolitan area. It would be daylight for most of his week's stay. Typically, the period known as "White Nights" ran from May through July when St. Petersburg's sky was rarely dark.

After unpacking and hanging up the one suit he'd brought with him, he locked his laptop in the room safe, grabbed his key card, and left the room. He headed for the opening ceremony and welcome address of the conference. Louis remembered that there was a conference dinner scheduled to follow the opening ceremony. The event was held in a large cavernous room located in the basement of the hotel where a sizable number of people were already gathered. Because the room appeared to be capable of accommodating another two hundred or so, it was not at all crowded.

Louis didn't recognize anyone nor was he familiar with the person at the podium who gave remarks in heavily accented English. He appeared to be a middle-aged, slightly balding Frenchman who read from a prepared script.

"In this new era in which technology has become a part of everyone's life, when it is ubiquitous, the theme for the ICOPE meeting of this year is especially timely. 'The Future of Education at the Human-Technology Frontier' is a theme that should resonate with all of us engaged in any aspect of education and education research. We are at a frontier, and the opportunities seem endless..."

Louis listed attentively for a few moments and then turned his attention to the unmanned table at the entrance of the hall. He read the names on each of the tags and found his own, which he scooped up along with a conference folder bearing his name. He looked some more at the remaining name cards and folders, and was shocked to see the name of a colleague from his own department. *No way!* he thought. Had Ron actually registered? He couldn't help shaking his head in disbelief. But yes, there was a name card and a folder that had been prepared for him. Louis thought this amazing because he knew there was no way that Ron would have actually made the trip to attend the meeting.

Louis allowed his mind to wander for a moment as he imagined what it would have been like if Ron had actually come. They would have palled around together no doubt, and it would have been nice to have someone else he knew to experience Russia and the city of St. Petersburg. But he also realized that the only time he ever actually socialized with Ron was once a year at the Gala they both attended as guests in exchange for their pro bono work as judges for the nation's premier high school science competition. Ron regularly attended with his wife Ann in tow, and the three of them usually spent the better part of the cocktail hour chatting before being seated for dinner. They used the time to talk about everyday life events that paled in comparison to the unexpected sometimes unpleasant things that also happened in their lives.

Last year, it had been the traffic accident that he had had just before coming to the gala. Fortunately, his car had sustained little damage, but he was anxious about the liability. In the accident involving his car, another car, and a truck which had stopped short ahead, he wound up damaging the fender of the car in front of him. He had arrived to the gala somewhat shaken and so had wound up consuming several of the event's specialty cocktails well before the cocktail hour ended. The alcohol warmed him as it loosened the tightly wound coils around, which he seemed to be wired. He recalled that Ron and Ann were attentive listeners and had expressed genuine concern as he recounted details of the accident to them.

That evening, when the bells sounded to signal the end of the cocktail hour, the couple made their way to their assigned table, and Louis said goodbye as he headed off to find his. He knew at that point as always that he would not socialize with them again until the following year. It wasn't that he didn't like them. Quite the contrary, he looked forward to seeing them each year at the gala.

That they would not get together to socialize in the time between the annual galas was something that he and Ron both realized but never actually spoke about. Ron routinely expressed his intention of inviting Louis over to his place at some point, and in the beginning, some five years ago when Louis arrived to the department, he believed him to be sincere. But the occasion never materialized, and instead, there were rain checks and apologies too numerous to count. He always nodded his understanding at these times and in doing so gave Ron tacit approval for the pretense he insisted on maintaining.

Louis's thoughts were interrupted. The Frenchman had finally finished speaking. He concluded his opening remarks and welcomed all the participants, inviting several other speakers who were each given an opportunity to address the audience. It was at this point that Louis quietly exited the hall, wandered down a hallway, and stumbled upon the hotel pool. It was closed and appeared to be under construction. Too bad; he consoled himself by acknowledging that he hadn't actually known that there was a pool at the hotel and hadn't brought a swimsuit.

Louis walked some more and came to one of the three restaurants in the hotel. At the moment, he realized that he was actually quite hungry. The last time he'd eaten was on board the plane a couple of hours after takeoff. Although another meal was served close to the plane's landing time, he was asleep at that point and so he had not eaten.

This particular restaurant seemed to pride itself on Western offerings, and he ordered a club sandwich. Louis figured he'd probably skip the conference dinner that evening. On the off chance that he had the energy, he might venture out to explore the area surrounding the hotel. He'd look around, see what was what, and maybe pick up some souvenirs.

The sandwich arrived. Atop the bottom piece of bread were several sliced hardboiled eggs, and although this was not something he would have listed among the most desired ingredients for a club sandwich, it was close enough. He took a bite. It tasted good and because he was hungry he ate everything on his plate.

Back in his room, Louis decided to shower and change clothes. The water pressure in the room left something to be desired, but at least the bathroom was clean. After putting on a tee shirt and a pair of shorts, he felt extremely tired and decided to lay down on the small twin bed.

Once again, he chose not to think about the fact that he was alone. He was tired and felt his muscles relaxing as the day's tensions receded. He slept on and off and found himself awakening every two hours or so.

At times like this when sleep is just beyond reach but close enough to sense, Louis allowed his mind to wander and flirt, indeed caress, his fondest memories of her. He was most vulnerable at these times when he thought most about their times together. Even though the impetus for the trip to St. Petersburg was the conference, they had actually planned to travel there together. Back then, the plan had been for them to take an extended holiday together.

The two of them had been intrigued by the city of St. Petersburg as much for its historical and cultural realities as for its geographical location. They had watched a documentary about Russia and found the part highlighting its history which took place in St. Petersburg to be especially fascinating.

The city, located relatively north, experiences sunlit nights (i.e., daylight for about twenty-two hours) once a year. During this time, the sun refuses to sink deep enough under the horizon for the sky to appear dark, and dawn makes only a brief appearance.

This period of "white nights," though not unique to St Petersburg, has been romanticized and heralded in fiction and film. Louis was excited to be experiencing it firsthand. Yet, because of the effects of jet lag coupled with the loss of sleep as a result of his journey, he was far less impressed than he had been when reading about the trip. The reality was that one of the very things that excited him about the trip, experiencing white nights, made it hard for him to feel rested. He noticed that around 4:30 a.m. when he woke up again that it had finally gotten dark, although not quite pitch black.

When he woke up again some forty-five minutes later at 5:15 a.m., it was completely bright again. This time, he decided to stay awake at that point. He did not feel at all rested, but he was tired of the challenge of trying to sleep.

At 9:00 a.m., Louis boarded a large tour bus with about thirty other conference attendees. The group headed out for one of several organized tours.

Their first stop after a relatively short bus ride was the St. Nicholas Naval Cathedral. They were allowed to enter the church and mull about quietly. Louis saw many gold gilded pieces of art, which represented Jesus Christ as well as the many patron saints of Russian orthodoxy.

Even as the members of the tour group milled about, people continued to worship at the church. While they were there, a priest recited a liturgy for the faithful in attendance. They were primarily elderly women, who prayed out loud and lit candles. Louis was taken by the beautiful wall plaques of the icons made on small blocks of wood that were meant to resemble the large frescos still visible on the church's walls and ceiling. He bought a small souvenir fresco and put it into the pocket of the light windbreaker he wore.

After boarding the bus again, the group headed to the Hermitage. The Hermitage is a national museum known as much for the size of its collections (it boasted the largest collection of paintings in the world) as for the value of its antiquities. The museum was founded in 1764 and retained a number of the original pieces she acquired at that time.

The group toured the Hermitage as if they were powered by a world wind. It reminded him of closing time in a toy store on Christmas eve. It was impossible to see and absorb everything, but the act of trying to do so piqued his visual senses. And while it may have seemed to be aesthetically overwhelming, it was an experience imbued with the extreme beauty that the museum's founder, Russian czarist, Catherine the Great, intended.

The museum contained original masterpieces and unlike the great museums of Western Europe (e.g., the Louvre in Paris and Madrid's Prado), at the Hermitage, one could photograph them for a fee. Louis photographed the two Leonardo da Vinci paintings of the Madonna after depositing the requisite rubles into the locked box next to the security guard. Clearly, the Russians were less concerned about the risks of photographic exposure on the quality of the masterpieces than they were of the potential profit they stood to make from charging people a fee to photograph them.

Inside the Hermitage museum's "Stolen Treasures" room, there were countless paintings by Renoir, Monet, and Cezanne. In a separate room unto itself was the museum's prized and most famous collection of Rembrandts. Although far from being an art buff, the beauty of the paintings did not escape Louis, and like the others in his group, he marveled at them. They were exquisite.

Louis spent the greatest amount of time looking at the Rembrandt painting titled "The Return of the Prodigal Son." He was familiar with the biblical parable in which the story is told of the son who squanders his inheritance, returns with a plea for forgiveness, and is forgiven. It was the details of the painting that mesmerized him. From the father's somber eye to the son's foot that was apparently missing its slipper, Louis was moved. It was amazing to realize that the talented artistry capable of painting such a picture nearly four hundred years ago rivaled what technology, in the form of the camera, could produce today.

An hour and half later, the group hustled out of the Hermitage and boarded the bus, hurrying so that they could be back at the hotel in time for the conference afternoon sessions. Once back at the hotel, Louis attended the first of three sessions, then went back to his room where he quickly fell asleep exhausted from the restless sleep the night before. When he woke up a couple of hours later, he decided to head out for some air.

Outside the hotel, he eventually found himself walking down Muscovy Street, the longest street in St. Petersburg. He passed a McDonalds and a department store that reminded him vaguely of a store he might see at home. It was not what would be considered one of the finer, luxury department stores but instead a middle of the road shopping outlet for a working-class community.

Out of curiosity, he entered the store and walked through the first floor. He didn't buy anything but couldn't help noticing that on the same floor where women's and men's clothing, slacks, undershirts, and T-shirts were sold, there was also a counter for firearms and another for laundry detergent. *Truly, a store that lived up to the goal of providing one stop shopping*, he thought.

Back at the hotel, the last afternoon session had ended, and the attendees were once again boarding buses. Louis met a tall man who immediately introduced himself as Niles Lewis. They shook hands as they made their way to an empty row of seats in the middle of the bus and decided to sit together. Louis took the window seat.

"Hey, good meeting you. I'm a long way from home. From Carleton College in Minnesota. What about you? Where are you from?"

"I'm from Philadelphia, and I'm just glad to have been able to make this trip."

"Really? Been looking forward to it for a bit, huh?"

"Yeah, that's an understatement," said Louis.

"I'd submitted a proposal for my work as soon as I caught wind of the conference. I've never submitted to ICOPE before. Have you participated in any of their other conferences?"

"Never. This is my first time, too! I only get a limited budget for international travel, and what with my heavy teaching load, it's nearly impossible to make these kinds of jaunts. But, hey, what can I say? It worked out this once, and I'm so psyched to be in mother Russia." Niles laughed at his own enthusiasm.

For the second time since arriving to St. Petersburg, Louis was convinced that he had made the right decision to travel there. He and Niles talked throughout the ride.

As they drew near to the stop where they would all get out to board the short boat tour, Niles pointed to a large open square they passed. He said, "You see that square right there?"

Louis nodded his head.

"Well, it may look like nothing to you now, but tomorrow at about this time, it will be filled with every item under the sun that can be sold for a price. And I do mean every item. I'm telling you, it's a sight to behold. The guidebooks refer to it as a kind of farmer's market on steroids, and that only comes close to what this thing actually is."

Curious about what it was, Louis agreed to visit the market the following day.

"I came in last week a little before the conference in order to look around and do some serious sightseeing. I just happened to stumble on this massive market on my way to one of the smaller museums not far from here. At first, I couldn't tell if it was some kind of a protest or a demonstration or what. I mean, it's unlike anything you have ever seen. You have got to check it out."

Louis was intrigued and promised to check it out. He wondered whether there would be anything he was interested in buying. Maybe he'd pick up some souvenirs. He could get her something too depending on how he felt then.

The bus delivered them to a parking lot not far from the River Neva where they would board a boat for a riverbank sightseeing tour. Everyone got off the bus and milled about the tour coordinators. After each member of the tour group was given a small card that represented tickets for the boat, they crossed the street and walked along the river's banks.

Their boat would travel the course of the river before arriving at Admiralteysky Quay, an area west of the city center. Louis was looking forward to the sights along the way. He was especially excited about seeing the Tsar Carpenter statue of Peter the Great, something that almost every guidebook or online travel site had recommended.

Even though there were parts along the River Neva where people swam in warm weather and children played in the sand, it was hard to envision either of these frolicking scenes at this particular place along the river. The water was dark in color, and it moved as if it were rushing for an appointment for which it was already late. It wended its way through the city running parallel to its major *prospekts* or parkways.

Excitedly, the people lined up and began boarding the large boat. Once aboard, many of the conference attendees stood along the railing in the ship's stern. They chatted excitedly and took photographs of the images that passed them by like still images in a slow-moving film. More than a few of the boat's passengers commented on the unique angle their view from the river below the streets provided.

"It feels a little weird looking up like this," remarked one man in heavily accented English. Louis hadn't met him yet and simply nodded. The man spoke to no one in particular and continued, "From down here, I say it feels a little wrong. Sort of like looking up a lassie's skirt," he sniggered.

"Well, just so long as you don't really look up anyone's skirt and keep your eyes on architect, that's what they want us to focus on, you should be okay," said another of the boat's passengers.

At that point, the boat's captain welcomed the passengers, making a special point of greeting attendees of the ICOPE meeting.

"Welcome aboard. You will ride now on the River [he pronounced it 'ree-var'] Neva. I'm am hoping you have an enjoyable time. To your left, please notice, the…" His scripted commentary droned on, and Louis turned his attention to the large Russian baroque and gothic style buildings bordering the embankment. The buildings made from simple brick masonry were grey and terra cotta colored and ranged in size from five to six stories. They were primarily apartment buildings, and because the facade of each of them was ornate, they reminded him ever so slightly of the Russian palaces and mansions of an earlier period. Louis couldn't help imagining what the occupants of the buildings were like.

It was the window in one such building that held his attention for several seconds longer than was typical, and which when looking back on the turn of events, he blamed for his inattention and inability to describe what triggered a catastrophic chain of events. A small child appeared to be perched, presumably on the inside, of the window's sill. But because it was at least five stories up, Louis realized that what he thought he saw, a small child sitting on the window's ledge, could very well have been something entirely different. The child could have actually have been sitting on the exterior ledge of the window; perhaps it wasn't even a child that he saw. Maybe it was a cat after all. Louis looked long and hard at the window.

Several moments later, there was the sound of the squeal of tires. Immediately, on its heels came a loud bang signaling the crash of two or more vehicles. Instinctively, Louis's eyes dropped from the window to the street alongside, which the boat traversed. When he saw nothing there accounting for the noise, he turned around to look at the street on the other side of the river.

By the time he realized that the sound stemmed from a car crash on the bridge overhead, which the boat had just cleared, the worst of the accident became apparent. Within seconds after the crash, a small truck similar in size to the shuttle bus that transported him from the airport two days earlier sailed over the bridge through the air, clearing all but a small section of the bow of the tour boat. It flew, like a projectile, as if it had been propelled by considerable force to do just that. That the truck managed to miss most of the tour boat, striking only its very front represented the worst of the tragedy for the unlucky conference attendees who happened to be positioned on deck at the most forward point of the boat's hull.

The terrifying screams followed the second loud crash that occurred when the truck made impact with the boat. And then came the sound of splashing water. As the boat shook and heaved strongly toward the bow and its starboard, a loud crack could be heard. It was the sound of the boat breaking apart.

The ship's passengers who had chosen to ride in the boat's stern saw this and within seconds grasped the significance of what had happened. They began to panic. One by one, like a chain reaction, the fear settled upon each of them like mites dropping from a plague's cloud. They were initially immobilized, but just as quickly, the motive to survive revived them. They were the lucky ones, and where possible, they frantically grabbed for life vests before jumping overboard into the river.

For its part, the River Neva beckoned them, and while she did not promise succor, she provided them with an escape from the ship now on fire and sinking quickly as if to follow its now invisible bow.

Those who'd chosen to sit and stand in the front of the ship for the tour were killed instantly. Among them, Louis could recall only the friendly Niles Lewis who he had befriended earlier on the bus ride at the outset of the tour. How unsettling it was to know that he was gone and that he had only had that one opportunity to know him.

With a life vest held in both hands, Louis jumped. At that moment, he thought of many things. He thought about the delayed flight and thought how it was that if the first flight had actually arrived too late for him to make his connecting flight, he probably never would have been in this predicament.

Louis also noticed how uninviting the River Neva appeared. He wanted nothing to do with her. Yet at the same time, he didn't want to die. These two incompatible thoughts were ultimately resolved when he made the decision to jump off the sinking ship into the river.

It was only with the shock of the cold water that his thoughts coalesced into a single, new one. He decided at that moment that if he survived, he would change his life, and that would inevitably involve returning to her. But if he didn't survive, it didn't much matter.

What took hold of him next was a sense of extraordinarily worry over who would actually tell her of his demise. When he left the US, she was fragile, and his trip to St. Petersburg, while not the cause of her vulnerability, had certainly compounded it. In this moment, he regretted his decision terribly.

Louis splashed about the river with the others who had also jumped in and quickly assessed the situation. He was keenly aware of the fact that he was in the water, and that the ship he was on just minutes earlier was now barely visible. The Neva seemed first to kiss the boat before heartily swallowing it whole. Within moments, the boat had succumbed, and it sank beneath the surface, out of view.

There were a number of people who were screaming. For some, it was because they were afraid of drowning, and for others, it was because they'd lost sight of friends and colleagues. And then there were also the people on land and on the bridge who screamed. Oddly enough, it seemed that their screams were in English, though this hardly seemed possible. Louis wondered whether death screams and screams of terror were language specific and decided at that moment that they probably were not.

The crew aboard the sunken ship who'd survived and those associated with the boat on land were all trying to be helpful, but in their agitated states, they'd reverted to Russian and so the largely non-Russian-speaking group of people struggling to stay afloat in the water understood little of what they were saying. They understood only that they needed to get out of water and away from the area where their ship went under.

Those who had made it to land as well as a number of bystanders were pulling people from the water. Louis was hoisted out of the water to the boulevard that ran alongside the river. Eventually, he walked along with the other survivors from his boat onto a waiting bus. He thought they would automatically be taken to a hospital to be checked out even if there were no visible injuries, and so he was surprised when he realized that they had been delivered directly to the conference hotel.

This was an example of how things differed as a result of the country in which one found oneself. *Had an accident of this magnitude occurred in the States*, thought Louis, *all survivors would have been taken to the hospital for examination.* Then they would have each been interviewed by representatives of the various government agencies and approached by any number of personal injury lawyers.

Here in Russia, there was a sense in which those he encountered immediately following the accident seemed to believe that he and the other survivors were lucky enough to have survived. Anything more than that, including medical attention or litigation, was simply more than they could fathom. It was not so much that they did not see his predicament as one that merited additional attention, but more so it was not something they could imagine in a world that still retained many of the vestiges of the era of Soviet life.

To be sure, Louis was happy to be alive. Yet, he could not help thinking about the deaths of the other conference attendees who just happened to have been unlucky in deciding upon where to station themselves aboard what was to have been a lovely sightseeing voyage up the River Neva. What of Niles Lewis? He would never get to know him beyond the short conversation they had on the bus that had ultimately delivered the poor man to his death. He had mentioned having a wife and a family back in the midwestern town he called home. Who would make that horrible call to them? Among the conference organizers, hotel staff, and others Louis encountered, he couldn't imagine a sufficient quantity of empathy to relay the devastating news in as painless a way as possible.

Back in his room, Louis took off his clothes and removed his waterlogged and now ruined camera from his pocket. He tossed everything in a heap on the floor and noticed a faint odor. Naked and stepping closer to the pile, he smelled a whiff of mildew, and there was another smell he wasn't able to identify. It didn't matter though, he planned to dump it all.

He stepped into a hot shower and stood under the faucet for a long time. He found the water comforting as it pummeled his head and ran down his face. The realization that he had skirted death became clear in much the same way as the shower water cleared his skin, hair and nails of any residual microorganisms that latched on to him as a result of his time in the river.

Louis began to cry. His tears mixed with the shower water and washed the soap and shampoo that ran off his body. *Too much water for one day*, he thought wryly. Tears, the river, and this extra shower made for far more time with water than he liked. He was as surprised by his emotional lability as he was affected by the events of the afternoon.

His thoughts eventually returned to her. The experience today left him feeling deeply wounded. At a very basic level, he wanted to be held. He wanted someone who loved him to take joy in knowing that he'd survived the ordeal of the boat. For now, he would just have to settle with being satisfied that he had not died on board the boat.

She had called him that day when everything seemed to have fallen apart for them. Louis remembered it clearly. He had been in good spirits, having just learned that a highly regarded European publisher would publish his book the following spring. When he answered the phone, she was crying. How had this happened to them?

Louis had left her only for a few hours each day following the delivery of the baby. As far as pregnancies went, hers was pretty smooth. She'd experienced some morning sickness the first month, but in the following months, she had none of that discomfort. Of course, she was sensitive to the weight gain she'd experienced and the other changes in her body, but she was even more lovely to him. He had always loved her but found himself feeling more loving toward her during the pregnancy.

When she delivered the baby, it was as if all their hopes and dreams for a child had rolled up into a great big, unyielding ball that lodged itself into her body. For nearly eighteen hours, she had struggled and sweated and screamed until at last the beautiful little baby, a girl, who would be their daughter, came out into the world. Babies are born around the globe at every second of the day, and yet the event itself was indeed a miracle. When Ava was born, they were over the moon and smitten with her.

Ava did not take to her mother's breast initially, which they were told was not all that unusual. Sometimes, it took a bit of prodding and time, and sometimes, infants never did. But what was unusual and in the end proved tragic was the baby's inability to eat and to regularly wake up. These were clear signs that something was wrong.

In those first three days before learning that something was terribly wrong, they'd agonized. It was an agony so profound that it rivaled the intensity of pain that came later when they received the actual diagnosis. Ava, their baby girl, had a rare, incurable genetic disorder called nonketotic hyperglycinemia that impairs the brain and leads to seizures, breathing and feeding difficulties.

They were devastated. Neither of them had any real idea about what to do when Ava left them just six days after her celebrated birth. Apart from the practical matters like what they would do with all the clothes, gifts, and furniture they'd amassed in the last nine months in preparation for her, there was the intangible and unexpected matter of having to reconfigure their relationship with one another and their identity as parents.

While it is true that couples don't truly fit into their identity of parenthood until they are actually with their baby or child, there is a gradual adjustment in preparing for the arrival of a child. Now, because their baby died within days of her birth, they had wrestled with their shared identity as parents of the deceased at the same time that they found themselves redefining their personal identities and relations with one another.

It was too hard to bear and their marriage suffered. They were on the older side of having babies, and although it was possible that they could conceive again, it would not be easy. They would have to move on and reach for each other again.

Trying to find the coordination to do so was hard because they each dealt with the hardship differently. Louis returned to work with an urgency he hadn't had in years. The distractions of work provided him an ameliorative remedy to his pain, and he relished the opportunity each day to leave home, and though he wouldn't admit it to leave her.

She had taken nearly six months off for maternity leave, and although there was no baby to care for, she used the time to remain at home. It was there that she found comfort with her constant companion of grief. She wept quietly at unexpected times and in the corners of the house that provided solace.

Although they were kind enough and spoke to one another in order to exchange information about the necessities of living together, after the loss, they rarely made eye contact, and they almost never touched one another. He remembered one morning walking behind her chair at the exact moment that she stood up and how it felt when they'd awkwardly collided with one another. They apologized like strangers on a train. It was as if the emotional distance that separated them had morphed into an actual physical gulf so that the experience of physically touching one another had caught them both off guard.

A few months later, he prepared to leave for the conference in Russia. As he packed his bags, it was understood that she would not be coming with him. When their lives were bright, and hopeful they'd planned the trip and laughed together about Russia being their baby's first international destination. They were so excited, hopeful and happy.

Louis realized now how profoundly he missed her and the comfort in being with her. He was ashamed that he had not given her more of himself in the aftermath of Ava's death. He wanted to tell her that, but he knew he probably never would. The most he could do was to be by her side. They would have to get past this pain together. He looked around his hotel room, for the first time noticing a phone. Louis decided to call and find his way back to her and their lives together.

THE FOOT MASSAGE IN THAILAND

The key turned easily in the door and with a slight push it opened. It was dark and the faint scent of bleach in the air reminded him for just a second of Saturday mornings in his childhood home. The memory was shrouded in haze, but the pungent smell of bleach brought him directly back to the periodic cleansing ritual he recalled his mother undertaking with fervor most Saturday mornings. Franklin maneuvered the doorway by turning slightly sideways in order to enter with all three pieces of luggage he carried.

For this trip, he'd splurged and purchased what he thought of as a proper set of luggage. It was the first set he'd ever bought for himself, and more than signaling maturity, it reflected a newfound sense of readiness to move, to travel and take steps in new directions. The matching pieces of luggage were sleek, midnight blue, and in the dark room, they blended in imperceptibly.

He felt around for a light switch to the right and then the left side of the doorway. He eventually found it. It was slightly above where he had anticipated it, and because of its bevel shape that was unlike the wall switches typically found in homes in America, it was unfamiliar to him. He eventually managed to switch it on and gradually, the room lit up.

That was also different. Instead of immediately being plunged into light and having to come to one's ocular senses quickly, the light came on gradually. Within a few moments, the small room he stood in was bathed in a reassuring yellow light that flowed from several overhead structures discretely tucked into corners of the nine-foot-high ceilings. As the light illuminated the room, it comforted him.

It felt good to be able to put down his bags and rest his shoulders and arms. The trip had been grueling, but at last he was here; wherever here really was. His guidebooks described Phuket, one of the many small islands of Thailand, as a gem within a crown of beauty. He had every intention of discovering all of what it had to offer during his stay. At the moment, however, with darkness surrounding him, it was hard to have much of an opinion.

His flight from Bangkok to Phuket International Airport had arrived at about 1:00 a.m., and that was after a long layover. He was a bit dazed not just because of the grueling nature of the long flight in premium economy, but also because of the fact that he was now on the other side of the globe. It drained him to think of the many miles he had traveled to get there. All in all, he had been traveling for close to twenty-six hours to get from Detroit, Michigan, to his arrival in warm, muggy Phuket.

In Detroit, it was a gloomy wintry February day when he'd boarded the jumbo jet to travel some six thousand miles across the globe to Thailand. That first flight was long, too long. He had upgraded to the so-called premium economy seat, which as far as he could tell looked and felt a lot like economy except his legs were only jammed into the rear of the seat in front of him when the person occupying that seat decided to sit all the way back. That was the upgrade. Had he been in regular economy, his legs would have collided with the back seat of the passenger in front of him even when they hadn't reclined their seat.

During the flight, he'd watched four movies, had a couple of beers, ate each time a meal was served, and napped. He had not been able to sleep very well. When the plane finally landed at Bangkok's Suvarnabhumi Airport, Franklin was exhausted.

As far as he could tell, the airport lacked any comfortable seats, and there was little that had been added to ensure the comfort of travelers. Although he wasn't really hungry, he had looked forward to getting some good Thai food during the four-hour layover he had before the flight to Phuket. To his surprise, not only wasn't there any Thai food to be had in the airport, but also the only food establishments that were there were Western chain restaurant troves.

Indeed, he was taken aback and disappointed by the number of American fast-food restaurants like Burger King, KFC, Starbucks, and Krispy Kreme that were there. Eventually, he gave in and purchased a chicken sandwich and french fries from KFC.

After eating, Franklin wandered through the airport noting its relatively small size. The airport itself seemed like the no frills equivalent of the budget airline he'd just flown. What little shopping existed was small and of the cheap variety. He saw more than a few "made in China" stickers on the items for sale that he inspected. After finding his way to the gate for the flight to Phuket, Franklin settled in for the wait for the final leg of his journey.

There were no television screens, and seating though sufficient was pretty basic. He was tired, bored, and anxious to be finished with this part of his adventure. He couldn't wait to get to Phuket.

Every few minutes, it seemed his mind turned to the events that had happened in the last year. He thought of the most recent passage of time in much the same way as one views a digitized movie in its reverse mode. By selecting "rewind," he saw the unfolding of each event until at last he'd arrived at what seemed to be the start for what followed. He couldn't help but shake his head at times, incredulous over the strangeness of it all. When the ordeal had finally ended, he was left not quite knowing what to do, where to go, or who to talk to.

Everyone he knew told him to pick himself up and start over again, make a clean start someplace else. It was a well-worn cliché to think that one could just pack up, leave, and start anew, but he thought seriously about doing so. Why not leave Detroit? It wasn't like he had any real emotional ties to the city any longer. He was divorced, he had no children, and his parents had long since passed away. His job as a mid-level manager in the regional office of a national insurance firm though manageable was something he had long since grown tired of doing. There was a certain tedium that characterized most of his days at work.

Franklin had taken a month's leave of absence before actually deciding what to do with the time away. Unable to sleep the first night of his self-imposed sojourn, he was up late one night mindlessly watching television when he'd come across a show on the travel network that featured several vacation destinations in Asia. He'd never been to Asia before and was drawn in as much by the beautiful landscapes and distinctive exotic cultures as he was by the fact of its unfamiliarity and novelty to him.

Franklin longed for the cover of anonymity. He was intrigued by the prospect of journeying to the other side of the world where he would be a stranger to everyone he encountered.

The next day, he began a thoughtful search online exploring Thailand and the island of Phuket. After figuring out what a trip would cost, he decided to do it. By that evening, he was confirmed on a Thai Airlines flight leaving Detroit the following Friday.

For the first time in months, he was actually looking forward to something.

While he was not happy about the long travel time required to get to Thailand, the actual flight and logistics of getting there were for him a part of the overall experience. He knew, indeed he sensed, that this would be a life-altering trip; one which he would come to look back on for years to come. He dreaded the return journey but decided not to think about it. The flight was just a part of it and as long as he survived, he figured it would be worth it.

Franklin knew that travel provided a way to put the breaks on his current condition, to step out and see the unexpected. He knew that if he was willing to imagine what an unknown place might be like, an actual trip there offered an opportunity to bring that image to life. Whether being there confirmed or disconfirmed his expectations, travel made incarnate imagined experiences and places.

He was here now and had one month to enjoy, explore, and expunge his mind of everything that had weighed on him and taxed him to the core in the last year.

It had begun with an innocent meeting online that had followed a virtual introduction that a friend of a friend (or so he had thought) had made for him.

Two years ago, Franklin had taken a continuing education course that his employer had paid for as a part of their commitment to professional development. The class met once a week on the campus of a local community college. In the study group he belonged to, he'd met a woman, Annette, who he grew to like a great deal. She was smart and friendly and seemed to be a straight shooter.

Although there were three other people in the study group, from the beginning, Franklin sensed a unique connection between the two of them. Consequently, Franklin was saddened to have to say goodbye to her when the class ended. He was pretty certain that he wouldn't see her again.

Of course, everyone in the group went through the motions of exchanging contact information and promises to get together. He remembered the last day of the study group when they'd had a potluck, and everyone shared what they had brought with one another. Annette had seemed to make a pointed effort to exchange information with Franklin, saying, "Hey, Franklin, as happy as I am to have completed this course, I am really bummed to have to say good-bye to everyone here, especially you."

Franklin had responded in his usual reserved way saying, "Oh, I feel the same way. I actually look forward to the class meetings each week in order to get together. I'm sorry it's come to an end."

That seemed to be fine with Annette because she had asked him for his telephone number. As she entered it into her cell phone, Franklin asked for hers and took the plunge by suggesting that perhaps they could get together.

"Maybe, we can find a time that works for lunch or a coffee," he said hopefully, though hoping not to sound too hopeful.

"Yes, or course, let's do that!" she'd said. She had given him her office number.

"It's been such a great experience. Not just the class of course but spending time with you and everyone." At that point, she'd gestured to their other classmates and turned away from Franklin.

He had remained hopeful in the immediate days following that last day. Franklin thought quite a bit about Annette and about the fact that he had her contact information, even if it was just her office number. He could reach her at work if he wanted to, but as time passed, his enthusiasm and hopefulness waned.

Franklin rarely initiated contact with others outside his immediate sphere of engagement. With the class having ended, the only people he actually spoke to each day were those at work. If it wasn't work-related, he usually opted out of social gatherings requiring informal interaction; and he never initiated contact. The divorce three years ago had done that to him.

So, it was a pleasant surprise when he received a phone call from a friend of Annette's several months after the study group parted ways and the class had ended. "Corinne" told him that Annette sent her regards and had forwarded his contact information because Corinne had recently moved to the Detroit area. She had just relocated from California and needed information about insurance options for a personal collection of antique goods and furniture.

Franklin was happy to answer her questions and took some measure of pride in being able to answer each of them with details that only someone who was extremely knowledgeable could do. Although it would likely have been boring to anyone outside his profession, he was excited to share his expertise with the intricacies of insurance coverage for valuable antiques.

As a result, his confidence was buoyed. Without even thinking about it, he found himself inviting her to his office to continue the conversation. She seemed to be happy with that and in accepting his invitation to visit the office, she went a step further and suggested they meet over lunch or later in the day for cocktails. Surprised but also pleased, he'd accepted her invitation, and the two met for lunch a few days later.

In retrospect and with hindsight, he realized later that he was more open and less reserved in his initial interactions with Corinne because she was a friend of Annette. Had she not been her friend, he probably would not have been as open, willing, and vulnerable. He hadn't treated her like a complete stranger because she was Annette's friend, and so he'd opened himself up to her and had instantly warmed to her attention.

Corinne was a self-described collector, though that did not explain how she supported herself in the absence of any apparent actual employment. He'd learned that over lunch that first day when he'd asked, "How did you come to acquire such valuable pieces? I don't know any individual who has such a valuable personal collection, though I have some experience in working with corporate clients who do. It's a remarkable collection."

Flattered, Corinne had explained, "Well, I never actually started out with any plans to be a collector. Even now, I honestly don't know if I am a proper 'collector.' I fell into this when my mother's mother passed away and left several Queen Anne pieces. They weren't really even left for me personally, but Mom died shortly after her mother, and there were no siblings. All of the pieces passed to me. God rest her soul." Corinne uttered these last words with such reverence that Franklin assumed much about the relationship.

He also assumed that Corinne came from wealthy stock. At that initial meeting, she had said or done nothing to disabuse him of that belief. It would be much later before he learned otherwise.

As Franklin wandered through the hotel apartment that he would call home for the next four weeks in Phuket, he looked closely at the details and personal touches that revealed something of the owner's style in decorating. The furnishings were contemporary, but it was possible to detect a hint of island flair. It was reflected in the small driftwood sculpture adorning the glass cocktail table in front of the living room's only sofa. The room was comfortably though sparsely furnished.

Franklin wondered who actually owned the rental flat. Was it a man or woman? Was it a Westerner or an Asian? Were they Thai? Or, maybe they were Russian?

He'd noticed quite a few Russians in the airport as well as in the lobby when he checked into the apartment hotel. It was hard to tell who the owner of the rental was; there were decorative touches that could be attributed to any one of the dominant ethnic groups he knew to comprise Phuket.

The apartment was a bit stuffy, and Franklin's first impulse was to open one of the shuttered windows, but as he approached it, he noticed the condensation on the glass and remembered the intense heat and humidity that draped the island even now well past midnight. He thought better of it and decided instead to adjust the air conditioning.

After doing so, he wheeled his luggage into the larger of the two bedrooms. He remembered the conversation he'd had with the travel agent who had essentially convinced him of the value of a two-bedroom rental instead of one. Now he was not so sure of that decision.

"Natalia" had said that the two-bedroom rentals actually wound up costing less than the one-bedroom ones because of the little-known tax system on the island that calculated taxes on the basis of a complex computation related to the number of people relative to the number of bedrooms. Somehow, as a single person, he actually came out ahead by renting two bedrooms rather than one. Like so many other thoughts that entered his mind as of late, this one immediately reminded him of the circumstances that gave rise to his now solo status.

His thoughts returned to that very first day when he and Corinne had met over lunch at a restaurant near his office. Because he rarely went out for lunch, the receptionist and several of his coworkers were aware of his absence during the lunch hour. Knowing that they knew he had broken from routine and was likely out with someone made him slightly sensitive to the time he spent at lunch with Corinne.

They'd met at one of the few upscale restaurants in the area. Most of the neighborhood eating establishments near his office tended toward the "Mom and Pop" variety—pure Midwestern Americana with grilled cheese sandwiches on sunny days, and pot roast and chili when the weather turned grim.

This restaurant was different. Rumor had it that a transplant from New York City was the restaurant's "silent" owner. The story was that he'd founded a dot. com company, made a lot of money, and sold the company before the market tanked. It wasn't clear if the restaurant would survive after its novelty wore off, but everyone who dined there during its initial period raved about it despite its relatively more expensive prices.

Corinne had arrived before him and was waiting when he arrived. As the hostess led him to their table and she saw him approaching, she rose gracefully from her seat and extended her hand to greet him. He was pleasantly surprised by her appearance.

She was slim and attractive, and her eyes seemed to sparkle. He put her at just over forty-five.

As an insurance assessor, he tended to be remarkably accurate in estimating people's ages. He would later learn he was spot on—she had turned forty-five on her last birthday! A nice age he had thought then.

At forty-nine, Franklin was slightly older than her, which meant that he was old enough to know and forecast the signposts of middle age that would appear along her path. At the same time, because he was a smart man, he knew that he was more of an emotional peer than an "emotional elder," and one that had as much to learn from her as he could possibly teach her.

His coworkers had said nothing when he returned from lunch that day, though they surely noticed his absence and amount of time spent away from the office. He had been gone for nearly an hour and a half. Although no one had commented or said anything about his absence, there seemed to be a current in the room that shimmered from their seemingly knowing silence.

Franklin and his coworkers were not especially formal with one another, but they were careful, and while they all wanted to know what accounted for his time away and why he seemed to step ever so slightly lighter upon return, no one dared to inquire. Not one of them thought it appropriate to ask. He knew this and appreciated them for it. And yet, at the same time, he desperately wanted to share something with someone about the tiny sparks ignited somewhere between his heart and his mind. He was attracted to Corinne.

What followed were several more lunches and then dinner, and within a few months, they were a couple. Corinne seemed to enjoy his company a great deal, and for his part, he enjoyed spending time with her. She was something of a risk taker and given that he was not, this characteristic of hers excited him.

He remembered how she had suggested one evening that they go to the big casino downtown, the MGM Grand Detroit Casino. Although he had lived in Detroit for as long as its casinos had operated, nearly fifteen years, he'd never ventured inside one. He never gambled and had never really had an urge to do so. But she was different, and because he enjoyed her company, he found himself not only doing things he didn't usually do, but also doing things differently from the way he'd habitually done them. So, one brisk autumn evening on a Friday, the two met there after he had left work.

For the first hour, he had watched intently as she played blackjack. She'd won and lost and won again something in the neighborhood of $5,000. He'd lost track after the first series of losses, and at the end of that time frame when it seemed that she'd lose all of it and more, she'd won again.

He'd struggled throughout the entire time as he found himself consciously restraining the urge to insist that she quit. His risk averse nature made games of chance like the one she was intent on playing as pleasant as a visit to the dentist. When at last she had quit, he was relieved. He was physically drained as a result of the time she had spent at the table.

Oddly enough, when she'd finished the game, it seemed that all the anxiety he'd experienced while watching her play had been transformed into some kind of heightened arousal. His libido, which normally existed at a fairly tranquil level, had run amuck. Franklin could hardly restrain himself. This was highly unusual for him. He was not the type of man who regularly displayed affection in public, and in private, he tended to be relatively reserved. It was strange. There was something about her gambling that he found to be as appealing as it was in some way appalling to him.

That same evening after they had made love, Franklin learned more about her finances and came to understand that not only wasn't she wealthy, but she also struggled financially. She regarded her winnings that evening as far more important than he had realized.

As she told him what her youth had been like, her countenance underwent a noticeable change. She described the circumstances of her youth, her childhood home, and her parents. As she continued speaking, he was struck by the simmering rage that seemed to percolate just beneath the surface of her relatively flat demeanor.

"My father wasn't much of a father. Aside from having knocked my mother up three times, he was no father to speak of. Each time he left my mother, she had a newborn to care for, and two of those times, she had small children as well. He didn't care much about us or her, and I never could understand why she'd always take him back. The first was a mistake, the second and third times were just plain sinful. As a child and then when I grew up, I never forgave either one of them."

Apparently, her father had left her mother for good when she and her siblings were quite young. Her mother never really rebounded. She was devastated by his absence and, according to Corinne, took his absence far more seriously than his character warranted. He was not a nice man, and she swore that she would never forgive him.

Corinne's recounting of her experience as a child spoke volumes about the way that childhood hurts could spill over and create an adulthood of painful longing. This was the first time that Franklin had sensed such disquietude with her. He wanted to take her pain away, but he wasn't sure that he could.

He had tried to hold her. But she had pushed away. On the surface, she seemed strangely flat, as if her emotions had left her in much the same way that her father had left her mother after the birth of their third child—unabashedly abruptly.

As he looked around the apartment, Franklin noticed that the television in the bedroom he had chosen to sleep in was the larger of the two in the apartment. Pleased with his choice, he looked around for the remote control and found it next to the phone on the small table by the queen-sized bed. He picked up the remote, deciding to postpone the task of unpacking, and sat down heavily on the edge of the bed with a sigh of relief.

He mechanically went through the channels noticing that very few were in English. He settled on the British Broadcasting Channel. They were airing a story about the problem in Syria that had now become a situation throughout the Middle East. It was rapidly spilling over into other regions of the world including Europe and America. Even though he followed global events sporadically, he sensed the urgency and impending doom. There would be a lot more bloodshed and war before anything good came of the current turmoil.

For a moment, he took comfort in his own personal crisis. Though no less important in its consequences to him, it was far smaller in that it had disrupted two people's lives only—his and Corinne's. He recognized the perverse value in peering in on other people's misery. It paled his own.

Franklin thought more about his experiences with Corinne and everything else that had happened. As he tried to replay events that might have been prophetic or otherwise significant, it felt like he was thumbing the pages of a book, only backwards as he tried to make sense of what had ultimately happened. He could not place his finger on the precise moment when things shifted in their relationship. Despite the bad feelings he was now left with and the pieces of his life now shattered which he sought to repair, he had to admit that in the beginning and for much of their time together, there was more fun and light than there was pain and darkness. Although he knew early on that she was not perfect, he couldn't help being drawn to her despite her imperfections.

It was only toward the end, though he did not see it as such back then, that things began to unravel. Just when he'd become comfortable with the rhythm of the affair—its predictability, comfort, and fullness—it seemed she experienced a very different set of feelings.

For no reason he could think of, she became agitated and edgy at unpredictable times. He could not soothe her mood when this happened. Eventually, he learned that what worked best was to be near her but not to engage her. It was like being a primary actor in the background cast of a drama he lived. It was a strange experience that only became downright weird later.

There were a couple of times in the beginning when the thought had occurred to Franklin that he was being followed. That sensation crossed his mind several times, and usually it occurred when they'd been separated because of work conflicts and other obligations for prolonged times. *But why would anyone want to follow me?* Franklin had wondered. He'd dismissed the thought.

Most recently at work, he had been responsible for handling the accounts of several important clients in a relatively short time period. It was during that series of work assignments that he'd found himself having to cancel two dates in a row with Corinne. Although he had rescheduled them, it was not without a fair measure of duress on her part. He was always conscientious enough to let her know well in advance, and she always seemed understanding. But the next time he communicated with her, she would be as distant and cold as an ice princess on Mars.

It was after the second time that it had happened that he had sensed someone's presence in a space that logic and experience told him was unoccupied. The first time it occurred one evening when he was leaving the office late. Everyone had left before him, so that by 8:30 p.m., when he looked at the clock and realized how late it was, it was eerily quiet in the office. He'd begun putting his piles of paper together and packing up when he thought he heard what sounded like footsteps in one of the adjoining offices. It was the office normally reserved for the firm's accountants, and he had called out, "Sam? Maria?" not really expecting to hear a response but waiting nonetheless. When no response came, he'd shrugged and finished packing his things away.

Later in the parking lot, which was fairly well lit, he'd heard a sound not far behind. When he turned quickly to look over his left shoulder in the direction of the sound, he thought he'd seen a shadow. The hairs on the back of his neck rose. He had stopped, looked around, and like a doomed character from a B-rated horror movie, he called out, "Is anyone there?" This time, he didn't expect a response, but for some reason, he couldn't stop himself from continuing to speak aloud in the quiet and darkness of the garage. And although the sound of his own voice did not provide the solace that another person's might have, at that moment, and just for that moment, he was reassured that he was okay.

He had actually dashed to his car, immediately unlocked the doors, started the engine, and taken off. It had spooked him.

How did it get to that point? he wondered, as he wheeled the largest of his two suitcases into the bedroom. At one point, they were in love. It had been mutual.

He shook his head as he remembered the ambiguity he'd had in knowing what to call her. He saw the two of them as too mature to use the term "girlfriend" and "boyfriend." That term implied a degree of frivolity that he had wished to avoid. When eventually he introduced her to his colleagues at work, he took pains to stress the seriousness of the affair. Doing so conferred a respectfulness on their liaison that he believed to be warranted. As he saw it, they were mutually consenting adults who were not only passionate about one another, but they were also very serious about being together. What he believed to have existed between the two of them was far more significant than seemed typical of the current generation's "hookups."

For their part, his colleagues were extremely gracious, and they genuinely welcomed Corinne into their fold. There were now invitations for social events away from work that included her. Since his divorce, these kinds of enabling attributes of being a couple were all new to him. If he was honest with himself, he had to acknowledge that he previously had only limited experience in being a part of a couple that others thought of as such when he was married because neither he nor his ex-wife were terribly outgoing. What's more at the time when he was married, he hadn't really established a work life that included people who genuinely cared about him or about whom he cared. Yet another way he thought, that he was a late bloomer. Perhaps if he hadn't lived his life so resolutely behind and far from the proverbial eight ball, he'd have seen all of it coming. Perhaps.

For now, he was left wondering how he had missed the telltale signs that would have warned him of her instability. He spent far too much time thinking of her now nearly a year later. In the aftermath of the nightmare and following countless hours of speaking with law enforcement personnel and psychiatrists, he faced a combination of feelings of self-doubt and anger.

She'd caused him to question his own judgment. He was now left not only with the loss and grief that accompanied the demise of any relationship gone bad, but he also faced a pervasive sense of uncertainty that affected all of his decision-making. Ironically, the only big decision he'd made as of late without tremendous angst was the decision to take the trip to Thailand. That was done in the course of twenty-four hours following a bout of insomnia spent watching the travel channel.

After several experiences with sensing that someone was following him and not actually seeing anyone there, he had relaxed. At the same time, work had slowed down, and they had resumed their normal dating schedule. When he wasn't spending the night at her place, she was at his. To be sure, they weren't always mooning over one another, and they argued infrequently over small things. But the times they spent together in bliss certainly outweighed their times apart or their times together in straits.

Franklin had been caught off guard one evening when his boss convened an unexpected meeting after work, which he was required to attend. He'd called her around three thirty when he first learned of the meeting. It was as much to let her know that he probably would not be coming to her place that evening as it was to vent about his frustration with his boss and the job.

"Hello, my love. I am going to be unexpectedly delayed this evening, and I won't want to wake you, so I am probably going to just go home. Once again, my boss has dumped yet another unexpected tasker on me. Can you believe this? Do you remember when I told you…"

He'd gone on a bit admittedly, but she didn't have much to add to the conversation it seemed.

It wasn't the first time that Franklin had shared his dissatisfaction about work with Corinne and had expected nothing more than her willingness to listen and sympathize with him. This time, Corinne did neither. Instead, she had stopped him abruptly while he was mid-sentence announcing that she had to go.

"Look, I have to go, Franklin. Thanks so much for letting me know how important you and your job are. When you have some time, maybe we can try to get together then. Goodbye."

She'd hung up.

Puzzled, Franklin thought for a moment about calling her back to explain that this really was out of his control. Didn't she understand the responsibilities he had at work?

But in the end, he'd shrugged it off and dismissed her reaction to some sort of distraction. Maybe she had something on the stove or was working on the computer. He'd turned his attention to his boss and the task at hand.

That night, after a long meeting with his colleagues and boss, at which time he learned of the plans of his firm's parent organization to merge with a rival firm, he left the office and headed to the nearby People Mover station. He had not driven in that day because the weather had been nice, and he had planned on getting together with her that evening. She would have had her car as she always did, and they would have eventually driven to her home together. There was no sense in having two cars and driving separately.

As he walked to the nearest stop on the monorail, he was consumed with thoughts about the upcoming merger. What would it mean for him? For all of his colleagues in the Detroit office? His boss had assured them that their jobs would be secure and that the merger would be seamless. But neither Franklin nor his colleagues were assured of this.

Though there had been no time to discuss this among themselves, it was clear from the stunned expressions on each of their faces that this was far from being the good news their boss had suggested in his request for the meeting.

Even though Franklin's thoughts were focused on what the merger would mean for him, he was mindful of the late hour and the few people he actually encountered while walking. Still, he couldn't stop thinking about his job and wondering how secure it really was now that his firm would merge with another. "Would he have his job in a year's time?" "Did it make sense to look for something else now?" "What could he expect when the merger actually happened?"

Within fifteen minutes, Franklin made it to the station. After checking the display of the time-table and proceeding further down along the track, he looked around. He saw only one other person at the far end of the rail platform on which he stood. He read the electronic sign in red detailing the esti-mated time of arrival of the next train. He sighed and walked a few steps to the nearest row of waiting seats. It would be at least seventeen minutes before the next train according to the sign.

Some sixteen minutes later, while preoccupied with his thoughts about work and the merger, the electronic sign flashed to indicate the train's impending arrival. Franklin had hardly noticed that the figure he'd seen at the other end of the platform was gone.

As the train rushed forward along the track, Franklin sensed someone's presence. Within seconds, he felt himself being violently pushed in the direction of the oncoming train. He reacted immediately, bracing himself against the pressure and stopping within inches of the edge of the platform as the train approached. He was able to stop just short of the platform. However, because the laws of physics dictate that mass and speed create momentum, the initial force that had propelled him continued and with it the person who had pushed him.

It was Corinne! "Dear God, what is happening?" Franklin asked aloud. In that instant, the moment when he could have grabbed her and saved her from the gruesome fate she intended for him, he had frozen. He could hardly believe that it was her. She screamed as she flew through the air and was hit by the train before being crushed underneath its metal wheels. The train squealed to a stop some yards ahead. Alarms sounded from the train, and shortly afterwards, the station sounded its own alarm, presumably to signal the disaster that had just occurred. Someone—Corinne—had been killed on the rail tracks!

In the moments immediately following her death, Franklin watched its aftermath as a detached observer. It was as if the event involved someone other than himself. Who could blame him? It was too terrible a sight for anyone to witness, let alone a person so deeply connected to the person killed.

When the police and other first responders descended on the scene, his emotional state had passed from horror to shock to grief. They began to question him almost immediately. A police officer who identified himself as Inspector Lawrence was the first person to speak directly to him.

"Can you tell me what happened here, sir?"

"Uh, yes, of course, I mean...it was Corinne," Franklin offered.

"Do you mean to say that you knew the victim? Were you together?" asked the policeman who did not conceal his surprise.

"No, I mean yes, yes, I did know her. It was Corinne. I loved her. But we weren't together. I didn't know it was her."

"Sir, I am going to need you to calm down and explain to me what happened here. You said you knew the victim, but you were not together?"

Their conversation continued, but it was difficult to make sense out of what had happened. Franklin tried to explain that he had been waiting for the train and that there had been no one else there on the platform until just moments after the train emerged from out of the tunnel.

But then, his memory and the act of retelling became confusing. He said as much to the officer, apologizing.

"Look, I'm sorry, but it all happened so quickly. I mean, I remember standing up and walking to the platform just as the train came from the tunnel. Then I was just a few feet from the rail tracks, and I felt a push from out of nowhere!"

Franklin explained that at that moment, he remembered only struggling for his balance. That effort had saved his life. Because of that, it was he rather than Corinne who was the one attempting to answer the policeman's questions.

He could hardly believe that she had attacked him and that she had intended him harm. Even more than that at the time that the police questioned him, he couldn't grasp the fact that she had fallen in front of the train as a result of his failure to save her and that she was now gone.

It was unbelievable. He had been preoccupied with the matter at work, but always, even then, she remained in his periphery of thoughts. She was deeply present because of what she had come to mean to him and so to fathom the world—his world—without her would take time. It was not something he could manage right then and there.

He was taken to the police station where he was interviewed and asked to provide an official account of what had happened. Although Franklin was visibly distraught and narrated a series of events that proclaimed his innocence, the police knew that as time passed, his memory would degrade, even the parts, if there were any, less tinged by emotion. He needed to be interviewed immediately.

In the meantime, the police and representatives of the monorail system culled recordings from the security cameras. Fortunately, it provided them with video footage of what had transpired in the moments before Corinne's attack and subsequent death. The video recording also showed when and where they had each entered as well as the direction in which they approached the rail tracks and proceeded upon arriving.

What they observed was consistent with Franklin's account. He was cleared of any wrong-doing. With this evidence, the police were kinder. They even apologized to Franklin for what he'd experienced.

Before he left the police station, Franklin was permitted to look at the CCTV footage. He thought he had managed it all pretty well, but when he saw the video, it was shock all over again. He watched Corinne, who on tape was very much alive. He noticed her hair. It seemed she'd styled it differently, and she wasn't dressed appropriately given the brisk clime that characterized Detroit at that time of year. He said as much to the police officer who showed him the footage.

"She doesn't look like herself. Her hair is differ-ent, and she isn't [he spoke as if she were still among the living] wearing a coat. It was cold today. That's weird," he'd said, as if that were the only thing that stood out about the entire course of events in the last few hours.

In addition to her clothing, the video was pre-cise enough and provided sufficient resolution to reveal something else unsettling to him. Depending upon the angle of magnification, one could clearly see evidence of whatever madness had consumed her. Frame by frame representations showed her face from the time she walked up to the rail tracks until later when the camera that recorded him standing still awaiting the train's arrival, picked her up as she advanced toward him. What he saw on her face was as frightening as it was inexplicable.

Corinne had become unhinged. The last shot of her face was of someone who saw him as a mortal enemy. It was clear that she wanted him dead and had timed her attack on him to coincide with the arrival of the number four monorail. The only thing unclear was her motive.

Had Franklin really heard something as she approached him? Or had it been a guardian angel's touch that had caused him to turn in the instant during which she lunged at him? It was impossible for him to say, but he was certain that whatever it was, it was responsible for him not dying that evening. Instead, in the split second during which he turned, it was with enough force to balance himself against the force with which she struck him. Ironically, the very force she had used to descend on him was the same force which propelled her past him and directly in front of the moving train.

With the distance and perspective that time provided, Franklin was able to examine the sequence of events that made up his life with her over the past year and a half; from their first date to all the moments in between. He loved her early on in the way in which he was capable. It was not the kind of love that poets would have waxed romantic about, but it was steady, passionate, and enduring. He had looked past the strangeness and weird episodes, chalking them up to stress, and saw a future of companionate affection. Indeed, he had planned not long after that first time at the casino to propose to her.

It hadn't happened. He regretted revealing his intentions to two of his more youthful colleagues in the office one evening. After the accident and Corinne's death, they'd felt so sorry for him that a cloud of pity hung over the office. When the dust finally settled, they had offered to share news of her death with the various social media popular among many. Although they were well-intentioned, Franklin had declined their offer. He told them that he had shared news of her death with the necessary outlets, but the truth was that he did not feel that he needed a digital footprint of his grief. Wasn't it enough that he carried it around with him in his heart?

Now, here he was in Phuket, nearly two months after it had happened. He was physically exhausted and emotionally drained. Franklin decided to shower before turning in for the night. He unpacked his toiletries and used the shower just outside his bedroom.

As he washed himself, he felt that he was not only removing the grime of the long journey to the other side of the world, but also that he was shedding something of the burden he had carried these last months since it happened. Of course, it would take more than a warm, soapy shower in the middle of the night to cleanse himself of the weight of the tur-moil he'd experienced, but he knew that being able to recognize what he was experiencing was a start to healing.

Surprisingly, he slept well. It was just moments after Franklin dried off, exited the bathroom, and climbed into the comfortable king-sized bed that he was asleep.

The next day, he awoke feeling refreshed, though he was still a bit groggy because of the jet lag. Although he had never traveled so far away from home before, there had been a few times when he had left the Detroit area time zone and experienced jet lag. He knew that his body was struggling to cope with being in a part of the world where his day was night and his night was day. Given that Thailand was nearly the exact "opposite" in time from Detroit, Franklin expected to feel less than one hundred per-cent and had wisely planned to take it easy his first few days "in country."

The day began with the sumptuous breakfast buffet held in the large tented building that was adjacent to the lodging structure. It was an attractive arrangement, and the dining building appeared half in and half out of doors. There were families with children, seniors, and couples. A majority of the clientele appeared to be Westerners, while the staff seemed to be comprised of an equal number of Thai and Russians.

The assortment of foods was dazzling, and Franklin dined on delectable pork-filled steamed

Chinese buns along with French crepes and American-style scrambled eggs. He washed it all down with fresh squeezed grapefruit juice while nibbling lightly on a plate of fresh fruit containing samples of the offerings indigenous to the region including mangoes, durian, papaya, and lychees. After feeling pleasantly stuffed, Franklin walked to one of the three pools available at the resort and stretched out comfortably on a pool-side lounge chair. He decided to rest by the pool until the midday's sun became uncomfortable.

A few hours later, Franklin returned to his room and changed his clothes. He set out to explore the neighborhood around the hotel. He was struck by how quiet it was. The night before when he arrived, it was noisy and busy, with bustling activity on every street. But now, at this time of day, the sun beat down on Phuket, and most of its residents adjusted their lifestyles to accommodate its rays. They spent the peak hours of sunshine indoors.

Franklin and a few stray dogs had the streets to themselves. When he wandered into various souvenir shops, it was usually him and the shopkeeper. The few other brave souls he encountered on his walk tended to be other tourists.

As he wandered the main street that connected to the resort's access road, Franklin saw multiple store fronts and stalls advertising "foot massage." At each place, there were three or four Thai women calling out to passersby as they advertised "sales" and "good feelings." He noticed that among the few shops he passed that had a customer, the customer was always a Westerner.

Whatever country they hailed from, they were clearly not Thai and had apparently decided to avail themselves of the "fifteen minute for 150 Thai baht" massage. What made these "massages" so unusual was that they were performed by thousands of tiny fish, which dwelled in large glass tanks. The customer would remove his or her shoes (everyone he saw doing it was male), which were typically flip-flops or sandals. The Thai shopkeeper would then rinse their feet with water from a nearby pitcher or bucket. Then the customer would take a seat on a bench directly above the large fish-filled tank and submerge his feet into the tank.

Franklin was intrigued. He passed several of the foot massage shops, and by the time he'd reached the fourth one, he decided to take the plunge.

The decision to do so was not unlike his initial decision to travel to Thailand. After he'd watched the travel show and explored what options existed online, he made the decision to go. He had the money and time, and was swayed by the various testimonials he'd read online. Just as he read their reviews and imagined himself in their shoes, he studied the other people he assumed were tourists who had taken off their shoes and put their feet in the fish tank. Franklin tried to imagine the sensation of having hundreds of tiny fish circling his feet and eating the dead skin away.

When he stopped at the next storefront, he signaled his willingness and handed over the fee for the massage. Once seated on the hard-wooden bench, he peered into the water teeming with hundreds of tiny fish. The fish, he thought, were in for a special treat. His feet reflected the mileage of a life lived more than halfway through the end of its allotment.

What would the rest of his time look like? He needed more happiness, and at that moment, he decided he would change. There was more to life to be experienced.

Corinne's love and death was huge, and it threatened to be the biggest thing in his life. If he did not do more; decide to live more on the outside of himself, he would have nothing more to define his life than the tragedy involving Corinne.

Although Franklin had no desire to minimize what he had just gone through (he knew he couldn't if he tried), he wanted to open his heart to the possibility of something more. Would he find it in Thailand? Who knew? He decided that this represented as good a time as any to shed whatever emotional and psychological burdens he bore as a result of the recent tragedy.

As the tiny fish descended upon his feet, Franklin couldn't help feeling as if they intentionally tickled him. Their tiny teeth gnawed away the dead skin. He had to consciously restrain the impulse to pull his feet out of the tank because of the curious sensation. But he stuck it out.

Franklin knew that after Corinne's death, he had retreated from everything and everyone. There was a certain degree of comfort in that retreat. It was not unlike the comfort that the nerves in his feet craved at that moment. But just as he forced his feet to endure the discomforting sensation of the foot massage, he would go after life outside the boundaries that were familiar to him.

Franklin knew that at the end of the fifteen-minute massage, the bottoms of his feet would be smooth with new skin evident. He also knew that because of the decision he had made to come to Thailand, his life would begin again. He would look back and remember fondly the foot massage in Thailand.

A DISAPPEARANCE
IN CAPE TOWN

The stories were horrible. They ranged from depictions of brutal assault and murder to organized theft and carjacking gone awry. As the date for their departure to South Africa drew near, it seemed that everyone JJ knew had a story to tell. Even those who had never left the States wanted to share what they knew of woe and alarm. Yes, it was true she knew that crime was an issue in at least one of the country's largest cities, Johannesburg. But she also knew that human nature led most people to fixate on sensationalistic stories. People found them most intriguing.

JJ was less worried because the bulk of their time would be spent in Cape Town, a city whose reputation was unlike that of Johannesburg. That said, she couldn't help ruminating on one story that a coworker had told her just weeks before the trip. Because she thought of her as a particularly reasonable person, she found her tale to be very unsettling.

As her friend Eleanor explained to her, "Last year in August, I went to Johannesburg to attend the

International Sociological Convention. It was a huge gathering of sociologists from all over the world, and it meets every four years. There were nearly five hundred of us who had traveled to Johannesburg for the four-day conference. It was a very conscious decision for us to have made the decision in the previous meeting to have the convention in Africa and in Johannesburg. You know, it was about recognizing the value of the meeting as an economic stimulus, and it was about being a part of a social and cultural milieu that was foreign to many of us. Eleanor was White like a majority of the other conference attendees.

"On the first full day of the conference, you know, after the orientation, welcome, and keynote, a number of attendees headed out. There were about fifteen people from the conference who walked out of the hotel, and within just a few feet of the hotel's entrance, they were assaulted and robbed. They were robbed of everything they carried with them including their handbags, briefcases, cameras, fanny packs. Everything!"

"Were you there, too? Had you left with the others?" JJ asked her.

"No, I was lucky. I hadn't gone out yet. But it put a major damper on the rest of the meeting. I think some people even cancelled their plans because a number of them had intended to stay on for a week or so after the convention to do sightseeing or more traveling within South Africa."

At that point, Eleanor must have realized the concern she saw on JJ's face because she said, "Hey, I don't want to alarm you or make you think twice about going. I just want to make sure you are careful. You'll be fine, just be sure to watch your back wherever you go."

"What was most disturbing about the whole thing was," she'd continued, "it all happened within minutes, and when it was over, what everyone couldn't stop talking about was the complete lack of a police presence. I mean there were no police to speak of and no hotel security. They were nowhere to be found when the armed attackers pounced on the conference attendees. So, just keep your eyes peeled and be careful."

That story stayed with JJ as she made preparations for South Africa and all throughout the planning of the itinerary for the time she would spend there.

Nearly a month later, in flight aboard the South African Airways jumbo jet, she thought again about that incident and wondered about the practicality of traveling there and bringing her husband and young son along. *Too late to back out now*, she'd thought.

The eleven-and-a-half-hour flight from London's Heathrow Airport to Cape Town was as to be expected, long and difficult. Because they could not get seats together, she sat with her daughter who was nine, and her husband sat two rows ahead of them.

In addition to the risk involved in traveling to a city that was annually rated among the most dangerous cities in the world, there was the matter of the ambiguity concerning her latest assignment. JJ was contacted earlier in the year by a private South African nonprofit organization. This was unusual as most of her typical employers were US government officials or state agencies, but the request itself was no less important. She had been hired to help create a short-term program to facilitate the expected reentry of some thousands of emigrants. Because of recent immigration changes that had taken place in the context of the economic boom, hundreds of thousands of South Africans who'd left the country in the preceding decades as well as immigrants from throughout the continent of Africa were entering the country's borders. She was being paid to help develop a policy to address a part of what would be necessary. Her job was to draft a policy that could be implemented to facilitate the least cumbersome migration for thousands of skilled African migrants into the continent's most Southern, current, economic oasis. It would be a challenging assignment, and whether it would even be possible to come up with a policy that made everyone happy or at least not miserable was debatable. She'd give it her best, but in the back of her mind, she had begun making preparations in the event that the worst actually transpired.

Because it was summer in the US and that meant her daughter was out of school and her husband could tap into his vacation reserves, she had opted to bring her family along. That meant that although her travel was paid for by her employer, her husband's and daughter's were not. Having them along, though costly, was something she valued.

JJ would also be attending a large conference sponsored in part by the World Bank that would convene in Cape Town before they traveled to Johannesburg where she would begin the assignment. She would attend the conference for a few sessions spread over three days. Her husband and daughter would spend the time at any one of the many attractions her tour books recommended while she worked. For his part, Mark, her husband, was somewhat ambivalent about the entire adventure. While he professed to enjoy the travel experience abroad and the views it provided of worlds unknown, his preparations for this particular trip were limited, indeed bordering on inadequacy. *Had Mark really wanted to come?* JJ wondered, but quickly dismissed the thought, the pilot was advising that they would be arriving shortly.

When the flight finally landed at the newly upgraded Cape Town International Airport, it was amidst a steady, cold rain, which she knew to be characteristic of winter within the southern hemisphere. Was the rain different here in this part of the world? Did gravity exert a stronger pull on its droplets given their closer proximity to the South Pole? JJ wondered if the raindrops fell heavier, or bigger, or rounder.

The forecast was for continuing showers throughout the weekend, and as they loaded the taxi van with all of their luggage, it was hard to imagine how different their surroundings would have appeared had they arrived on a sunlit day.

Sunshine always made JJ feel better. Indeed, the sun's shining rays molted the melancholy she often struggled to keep at bay. When she stepped into it, she was immediately buoyed by its welcoming warmth, and although it tended to blind the eye, it did so in much the same way that she consciously chose not to look at the negative side of things. For her, the sun's rays shielded the rough edges and despair that were so visible when it was absent like it was today.

They drove for at least forty-five minutes on a three-lane highway and passed what she later learned was the *Joe Slovo* settlement, a sprawling slum near the airport. There were hundreds upon hundreds of small corrugated shacks squeezed tightly together with what seemed to be their back sides facing the highway. It was as if a collective disdain for their predicament shielded them from the unwanted attention of passersby. How was it that so many people continued to live in such deplorable conditions in a country with such abundant natural resources? She was well aware of the tortuous history of apartheid in South Africa and questioned how much progress had actually occurred in the twenty years since the end of the regime legalizing discrimination and subjugation of the majority Black population. JJ also thought about the challenge of carrying out the work that she was there to do. There were already so many migrants living in substandard conditions, how would they meet the demands of even more who were expected to arrive over the course of the next year?

The taxi van pulled up to a parking lot filled with cars in a building complex with several business establishments including the hotel where they would be staying. The hotel was called the *Hollow on the Square*, a unique name for a standalone hotel that was not part of an established chain she had heard of before. The hotel's facade looked welcoming enough, though it failed to catch one's eye. If she hadn't been looking for it, she would almost certainly have passed it by. After unloading all of their bags and greeting the doorman and various hotel staff upon arrival, they checked in. For the most part, she took care of that process while her husband and daughter checked out the hotel's small lobby.

The two clerks at the front desk, a young man and woman who were Afrikaners—the blanket term used to refer to the group of White natives in South Africa—were quite friendly and engaging. She noticed that as she responded to their joviality and allowed herself to be pulled in despite her fatigue, the woman's already friendly face opened up even more. This, JJ figured was the countenance of authentic friendliness revealed only when the recipient responded in such a way as to ingratiate its display. The other, the first face she presented and wore as a matter of course, though pleasant enough, seemed to lack the depth of expression the clerk reserved only for those who responded openly. JJ was glad that she had done so.

The woman had engaged JJ in a friendly, if somewhat inquisitive, conversation.

"Where are you from?" she asked, as JJ filled out the initial guest information form.

"The US," said JJ, somewhat reserved.

"Where in the US do you live?"

"We're from the DC area, the Washington DC metro area."

"Oh, are you here for work or for pleasure?"

"Well, I am here for a work-related reason, but I certainly hope to find some pleasure in being here," JJ responded smartly.

The woman's curiosity was not to be deterred, and she'd followed up with yet another engaging smile and asked, "Oh, what is it that you do?"

JJ paused for a moment before offering her standard "You really shouldn't be so nosey to ask this, so I'll be as opaque as I can be" response.

"I work for a company that specializes in economic development."

That seemed to satisfy the woman, who simply nodded. JJ had elicited that type of response from others before, and she was pretty certain the woman was chewing it over wondering what that really meant. Fortunately, she'd completed the form, and her credit card had been scanned. The check-in process had been completed.

Accompanied by a hotel bellman who pushed their luggage on a large cart, they settled into their spacious room. It was a junior suite, which they would call home for the next week before departing for Johannesburg. They had agreed that the week spent there would be largely leisurely before they were beset by the business of Johannesburg requiring her presence. For her part, she had packed a combination of business and leisure attire. She packed comfortable sports clothes for her daughter that included a mix of cool weather and rainwear items. Inside their suite, she immediately set upon the task of unpacking and hanging their clothes in the freestanding wardrobes, which the room contained.

Buoyed by the excitement of arrival in a new place far from home and the familiar, they decided to head out for a light dinner and a quick walk around the hotel. After circling the block, they walked the short distance to the neighboring larger and more expensive Westin hotel and decided to have dinner there. The Westin was a tall, shiny very modern-looking hotel whose eastern side had bay views.

As it happens, the hotel's main restaurant turned out to be mediocre, and she assumed it was in part due to the apparent popularity of the restaurant. They appeared to be short staffed and unprepared for the evening's volume of diners. There were many people in town for the conference she would be attending the following day, and they all seemed to be dining at the same time and place. The three of them milled about the hotel lobby, watching people as they passed by and settled in to wait in front of the hotel's expansive indoor fountain. They were eventually seated after waiting for about twenty-five minutes for a table. After dinner, which they enjoyed, they headed back to their hotel, finished unpacking, and prepared for bed.

JJ noticed that her husband Mark was unusually quiet that evening. After Andrea had fallen asleep, she asked him whether there was something bothering him.

"Something wrong? What's up?"

"Nothing, nothing is wrong." He'd plugged in his headphones to an iPad and proceeded to search for something to watch.

"Well, it seems like something is bothering you, because you haven't said much of anything to us this evening."

"I don't have anything much to say. I'm going to watch a little more of the movie I had started watching and then I am going to sleep. Okay? No worries."

Although JJ was not satisfied with his response, she decided not to push it. It was easier not to. If she did, she knew that an argument would ensue. There was enough blame and disappointment between the two of them to go the distance. And it wasn't like they hadn't done this before. No, this was not new. They had talked and talked and talked and gotten nowhere. It was so tiring. She stared at Mark another moment before shaking her head and turning away. She showered, brushed her teeth, and got in the bed. Within minutes, she was asleep.

The next day, JJ arose early while Mark and Andrea were still sleeping. She would walk the block and a half to the conference venue, register, and attend a morning session. By noon, she would return to the hotel and the three of them would set off for the day. Mark and Andrea would eventually rise and have a light morning snack in the hotel's restaurant located in the lobby. While there they exchanged pleasantries with the concierge who provided a colorful description of local sights, he assured them would be worth seeing. JJ had returned to the hotel when they were finishing up, and they decided to venture out. At the hotel entrance, the concierge who they had chatted with earlier waved goodbye, saying, "Enjoy the day, keep your eyes alert! You don't want to miss a cheetah!"

JJ smiled and waved. She knew that he had added that last bit about the cheetah just for Andrea's sake. Mark explained that Andrea had asked inquisitively about the prospect of seeing cheetahs, as if they might be roaming the streets of the city or lingering around the corner under some streetlight. She was obsessed with the fast felines and more than anything that South Africa could provide, she was most excited about the opportunity to see a live cheetah up close.

They headed away from the hotel toward the tour bus stop. There was a light rain today that fell intermittently. Once at the bus stop, they folded their umbrellas and hopped aboard a free shuttle. Her daughter was delighted to be aboard the big red bus and immediately scampered up the stairs in order to snag the front seat on top. From their vantage point at the top front of the double decker bus, they towered over the streets below. Their view allowed them to see the cityscape far ahead as well as the minute details of the facades and rooftops of the buildings they passed. They saw the neighboring entertainment complex called Canal Walk Shopping Centre long before they actually arrived at it. It stood out like a beacon of sorts amid the coastline where one and two-story upfront residences and hotels were located.

When they disembarked, they mingled with a crowd headed for the center that seemed to include a diverse group of other tourists, shoppers, and local clientele. They decided to shop for a few souvenirs and gifts for family and friends back home. Typically, on trips like this to foreign countries, she picked up small odds and ends. In the past, JJ made a habit of doling out the foreign treasures she brought back from travel to her intended recipients on birthday and Christmas celebrations. She learned many years ago that these kinds of gifts brought as much pleasure to those she shared them with as it did for her because the item invariably prompted recollection of the travel experience. As she fingered these gifts several months or in some cases an entire year later after purchasing them from some foreign merchant, she would psychologically revisit that particular experience abroad. That kind of journey, which took place within her mind, always left her feeling heady and anxious for the next trip.

After shopping, they visited an arcade with games and small rides, which her daughter spotted the moment they turned the corner. Most of the attractions there cost fifteen rand, just under one US dollar. Andrea, her daughter, rode two of the three small rides there and played several games including one which was apparently one of her favorites from the States. She hovered over her throughout their time in the arcade because she was adamant about her not playing any of the games that used guns or other shooting weaponry. It was a bit of a challenge because so many of them did it seemed, and because her husband Mark was far less vigilant about monitoring Andrea's play.

In the beginning, JJ had expressed her opposition to toys that resembled and mimicked the deadly force of guns and other firepower. Mark had agreed in principle, but she quickly learned it would be up to her to enforce the rule. Over the years, that had meant donating certain gifts from relatives and on some occasions bucking the tide and openly telling others that they forbade guns as toys. At these times, her husband's discomfort, likely stemming from his ambivalence about guns, was palatable. Yet, even when there were no guns to rule against, he tended to carry out his parental duties in a way that was more like what you'd expect from an older sibling or teenage babysitter rather than a parent. If he had actually had a child from his first marriage of many years ago, she would have understood his lack of engagement better. But because his previous marriage resulted only in recriminations and no children, she blamed him for his character rather than his past. How much better it might have been for Mark and for their life together with their daughter if he had some previous experience in parenting.

After leaving the arcade, they had lunch at a restaurant that stood out to them because it's menu boasted the "rainbow" cuisine typical of South Africa. In deciding to dine there, JJ was curious about what this actually meant in a place as diverse and histori-cally contested as the country of South Africa. Because of the variety of cultural and national influences from the indigenous people of Africa, the White European settlers including the Dutch, German, Italian, French, and British, and that of their servants from Asia, South African cuisine tended to be a blended melee made up of distinctive meats, stews, vegeta-bles, and sweets.

When the meal arrived, JJ and Mark ate enthu-siastically sampling several different dishes. He ordered ostrich, a local specialty enjoyed by many in the country. Andrea would have none of it and expressed her dismay. She was not at all pleased that her parents were eating a bird traditionally depicted in US television shows and books as a friendly or goofy bird. The ostrich tasted a little like beef, and although JJ found it tasty enough, she too found it difficult to eat the big bird with large floppy feet and lots of feathers. There was a considerable amount of leftovers, which were boxed for them to take away.

After eating, they paid the check, walked out-side to the marina, and decided to head back to the vicinity of their hotel. On the way back, they walked throughout the neighboring area surrounding it. The complex in which the hotel was located included a number of other commercial properties, and so there seemed to be a perpetual flurry of people milling about. JJ carried their leftovers from the lunch they'd had. Her daughter did not eat all of her cheese sandwich, so the sack they carried contained half of her sandwich in addition to the remains from the other dishes that the three of them had shared. They passed a number of people while walking, and everyone it seemed had a determined purpose. It was late in the afternoon on Friday, and she noticed that there were several people who seemed to be panhandlers or even worse off, homeless.

As they neared the hotel's entrance, they passed a man seated on a bench who called out to them. He did not speak in English, and so it was not clear what he said. But with his outstretched hand, it was safe to assume he was asking for money. Andrea noticed him first and seemed to be drawn by him. She approached the man who continued to keep his hand outstretched. Although she clearly didn't understand what the man was saying, she sensed his need and looked back at her parents. Her father, who was somewhat alarmed, ordered her back, but compliance was not a strong suit for the little girl, and she continued walking closer to the stranger as if closer proximity would allow her to better understand the foreign words he spoke.

When she was standing directly in front of the man, she looked over his shoulder at her parents and said, "I think he is hungry and would like something to eat. Can I give him the other piece of my sandwich from lunch?" Touched by her compassion and speechless for a moment, JJ simply nodded her consent. The little girl hurried over to her, grabbed the bag, rummaged through it for the sandwich, and then handed the bag back to her. She ran over to the man and handed him the food. For his part, the man, surprised at first, accepted the offering with gratitude. He seemed pleased and nodded at the girl, and then turned and smiled at them. Pleased to have helped the man, Andrea ran back over to her. They continued on their walk back to the hotel.

If she hadn't seen the slum on their approach into the city, she needed only to have experienced this incident to know that there were hungry and home-less people in Cape Town. But whereas the slum she passed on the way may have been largely populated by South African Blacks (she believed this to be the case based on what she'd heard about the settlements and townships that characterized the post-apartheid res-idential landscape), the homeless people who milled about the hotel in downtown Cape Town and the hungry stranger who gratefully accepted her daugh-ter's leftovers appeared to be something other than Black. Indeed, the man who spoke to her daughter was Caucasian, an Afrikaner.

As they walked, Andrea, who was pleased to have done something kind for someone else, skipped along. JJ appreciated her gesture and wanted to encourage her to always be kind and to show compas-sion for other people. Was that what spurred her to help the stranger, or was it more likely a natural reaction, an unlearned behavior, that stemmed from her youthful innocence and sympathy? Unfortunately, her husband was less convinced of the value of their daughter's gratuitous beneficence. That grace, which came naturally to the child, was in short supply when it came to the man. She'd actually had to restrain him from telling the child no when she asked if she could give the stranger her leftovers. It wasn't that her husband was unkind or unfeeling. He was in fact quite the opposite. But he was also wary of strangers and less willing to consider the sad stories that characterized the experiences of the less fortunate and indigent of society. So, it was with reluctance that Mark permitted Andrea to give the man the food.

JJ thought about her husband and compared him to the person she had married some ten years ago. His most enduring quality was that of predictability. Mark was as predictable as the ebb and flow of the returning tide that crashed on the coast's shore each day. It made for a certain ease in planning at the same time that it risked perpetual boredom.

Mark took pride in his predictability and wore it as a badge of honor. When JJ suggested that this might be less than ideal, he said that she should be glad because had he been anything other than that, his commitment to her and to their life together might well have wavered. Although her feelings were hurt by this (as she knew it was intended to do), she left the issue of his predictability alone after that. His retort sounded a lot like a veiled threat.

JJ hadn't married Mark because she adored him. She had married him because he loved her and because the others before him had not, and had broken her heart in irreparable ways. For JJ, their marriage lacked the passion that had absorbed her when she was young and with other lovers. What she had now felt a lot like living a lifetime in the middle of a winding road. In the beginning, she wondered whether it really mattered, and now more than ten years later, she was convinced it did. She had resolved herself to the stasis that characterized their life together.

Still, she wondered how their marriage would have fared if he were a bit more like the unpredictability of winter storm weather. With the winter season in the southern half of the globe, one never really knew what was coming until it had arrived. She glanced at him, and as she caught his attention, he turned to look at her. He smiled briefly, never imagining what she was thinking. She didn't smile back because she didn't feel up to it. If she had, she would have risked conveying something she wasn't actually experiencing at the moment. Instead, she shifted her gaze elsewhere and feigned distraction. For some reason, it was important for her to make sure that he did not think that she was happy at that moment. It was too far off course from where she was. She was feeling somewhere in the melancholic midrange between just fine and disappointed.

When they returned to the hotel, the concierge greeted them warmly as if they were dear friends who had been missed for long. It made returning to the hotel and their temporary digs a pleasant-enough experience for everyone, and it seemed to offset many of the challenges that came with being away from home and out of their comfort zone. For her part, JJ was happy to be exactly where she was at that very moment. Being thousands of miles away from her regular routine enlivened her spirits and took her away from a tendency in which she shamefully acknowledged engaging. In her regular space, apart from the global landscape she visited periodically on trips like this one, she coveted the lives of others in much the same way that a child envies a classmate's bike.

The lives she envied appeared full and rich on the outside. They were the lives of single friends who globetrotted and rubbed shoulders with royalty. They were the lives of couples she read about with a multitude of healthy and attractive children, rich and rewarding careers, architecturally smart modern homes, and vacation retreats. On occasion, she even envied the lives of strangers she glimpsed momentarily on a train or airplane. She imagined what it would feel like living in their lives. She would have nothing to do with "the grass is always greener" adage and instead pined, however reluctantly, for the trappings of others. She was always aware of what others had and did in comparison to what she herself owned and did except when she was traveling abroad. It was only when she boarded a plane and left the States that she stopped wanting what she thought other people had.

Then, like now in Cape Town, she counted herself among the enviable and felt smugly satisfied.

The three of them trudged upstairs to their room and kicked off their shoes. Andrea ran to the bathroom, used the toilet with the door slightly ajar, flushed, and washed her hands. She settled into the sofa and reached for her handheld electronic game. Mark turned on the TV, which was set at an international news station. Apparently uninterested, he changed channels until he reached a sporting event; it was soccer, which he was interested in watching. JJ sighed absentmindedly, sat in the chair at the desk, and opened her iPad to check for emails.

In many ways, she considered herself to be a citizen of the world. True, she was an American, but she was not one to view her own country through rose colored lenses. She saw her native land objectively, recognizing its bounty and its shortcomings. She had come to think of her wanderlust and desire to travel abroad as a way of sampling what other countries had to offer, as well as coming to terms with what it was about her own country that might have been better. When it came to South Africa, the only thing about which she was definite was her ambivalence.

She'd known about its political history and learned early on about the unique system of apartheid that dictated inequitable social and race policies in the country for nearly fifty years. As an American, she was acutely aware of the injustice that prevailed until 1994, and she had always been curious about the way that the past affected current relations. When she learned that she would be attending the international meeting in Cape Town as well as consulting in Johannesburg, or Jo'burg as the locals called it, she was excited about having the opportunity to see firsthand what she had only read about previously. Apartheid had ended more than twenty years ago and from what she had heard, relations between the different social groups that comprise the society were still a work in progress. Power had shifted from the small minority to majority rule, and in addition to resentment harbored by members of the minority, there were the growing pains that the newly empowered electorate and administrative governance endured.

This necessarily made for an interesting mix and backdrop against which to view current affairs. One of the reasons she had decided to tack on attendance at the International Development Conference underway in Cape Town was to learn more about the country's long-term economic plan. Because the work she would undertake in Johannesburg involved coming up with policies that could be immediately implemented, she knew that it was critical to understand as much as possible about the government's economic strategy.

The next morning, JJ arrived at the conference registration queue early with enough time to review the program proceedings and scout out an ideal seat for the special ceremony. The large auditorium was packed to capacity with nearly two thousand delegates from around the world. For all the changes that the country itself had undergone with respect to race relations, JJ found it somewhat unsettling to see very little racial diversity in the hall and anything that belied the Black African majority of the country.

The lights were dimmed as the ceremony got underway. The hall reverberated with the sound of loud drumming that was quickly followed by the entry of some twenty or so dancers who were dressed in the traditional garb of various South African tribes. They danced down the steps of the great hall and then onto the stage. For the next thirty minutes, the audience was treated to at least three different dances that varied in style and gender composition. What they shared in common was an exuberance and apparent passion for the traditional South African style of dance in which they performed.

When the dancing ended, the event's master of ceremonies introduced the keynote speaker whom she knew was responsible for the large number of attendees. It was a huge crowd that had turned out to hear the Noble award-winning, world-renown, and highly respected keynote speaker. Those in attendance who had the misfortune of arriving too late to garner a seat in the hall had to find solace in the glimpses provided them via the satellite television arranged in an overflow room. As the small man made his way to the stage, he appeared frail. JJ imagined that there were others in the audience who like her took comfort in knowing that there was someone escorting him, indeed supporting him, down the aisle to the stage and up the four steps required to reach the podium. Because he was a short man, there were a few moments spent adjusting the microphone in order to fit him.

His Grace, the Honorable Bishop Desmond Tutu, spoke eloquently about his humble roots and delight in being honored by the group. The remainder of his remarks, which lasted about fifteen minutes, focused on the far-reaching value of attention to the people and plight of South Africa, as well as its role in the global arena. In regards to the latter issue, he was matter of fact about the prominence of South Africa politically and economically relative to its neighbors on the continent. What it stood to gain and what it most needed to do was to elevate and hold dear the principle of social justice. That would be the only way of ensuring that everyone in South Africa's rich and diverse society would have access to the resources necessary for an acceptable quality of life.

When the session ended, JJ felt renewed and reinspired. She happily headed back to husband and daughter who would now be waiting for her in the hotel. They had made plans to rent a car and head out for a visit to a nearby animal reserve park where there was likely to be at least one cheetah sighting. She had arranged this through the hotel's concierge and was looking forward to the adventure. She spotted them first as they waited for her in the lobby. After greeting both of them warmly, she dashed upstairs to quickly change her clothes. Ten minutes later, she joined them downstairs, and they were off.

KELLINA CRAIG-HENDERSON

The car rental company had delivered the small car to them. Fully loaded with GPS, maps, and umbrellas, they waved goodbye to the concierge and drove away. Mark was at the wheel.

It would be a good day. The rain had stopped, and the sun hinted at its full arrival. The temperature was warmer than it had been, and it seemed they were each looking forward to the afternoon ahead of them.

JJ thought about how much she had talked about this day with Andrea. Indeed, so many of the preparations for the trip to South Africa had included discussion of the opportunity it would provide them to see a real live cheetah. It was hard to believe they were finally headed to see this particular marvel of the animal world. The fastest land animal in existence, a fact her daughter enjoyed pointing out, the cheetah could run up to sixty miles per hour.

After driving for an hour, they decided to stop for a quick break at a rest stop that resembled similar places along the road in the States. They were about halfway from the reserve park. The place they stopped at was attached to a petrol station called Engen. They'd seen other stations bearing names more familiar to them like Shell, Total, and BP, but by the time they found themselves actually wanting to take a quick break for a snack and drinks, Engen was the only station they saw, so Mark pulled into it. Not needing fuel, they pulled over slightly to the side of the station's entry. There were no other cars at the station, and for a moment, she wondered if the shop was even open. Of course, it was. It was a little after two on a weekday, so why wouldn't it be open? The three of them exited the vehicle and made their way to the shop.

Inside the shop, there were many things to choose from. There were Bobotie, pickled fish, samosas, Gatsby served with chakalaka, Hoenderpastei, along with what appeared to be ham and cheese rolls. Andrea, ever the picky eater, opted for the latter when it became clear that there was no peanut butter and jelly to be had. After a brief exchange with the young Afrikaner who manned the register (he'd asked where they were from), she chose a yogurt, a pack of nuts, and a hot cup of tea for herself while Mark went for the Gatsby, a dish popular in Cape Town consisting of a long roll filled with meat and served with hot chips. Mark and Andrea chose small bottles of orange juice to wash down their food. They each used the rest room and then headed back to the car with their purchases.

JJ carried most of their items in a large sack, and Mark absentmindedly opened the car door for her and then Andrea while presumably checking the navigation feature on his cell phone. Andrea, now comfortably seated behind her, chatted excitedly about the animals they hoped to see at the nature and game reserve. While JJ listened to her, she opened the dashboard in search of the car's cup holders she would need to hold the hot tea that she was looking forward to drinking.

She didn't notice her husband's absence until the seconds seemed longer than they should have been. How long does it actually take to walk around the back of a car? One second? Two seconds? When it dawned on her that he was not in the car, that he wasn't pulling on the driver's side of the car door handle, she turned and looked over her shoulder toward the rear of the vehicle. She expected to see him there, perhaps opening the trunk or having stopped to more closely inspect his phone, standing in front of it. But he was not there, and suddenly, she was alarmed.

Once again, JJ looked in the rearview mirror and then the side mirror. She still could not see him. She said as much aloud and caught her daughter's attention. It was not so much what she said, but the tone of her voice that signaled something was wrong.

"Where is he? What's happened?"

The little girl caught the inflection in her voice that sounded of fear. JJ impulsively reached for her own door handle, opened the door, and quickly got out of the car. Before she could tell her to stay put, Andrea did the same. Running a step behind her, she asked, "Where's Daddy, Mommy?"

"What's wrong? What's happening?"

She ran to the rear of the car expecting to see Mark sprawled out on the ground hurt, injured or unconscious, what she could only imagine being the worst at that point. But he was not there. She was viscerally relieved. He hadn't suffered a heart attack, stroke, or anything else that would have resulted in him passing out on the ground behind the car, out of her line of sight. Yet, her relief lasted only for an instant because after running around the car, she realized that his absence meant something even worse than what she had first imagined. With him not being there, she knew nothing about what had actually happened to him. Where was he?

Andrea, similarly confused and now alarmed, began crying.

"Where is Daddy?" she asked through tears.

JJ grabbed her bag and the girl's hand, leaving the car doors opened. They rushed back inside of the Engen station. She thought it highly unlikely that he would have returned to the station without telling them, but she told herself that there could be no other explanation for his absence. Perhaps he'd forgotten something. Had he left his wallet? The car keys? No, he couldn't have left the keys in the shop because he'd opened the car doors for them with the keys, and she had paid for all of their purchases so he'd never even removed his wallet. Nevertheless, she hurried into the station, ran to the manager who helped them previously, and asked him if her husband had returned to the shop.

He had not. The young clerk appeared surprised by the intrusion. He was focused on shelving items and seemed to be put off by the interruption. He made a show of turning off his earphones or whatever it was he was listening to before removing the earpiece from his ear. When finally JJ succeeded in getting his full attention, it seemed it took even more time for him to grasp the significance of her interruption. She explained that they had just left the shop together a few minutes before. Only then did the clerk show a hint of recognition. She saw a faint note of concern flash across his face, but that was quickly replaced by something she had difficulty reading.

He suggested that perhaps her husband had gone for a walk or wandered off briefly to explore. She insisted that that hadn't happened and quickly became exasperated by his suggestions. JJ's voice became louder and shriller until she realized that she was becoming increasingly unhinged. Andrea's grip on her hand tightened. Her reactions mirrored hers and a dark combination of fear and sadness washed over the little girl's face. She looked at her as the silent tears continued to flow.

By now, a few other customers had come into the shop, and the clerk's attention shifted. Although he was willing to be helpful to her, he also wanted to carry on with his duties and that included assisting the other customers and stocking the shelves. Later, JJ would acknowledge not remembering whether he had suggested calling the police or whether she had decided on her own, but that is precisely what she did next.

In the moments following her phone call while she waited for the police, JJ instantly felt relieved in knowing that she had done something and that she would have help. But as she turned to look out of the petrol shop's window and saw the empty car with two of its doors open, she was struck by the horror of what had occurred. The very person who was closer to her than anyone else on earth was gone and in place of him was a sinking feeling of dread, unease, and fear. How amazing it was that one could replace the other so readily, she thought.

Within ten minutes, a South African police car pulled up to the shop. Two officers who were Afrikaners got out of the car after briefly looking around. They conferred among themselves and apparently decided that one of them would inspect the vehicle. The other officer, the more senior of the two as she would later learn, came inside, and she immediately walked over to him. He was a tall Afrikaner with eyes so blue that little else about his face was memorable. JJ placed him at about thirty-four, and when she spoke, she noticed that he gave her his full attention. Indeed, his gaze was intense. Good, she thought, hopefully he would attend as carefully to the matter at hand, her husband's sudden disappearance.

Because his cadence and tonal inflection was characteristic of South African English, she stumbled initially in understanding exactly what he initially said. His language, though familiar in content, lacked the cultural nuances with which she was familiar. As it was, she was experiencing increasing anxiety coupled with disbelief. It took a bit of willful volleying to control her emotions and reach a normal state of comprehension.

Like the shop clerk, the officer suggested that her husband had gone off to explore. When she flat out rejected that as a possibility, he suggested something that for her and for them as a couple struck her as even more preposterous. The officer asked her whether it was possible that he had jumped ship, left her, and walked away from their marriage. She hesitated for a moment only because of the sheer impossibility of it, and she told him that it was not possible. Looking knowingly at her as if he understood volumes about her and the circumstances that brought her there, he then suggested that perhaps her husband had wanted to surprise her and had wound up getting lost.

Here was the moment she felt something akin to pride in her husband's predictability. Because he was so very predictable, she said as much to the officer who was questioning her. She was completely confident that something had happened to him. There was no explicable way that he could or would have gone off on his own. No, something or someone had spirited him away, and she fully expected the police officers to figure out what that was. JJ's voice crept up a notch as she said this. More and more of the customers were looking at them.

The officers took notes and seemed to make a show of inspecting the petrol shop and its surrounding area. The two of them returned to the vehicle and inspected it again, now more carefully looking underneath it (no, he was not there), inside, and outside it. When they had finished their inspection, they questioned the store clerk who by now seemed to understand that something serious had happened. Because this likely represented something that the young man had never experienced before and involved interaction with the police and a family of Americans, JJ knew he would retell and embellish the incident for days to come. In fact, she was sure that the story of her family's despair was within seconds of being texted and posted on some internet site if it wasn't there already.

The officer who was the first to approach her and consequently the one she spent the most time talking with was now back in the shop. He explained that there were several forms that needed to be completed in order to initiate the process of actively and formally searching for her husband. In earnest, he then began working with her to complete the paperwork detailing the incident. He mistook her anxiety for exasperation, though she was struggling to remain patient.

As JJ succumbed to the weight of realization that something had gone very wrong, she allowed herself to think carefully about the implications of her husband's disappearance. Neither the officers or the store clerk had said what she had begun thinking and wondering about. Had her husband been kidnapped? She had heard about gangs in foreign countries like Colombia, Iraq, and Mexico that captured adults and then extorted huge ransoms from their family members. Some of the stories she had heard about had ended tragically when the family unable to muster the large sums of money demanded received gruesome evidence of their loved one's murder.

She asked the officer who was helping her with the requisite forms documenting the incident and authorizing a search for Mark whether this was likely to be a kidnapping. Although he initially hesitated in his response to her, he made light of this possibility. This was not something that typically happened in South Africa, he assured her. No, what had most likely occurred was that her husband had wandered off and gotten lost. She was unable to convince him that her husband just wouldn't do that, that he was not the type of person to wander, period.

After all the forms were completed, and she had provided them with information about the rest of their plans for their stay in South Africa and travel to Johannesburg, there was the matter of what to do. Her daughter was visibly distraught, and she was extremely unsettled, so it appeared that their trip to the game reserve would have to be postponed. Indeed, she knew that in light of the circumstances, it probably would never happen. The officer asked her whether she could drive back to their hotel.

"I could if I had the keys," JJ responded.

"You mean, your husband has the keys? How is it that happened?" he asked, truly perplexed.

"My husband drove us here and was supposed to do the driving. He had the keys when he opened the car doors up for us. Do you understand that he disappeared immediately after he opened our doors and headed to the driver's side of the car?"

The expression on the officer's face suggested that he did not. JJ tried again.

"He drove us here, and we were planning to continue on to the animal reserve. When we left the shop (she gestured at the Engen station), he had the keys in his hand and opened my door and the door behind me for our daughter. We got in the car and expected him to open and enter the car from the driver's side. We, my daughter and I, were talking and so we were a bit distracted. I did not realize Mark hadn't actually gotten in to the car until some time. I'd assumed he was looking at his cell phone in the back of the car after he opened the doors for us. When he didn't get in, I turned my head around expecting to see him in the back of the car. I never saw him again.

"Yes, I understood that when you first explained this," the officer said. "What I didn't get was that he had the actual keys. I thought that they were in the car with you. Now, we will have to summon a tow vehicle to get the car."

"It's a rental car," said JJ. "Do you think it would just be easier to ask the rental company to bring an extra key?"

"Yes, you should do that. It may be that they will come, but it's likely to take some time."

"Are you able to drive if they bring you keys for the car?" he asked.

"Yes, I am," responded JJ rather tersely.

His question seemed to be at least one part genuine concern about her well-being but also inquisitiveness about whether she was capable of driving. It would be challenging admittedly since they drove on the other side of the road than she was accustomed to, and she was upset. But she refused to fall prey to what she thought of as weakness, and she had every intention of driving the car back to the city and their hotel.

She assured him that she would be fine, and after explaining to Andrea that they would need to reschedule the outing to the nature reserve when Daddy came back, she contacted the rental company and confirmed their willingness to bring another set of keys to her. The police officers left a few minutes later, and she and Andrea waited in the car. How sweet the innocence of childhood was. Andrea had quietly fallen asleep. She listened to the soft sound of her breathing.

JJ's mind raced as she waited. What could have happened to Mark? Where was he? Had he been kidnapped? Did he willingly leave? No! That was impossible. There was no way he would have decided to leave them. But what explained his disappearance? Mark, where are you?

The rental car company had arrived. Thank goodness, she thought.

There was paperwork to be signed, and following that, she was handed the set of keys to the vehicle that the company representative drove. Because they could not be sure of where Mark was or the circumstances under which he had disappeared, they wanted to take the car back. They did not wish to end the agreement and break the contract with her prematurely. They offered her the other car, which was similar make and model. JJ took the new car.

With Andrea safely ensconced in the back seat of the new car (the sleepy child had awakened only briefly to get out of the other car and climb in the back seat of the new car), she set out for the return drive to downtown Cape Town. It bothered her that she was in a different car than the one that they had driven. She knew that it did not make sense, but she couldn't help thinking that she should not have gotten another car because Mark would not know how to find them.

As she navigated the car in the direction of the expressway entrance, she thought momentarily about continuing on with the day's plan. What prevented her from proceeding with the visit to see the cheetahs and other wildlife was not the duress she had experienced as a result of the disappearance of Mark, but it was more a matter of the optics of doing so. What would it look like for the two of them to continue on with a day of fun when they may have lost a third part of their family?

As JJ drove along the road, she gripped the steering wheel tightly as if that would help her to stay on the right side of the road. Now, she had an even greater appreciation for Mark who she recalled having commented on the challenge of driving on the other side of the road but had made it look easy enough to do. She focused attentively upon the car immediately in front of her, and when it exited, she sought another car to follow behind, which was no small feat given that the road itself seemed largely deserted.

Later, she would replay the entire sequence of events in her mind like a slow-motion recording of a low budget film noir. She remembered the clarity of expression on the tollbooth attendant's face as she handed him a 20 Rand banknote and waited for the change. She heard her daughter's gentle snores; she had fallen back asleep and seeming to be sleeping peacefully.

Nearly an hour and half later, she pulled into the parking lot of their hotel. The concierge who had helped make the arrangements for the car and provided them with detailed information and instructions about getting to the game reserve was still on duty as she and Andrea entered the lobby. He did not conceal his surprise at their early return and asked whether everything was okay. Perhaps he could tell from the looks on their faces or the way they carried themselves like balloons gradually losing air or flowers wilting in heat. She explained that her husband had disappeared.

It all seemed surreal. The concierge was immediately alarmed, but what she was most grateful for was that he did not make the ridiculous suggestion that her husband had wandered off to explore and gotten lost, nor did he suggest that he'd run off somewhere. No, this concierge was smart and he, like her, speculated about whether her husband had been kidnapped, though this he had said in hushed tones so as not to be overheard by other guests.

JJ told the concierge that the police would be coming to the hotel to continue the investigation. She also told him about the steps that they had already put in motion. She realized that she was exhausted and when he assured her that he would call immediately when the police arrived, she and Andrea went upstairs to their room.

As she turned the key in its lock (this hotel had apparently not made the leap into the future where key cards had replaced hotel room keys), she took a deep breath. This was going to be harder than she imagined. They walked into the room, and she appreciated the sunlight that had managed to wrestle the room's thick window curtains in order to enter. The room was bathed in the soft light of the southern hemisphere's afternoon sun.

JJ removed her shoes as she entered the room and, without thinking much about it, ambled over to the desk. She put her purse down and only then realized that she'd been tightly gripping the paperwork containing the police report since exiting the rental car. She placed it next to her purse. As she turned to her daughter, who was seated on the sofa in front of the large television, she noticed something on the bedspread on top of one of the bed's pillows. It was an envelope.

She went to it immediately and picked it up. It was sealed and addressed to her. It was written in her husband's distinctive handwriting. *How strange!* she thought. He was not the note writer; that was what she did. When she left the house for work, she'd leave notes reminding him of her plans to work late, or that the tickets for some event needed to be picked up, or that they were obligated to attend some function. At that moment, she couldn't think of a time in the ten years that they had been married when he had actually left her a handwritten note.

She opened the envelope and unfolded the single-page letter inside. There was no "dear" in the opening salutation of the letter. He had begun with her name and followed with a brief explanation for his disappearance. He had decided to leave their marriage. It was good that the bed was there to catch her because that sentence alone knocked the wind out of her. She put the letter down not reading the rest and breathed deeply. She looked across the room at the sunbeam's stretch on the room's floor. There were dancing dust particles that seemed to magically inhabit the beam, and she wondered what happened to them when the sun's light shifted, or the curtain was securely closed, or the night replaced the day. This was the kind of mystery she could focus on and to which she might try to find answers.

Why her husband had left, by what means he had done so and where he had chosen to go, these were questions whose answers would require far more wisdom and presence of mind than she could possibly muster at that moment. She glanced once more at the sun's rays that entered the room. She knew that it would provide the backdrop against which she would always remember the moment at which she learned that her husband had been anything but predictable.

THE TROUBLE
IN GREECE

There was something very odd about the landing. The plane's descent into Chicago O'Hare's Airport seemed hesitant. It was almost as if the pilots, who were seated comfortably in their post-September 11, 2001, secure cockpit had changed their minds. Were they conferring among themselves about an alternate course? When would they let the crew and passengers in on this last-minute change?

Kyle Winters knew that it was ridiculous to be wondering about this, but he couldn't help himself. Ever since a German pilot had committed suicide and plunged a plane filled with passengers into a mountain and immediate death, he was prone to dark thoughts like this while aboard a moving airplane. Had it not been for the interruption of an announcement on the loudspeaker, he would have continued to ruminate about alternative scenarios to the planned safe landing at O'Hare.

The Air Italia flight was the only one that had seats available at the last minute. He had snatched one of three of the remaining ones for the nonstop Athens to O'Hare flight. He would spend the weekend there visiting his parents, and on Monday morning, he would board a United Airlines flight home to DC. His visit had come as a surprise to his parents, who were now in their midseventies. He knew that they would be happy to see him, and so he had taken special pains in his last day in Athens to pick up souvenirs with them in mind.

Because it was an Air Italia flight, the first set of announcements were in Italian. It was purely background noise to him. He'd never given a thought to learning Italian, and so he could decipher nothing that was being said. When at last the initial round of announcements had ended, the flight attendant repeated them again in heavily accented English.

"Folks, from the flight deck, this is your captain speaking. Air traffic control has placed us in a holding pattern. Apologies for the delay, but it looks like we need to circle a bit more before we can proceed with the descent."

So, that's what it was. Too many planes trying to land. Now, there was a bottleneck of planes awaiting permission to land at once.

Kyle was willing to bet that something had gone awry as a result of the unpredictable weather patterns hundreds of miles away in the southeastern region off Florida's coast. He'd seen a BBC weather report the night before in Greece and recalled the foreboding warning of potential hurricane activity brewing in the Atlantic. It must have progressed.

There were nearly twenty jets from almost as many airlines vying for permission to land. They would have to wait their turn. He settled in for the wait.

It had been a long trip and not one that Kyle wished to repeat. Indeed, it was safe to say that he hoped never to have a similar experience like that again. How unexpected this was for him because the trip to Athens had begun as a business trip that he had actually looked forward to taking. He had been asked to travel there because, among the small group of employees with whom he worked closely at the Smithsonian in Washington DC, he was uniquely qualified at chemical authentication analysis. As one of several scientists at the Museum's Conservation Institute, his job required the use of chemical analysis to authenticate works of art. Kyle possessed expert knowledge of the materials and methods in use during relevant periods in history.

Apart from his boss, Kyle was the only one on his team with the training and expertise to confirm the provenience of the recently excavated objects d'art and antiquity in that region of the world. He knew the work would entail long hours, but as he made all the necessary preparations to go, he was looking forward to what he anticipated being an exciting stay in the ancient city of Athens. He had been confident that it would make up for the relative inconvenience of living in a hotel for six to eight weeks away from the comforts of home. And because he was not seeing anyone seriously at the moment, there had been no issues with his last-minute departure for a long-term stay in Greece.

If it turned out that the objects in question were truly of the Mycenaean or Bronze period as the Greeks insisted that they were, it would provide additional confirmation of what previous historical accounts only suggested. Indeed, if the story was to be believed, there would likely be some historical revisioning in order to account for this new evidence. This meant that there was no margin for error, and Kyle knew his role to be of grave importance. If he, as the in-country representative for the Smithsonian, could confirm through sophisticated chemical analysis that the objects in question came from when and where they were believed to have originated, doubt would be expunged and the matter would essentially be settled. Sure, there would always be some skeptics, but as far as mainstream archaeology was concerned, his endorsement of the Greeks' findings and account would nail it.

Kyle's job was to help provide expert chemical analysis of at least ten objects excavated from a site recently unearthed by the construction team of a Greek oligarch's builder. There was some urgency because the builder, already behind schedule, intended to construct a twelve-story luxury hotel. There was quite a bit of national as well as municipal attention directed to the site because buildings in Athens were restricted to twelve stories in order to prevent obstruction of the view of the Parthenon.

The site where the objects were allegedly found (it rattled him to use terms like "allegedly" because he was initially convinced of their authenticity) was believed to be the site of a former cemetery with roots in the Bronze Age.

The plane shook unexpectedly. Kyle opened the window shade and peered out of the window. Seeing only clouds, he leaned back and thought again about his first day at Greece's National Archaeological Museum.

The museum boasted the largest of the oldest collections the country possessed including objects from the sixth millennium BC to 1050 BC. When he arrived, Mr. Stanislaus Theopolous had greeted him warmly and introduced him to the staff there.

"Welcome, my friend, so good that you have come to visit with us," Stanislaus had said.

"Thank you, I'm glad to be here, and I look forward to working with you," said Kyle in response. Mr. Theopolous had gently put his hand under Kyle's right elbow and navigated him to the open floor work space just off the elevator. Together, they walked in just passing the doorway and stood there briefly. It seemed the pause was intended as much for him (and Kyle) to take in the entire view of activities on the work floor as it was an opportunity for those working on the floor to sense his presence and turn their attention to him and his guest.

"Everyone, please say hello to a new member of our team. He is a special guest from America. He comes all of the way from the US Smithsonian to assist in dating the new objects we have acquired. He has some special tools to help speed up the time it will take us to properly date the items. Mr. Kyle, this is our team. Please, everyone, help him to feel welcomed."

Kyle saw that everyone in the workshop area had indeed stopped working or talking, and was now paying attention to them. He also sensed a level of reserve in their first response to them. Only one person came forward to shake his hand, but because the others affirmatively nodded at him when he made eye contact with them, he assumed the norm to be one of reserve rather than outspokenness. That had been his first introduction to the team.

It was Mr. Theopolous or "Theo" as he insisted on being called, who had reached out directly to Kyle's boss at the Smithsonian. Although his boss could not travel there to confirm the provenience of the items excavated, in the end, it had worked out because he had agreed to send one of his most trusted staff. By agreeing to send someone for so important a task, he had also implicitly agreed to provide the necessary financial assistance in order to support the activity. By contributing financially to the venture, there now existed a shared understanding that the Smithsonian could expect to exhibit the objects in question at some point in the not too distant future. Kyle had the two of them to thank for everything that had happened in Greece.

In the beginning, his days in Athens were routine. Each day, he walked the six blocks from the small budget friendly *Kapnos* hotel to the museum and entered the employee entrance around 10:00 a.m. It was summer and hot, with temperatures ranging from eighty-five to ninety-five Fahrenheit most days. He learned after the first couple of days to walk with measured steps and to avoid rushing when possible because he tended to sweat a lot. He had noticed that the locals who presumably were accustomed to the heat did not seem to sweat at all. Were it not for the fact that because most did not wear deodorant, their bodies revealed their sweat in "less visual, more olfactory" ways, he would not have known of the heat's effect on them at all.

On his first working day, he had shown up at eight thirty and couldn't get in the building even though he'd been supplied a temporary visitor's badge. There were no guards there at that time to open the door. He quickly learned that the Greek custom dictated a start time considerably later than what he was used to. They also tended to stay later as well. It was not unusual to work from 10:30 a.m. to 8:00 p.m. After that first day, when he'd spent a couple of hours walking around the museum's surrounding neighborhood while waiting for the employee entrance to open, he reported to work each day at ten fifteen. It was just late enough for all the guards to be in place to open the doors and early enough that he tended to be the first among Theo's team present.

As expected, the first two days included quite a bit of preliminary analyses, back-checking, and verification of what Theo's team had already conducted.

Shortly after enough time had passed so that everyone on the team knew who he was, Kyle realized that several members of Theo's team viewed him skeptically, and they seemed to be somewhat defensive around him. Despite the fact that they wanted the additional analytic technology and expertise that he could provide, a few members did not hide their resentment of the "American" coming to test the veracity of their claims. Kyle was sympathetic and sensitive to their feelings, and he took pains those first couple of days to assure them of his commitment to the integrity of the process as well as his support of their particular perspectives.

The work required time and precision, and he learned quickly that because his Greek colleagues were strapped by some fairly basic limitations in equipment, large reserves of patience were also needed. He grew to admire his new colleagues as much for their proximity to the history they studied—they lived among the antiquities, as for their fortitude of spirit—they were not easily discouraged by the adversity of the economics that dictated their lot.

The plane had begun its descent. Nevertheless, the flight attendants made another sweep through the cabin, offering a last round of drinks and coffee to the passengers. Kyle signaled and then requested another black coffee. He figured he'd have to drink up quickly if they really were preparing to land. The flight attendant handed him the small cup of steaming coffee, and he grimaced when he realized just how hot it was. It was bad enough that it left much to be desired in taste, but it was also extremely hot. He blew the steam from the coffee and gazed out of the window. He was still limited to seeing only clouds.

His thoughts returned to Athens. After a week or so, although he was convinced of the authenticity of the objects he assessed, he remained uncertain of their precise dates of origin. They included objects that were valued by either those who died or those who had buried them. Some of the items were ceramics that the early Athenians who lived in that period fashioned to decorate their surroundings, but most were basic utility items used for cooking and transporting water. There was also evidence of certain burial customs, and because it was possible to identify many of the pieces of items they placed with their dead, they learned something of the early inhabitants' lifestyle. Their analyses confirmed that the foundation of the luxury hotel scheduled to be built there would be on or very near an ancient cemetery.

Most of the work that Kyle accomplished was with his own equipment that he brought with him from the United States. It was part of the arsenal of tools provided him in his capacity at the Smithsonian. Each day, when he reported for work at the National Archaeological Museum in Athens, he carried with him the small briefcase on wheels containing his laptop, printer, and the very new portable X-ray fluorescence analyzer (pXRF). All the analyses he was able to do onsite would be looked at more closely once he returned to the Smithsonian's headquarters, but it was useful to have this piece of equipment with him. The technique made possible with the pXRF allowed for analysis of the chemical composition of materials, which in turn shed light on an object's origins. By using the pXRF, Kyle could accurately determine the time period and environmental setting and conditions in which an object had been made. His colleagues at the museum in Greece were impressed by this relatively new technology he brought with him. On more than one occasion, they expressed disbelief while waiting anxiously for the results it produced.

Among the many objects he tested during those first couple of weeks, one object—an amphora—appeared to be from a completely different, more recent period. It was not inconceivable that this would have occurred given the years that had passed and the extent of building and human traffic in that area, so he was taken aback by the reaction he got from at least one member of the team—Agata—when he said that this might be the case. She expressed strident opposition to his suggestion that the object (it appeared to be a medium sized nearly intact container that could have transported or held water), though valuable, was not as valuable as the others, which were likely to be from a much earlier period. Their exchange had been heated.

"You cannot just come here and say to us that you know better," said Agata to Kyle.

"Look, I have no intention of doing that. I'm just following protocol based on the analyses."

"Well, everyone knows that the analyses are only as good as the person performing the work."

This last comment had taken him by surprise. She'd glared at him, and although he'd recognized the anger that shined brightly from her eyes, he had not expected so definite a rejection of his analysis. Because he was taken aback, he hesitated, and in not responding immediately to her, he deliberately paused for another moment. He glanced around the room, casually taking in the reactions of the other team members who were listening to the two of him. They were intently focused on the two of them and made no pretense of disinterest. It was a heavy moment. Kyle knew that whatever he said next would determine how everyone else would treat him from that point forward. Their loyalty to Agata exceeded their concerns about the authenticity of her claims.

For better or worse, he had decided not to pursue the conversation. Was it really a conversation? It had been an argument, hadn't it? He had let it ago, and he had turned away from her. Yet, it was also at that moment that he had decided to continue with the analysis. Perhaps it was this decision that had sealed his fate. Looking back on the events now, it was hard to see it differently.

Kyle had learned later that because Agata had personally retrieved and tagged the item, she had come to feel some sort of personal connection to it. While he did not question that she had actually unearthed the item when and where she said, he was struck by the anomaly of that particular item being found in the grave site of this particular cemetery. From all the other items unearthed so far, a picture emerged of a cemetery for ordinary ancient Athenians. It was very unusual to find so valuable an object as the amphora was assumed to be buried among the belongings of the ordinary classes who tended to lack elaborate or particularly valuable items among their remains. For this reason, it stood out, and Kyle's suspicions were raised.

When he analyzed it using the pXRF to determine its chemical composition and trace elements, he found that it had roots in Western Europe within a far more recent period dating back to sometime around 800 BC, and its clay composition was entirely inconsistent with what would have resulted from the Mediterranean. The other items which other members of the team had unearthed appeared to be more closely aligned with the estimated 1800 BC time period. While the amphora was quite old and valuable, it was almost half the age of the other less well-preserved items found.

Unfortunately, Theo's team had grand plans for the amphora. Because it was large, intact, and quite beautiful, they hoped to use it as a signature piece for an upcoming exhibition and series of archaeological events highlighting the Mycenaean period, the older period that characterized most of the other items found. The amphora was not of this period, and efforts aimed at making the dubious claim "that it was among the oldest and most valuable objects from antiquity existing in modern Greece" were scandalous.

This was a matter of integrity and potentially one of fraud. The museum could not present or display the amphora as representative of the Mycenaean age when it was in fact a product of more modern inhabitants of Germany. Its reputation would be destroyed if it did so.

After the heated exchange he had had with Agata, Kyle had kept his distance from her. Although the two maintained an air of professional courtesy when communicating, there was clearly a strained undercurrent to their interactions. It troubled Kyle that when he happened to approach a group of colleagues and she was among them, they quickly fell silent with superficial smiles affixed to their faces. Most other times, however, he simply wrote off the strained relationship with Agata as a loss. As he saw it, the animus that she clearly felt toward him resulted from his professional standards and unwillingness to bend the rules.

Later in the evening of the same day of the incident, Kyle had entered details of the assessment into his laptop. He had recorded all the necessary information about the object including its physical and chemical features, as well as where and when it was retrieved. After reading what he had written back to himself, he'd decided to go a step further and describe the context in which one of the museum's staff members (Agata) contested his initial analysis. Although he knew he would not forget the argument he had

had with Agata, nor the emotions with which she'd expressed herself, he followed the rule of law. That meant documenting the entire exchange and ending the entry with a note about having documented it. *A bit over the top*, he thought ruefully, *but at least there would be no gaps.*

About a week later, Theo pulled him aside to reassure him that he remained confidant in his judgment, and that he was glad to have someone like Kyle on his team who was as careful and meticulous as he was. He had said nothing specific about the amphora, only that he hoped that Kyle had not been too put off by Agata's dedication and commitment. He'd even made a joke about the passion of the Greeks.

Nevertheless, there was something about Theo's reassurance that made Kyle wonder if he genuinely felt that way. It wasn't that he was normally given to such paranoia, but he increasingly found himself ruminating over the professional conversations he had with other members of the team. There had been several other instances in which there had been a difference of opinion, although none had resulted in as much dissension as the incident with Agata.

The difference in estimated dating for the object in question was considerable—at least a thousand years—and given that the Greeks planned to showcase the object extensively as they kicked off the upcoming exhibit, there would be financial repercussions to any change in dating. He knew what was at stake, and he knew what the museum planned for the archaeological program.

Kyle glanced at his seatmate who was signaling the flight attendant. He had exchanged few words with him since boarding partly because he had been so absorbed with his thoughts about leaving the museum and Greece so suddenly, but also because his seatmate, a middle-aged businessman, slept almost immediately upon settling into his seat. When he'd awaken, they were in US airspace and beginning their descent. Kyle listened attentively to the man's exchange with the flight attendant as the two spoke in Italian. He assumed the man was Italian. On the other hand, he knew that unlike Americans, most Europeans spoke more than one language so he could very well be Greek. He looked at the man more closely. He was hirsute with dark-brown hair cut short, and he wore a slightly tight suit. He could be Greek or not, it was hard to tell.

Kyle turned his head, and his thoughts returned to the museum in Greece and the pressure he'd felt to date the object inappropriately. In the past year and a half, several high-profile cases of scientific fraud involving intentional and inaccurate dating of archaeological discoveries had been publicized. While these kinds of cases tended to be known only by those who were members of the scientific silos in which they occurred, one of those cases—there were three—had actually garnered attention in the *New York Times*. The notoriety of that particular case was due as much to the claim (it was alleged to have preceded the arrival of the Romans in Rome!) as to the circumstances under which the objects in question had been discovered (they were found during a private developer's covert removal of the burial site of indigenous people's remains). When the headlines hit, it was not a good day for public trust, but the silver lining if there was one to be found lay in the newly found infamy of the obscure and previously little-known field of classical archaeology. The specialty area enjoyed fifteen minutes of fame when several dozen zealous representatives of the field descended on the site to document the origins and to the extent possible, identities of the many remains uncovered at the developer's site.

After a little more than one month in Greece and working in the museum, Kyle had decided to regularly leave his laptop in his hotel room. He no longer carried it back and forth to the museum each day. Instead, he regularly recorded all of his notes and transmitted data from the pXRF to it each evening when he returned to his hotel room.

One fateful day, just weeks into his stay and more that several weeks after the incident with Agata, Kyle had left the hotel after logging off his laptop and shutting it down. As a matter of habit, he had placed the laptop in its carrying case. He'd left the carrying case on the small table on the left side of the bed, turned out the room's lights, and left.

That morning, work proceeded smoothly, and immediately following the lunch break (although there rarely seemed to be a time when everyone on the team stopped midday to eat a meal), he was pleasantly surprised when one of the team members invited him to join a group of them for drinks after work. He thanked her and agreed to join them. He remembered how his mood had shifted following the exchange with the young woman, Galena. It wasn't that he was attracted to her or sensed that she was attracted to him. No, it was that the invitation itself engendered a feeling of worth, one that he hadn't even realized he was missing. Now with the invitation, which he had happily accepted, he had a little extra pep in his step that afternoon. And because he was looking forward to the evening, the afternoon work hours seemed to drag along more slowly.

Finally, the workday ended shortly after 7:00 p.m., and he hurried along to meet the group at the tavern that Galena had described to him at lunchtime. Apparently, many of the team members met regularly at the restaurant with a small bar and an outdoor seating area that was within walking distance of the museum. It was nearly eight when he arrived with several others from the group. The workdays in Athens ended later than he was accustomed to in the States. It was nearly nine before everyone who was coming was settled into a large booth surrounded by several plates of mezedes, salads, and drinks.

It was a noisy place, but Kyle enjoyed it and found himself lulled into the warmth that came with good food, alcohol, and laughter. The conversation was light, and the banter was peppered with work-related references, which because he understood them, served to make him feel included and a part of the team. He remembered thinking at one point that he was glad that Agata was not there because had she been there, he most surely would not have sensed the camaraderie or the degree to which the others so obviously appreciated his presence. That night, he learned that the gathering met weekly and that an even smaller circle of those present met twice a week. He assumed that after that evening, he too would be a regular member of the "after-work guild."

They were a tightly knit group, though there were apparent snags and hitches in the group's social fabric noticeable only to an insider who happened to look especially closely. Kyle sensed that there was also some sexual tension in the group between the woman who'd actually extended the invitation to him to join the gathering and one of the younger men on the team who he had spoken to before only briefly. It wasn't clear whether they were actually a couple who'd fallen out or whether they'd never ever actually gotten together, but there was definitely something there. Kyle sensed that he wasn't the only one who was aware of the energy with which the remarks and eye contact between the two seemed to be charged.

The gathering broke up a little after midnight, and he realized as he stood and began saying farewell that he was slightly drunk. There were at least two rounds of ouzo during which time they toasted their team and friendship. He'd participated in both toasts, even saying a few words in garbled Greek about how much he liked working with them. When he wasn't toasting with ouzo, he was drinking beer, a Greek brand—Septem ACE. It had an earthy sweetness to it, and it was only after he'd begun the third one did he begin eating.

Although he'd eaten, he realized as he prepared to leave that it probably wasn't enough. Everything he had ordered to eat had been consumed by the group, a fact he noticed after the second time his stomach grumbled. He assumed that it was their routine and hardly noticed that no one else seemed to order food. He'd made a mental note to drink copious amounts of water when he returned to the hotel. It was a weeknight, and he planned to be at work at the start of the workday so he didn't need a hangover dragging him down.

As he walked alone back to the hotel, he thought about the evening and was pleased to have been invited. At the same time, it was not without a touch of disappointment that he realized that this represented the first time he'd been asked to join the group. He only learned today that almost all the team members met regularly, and now more than four weeks working at the museum and with the team, this was the first time that anyone had reached out to him with an invitation to socialize! It made the fact that he had spent so much of his time alone after work and on the weekends in the preceding weeks that much more apparent.

Usually, on weekday evenings, he typically ate alone. It wasn't as depressing as it might have seemed because he made a point of dining in a different restaurant, or "estiatorio" as they were typically called in Greece, every night. Every night, he felt like a tourist, and although there were a few moments when he wished he had had someone special to share it with, he never dwelled on this. In those moments, he'd look out in a neighborhood or at a location he hadn't previously visited and feel very little in the way of loneliness. It was only now when he reflected on the evening spent in the company of others that he realized how much time he'd spent alone. When he ventured out after work, he would often pick an activity or sight recommended by one of his two guidebooks. He relished these opportunities to explore the beauty of Greece and reminded himself of this as he rounded the corner of the street where his hotel was located.

Another set of announcements were being made in Italian, this time from the plane's captain. Kyle listened intently as if he could decipher something of his message by its tone and inflection. He didn't need to hear the particulars to know that it was not good news because after the captain had finished, there were audible outcries of displeasure and various moans and groans from the plane's passengers. Something was not proceeding as planned. When the captain had finished speaking, one of the plane's flight attendants translated his message in English. Sure enough, the flight attendant announced that because of the unexpected sudden change in weather conditions in the southeast region of the US, there were now more planes attempting to land at O'Hare than could be accommodated. As if to verify this state of affairs, Kyle peered out of the window. On both sides of the jet, he saw several airplanes hovering at about the same altitude. They were all waiting to land.

Waiting was something he did a lot while in Greece. He remembered the weekend excursion he had planned his first full week in the country. He considered himself to be relatively capable at planning and navigating the foreign tourism industry throughout Europe, but he had heard that there tended to be a different sense of time and urgency in Greece. It might be helpful to employ the services of a travel agent for trips he wished to take throughout the country. He had contacted a local travel company based in Athens and arranged a weekend trip through them.

The trip included passage by ferry to the tiny isle of Patmos, the northernmost island of the Dodecanese complex. The island located in the Aegean—a place of grave biblical significance for Christians because it was the place where the apostle John penned the Book of Revelations—could be accessed from Athens, which was some 325 kilometers away by boat only. Kyle's travel agent had recommended passage on the Blue Star Ferry, which would take seven hours to make the journey.

On the day of the scheduled departure for Patmos, he woke up around seven. He spent the morning catching up on emails and data analyses, and after having a light lunch at a nearby café, he prepared for his excursion to Patmos. It was a hot day, made hotter by his decision to pack and carry an overnight bag. He left the hotel and walked the four blocks to the subway. There, he boarded the green line from Omonia to the Piraeus port of disembarkation. Because the travel agent had instructed him to be there an hour before the 3:00 p.m. departure, he arrived well within the hour and stopped at a grill shop along the way for bottled water. When he finally arrived to the gate, he saw that there were many other people who were waiting. They had arrived some time earlier and had managed to be seated in the limited shaded area. Kyle squeezed into a narrow space on a bench that separated two families. At around three thirty, he noticed the restlessness of his fellow travelers. He eventually asked an English-speaking couple about the delay, and the man delivered the bad news. The boat would not be there until five thirty. Kyle hunkered down for the two-hour wait.

That wait stretched on until six thirty when at last the Blue Star Ferry moved slowly into the port and was docked. The little mob of travelers, which Kyle now belonged to because they had all endured the wait together, pushed its way on board. Kyle found himself buoyed by the crowd and marveled at the pandemonium. At the very same time, the passengers, cars, trucks, and mopeds who were on board struggled to disembark.

On board, he made his way to the economy class seating section. The area was musty, and although the seating looked inviting from afar and from the glossy brochures the travel agent had shown him, upon close inspection, he was dismayed to see the streaks of dirt covering each of the brightly clothed seats. The air in the boat was foul; a heady stench that reeked of cigarette smoke and body odors. Yet he remained excited and couldn't wait for the boat to push off to Patmos. Unfortunately, it would not be until the wee hours of the next morning that he would actually see the island because the ferry did not push off from the Athens port until well after 9:00 p.m.!

All the travelers he spoke to seemed to share his sense of frustration, but nearly all of them also shrugged their shoulders in resignation and acknowledged it was Greece. As if that explained everything.

Now more than five thousand miles away and nearly five weeks later, he totally understood it. He got it. There was a difference in the relative sense of time, and the more time you spent in the country, the more you understood and came to expect this. Kyle doubted that he'd ever really accept the fact that ferries, flights, and trains generally ran off schedule throughout the country, but at least he was no longer bowled over when they did. Waiting was something you were expected to do in Greece from the smallest transactions to the largest ones. He figured it would be a small miracle if the Air Italia jet he was now on board that had left Greece some thirteen hours before landed on time.

The plane shifted noticeably, and it seemed that it had begun its actual descent. Kyle looked up and saw that the "fasten seat belt" sign was on. It had been on for the last hour or so since the plane was in its holding pattern to land. He decided to risk the flight attendants' likely censure and rose, climbed over his seatmate's legs, and made a quick dash to the restroom. As much as he detested plane toilets, the need to relieve himself had become urgent. After completing his business and hastily washing his hands, he walked quickly back to his seat. None of the flight attendants seemed to have even noticed.

He settled back into his seat, and his thoughts turned once again to the evening out with the museum team members that changed everything that followed. No matter how often he replayed the events, he couldn't figure out how it had happened. From a logistical perspective, he could make sense of it and see just what the sequence of events were, but from a profoundly human position, he remained flummoxed by the audacity of the people he had grown to trust.

That night, after the last round of toasts and extended farewells, which any observer would have questioned knowing that they would all see each other the following morning at work, he'd walked back to the hotel in good spirits. He entered the small lobby of the hotel and acknowledged the hotel staff person at the front desk with a slight nod. She smiled and greeted him with a polite "yassou" in return. Boarding the hotel's only elevator, which was tinier than any elevator he'd ever seen in the States, he wondered as he did every evening how people in Greece managed with such tiny elevators. That night, he rode the elevator with a young couple. Because the elevator was as small as it was, there was no way to avoid each person touching the other. Not unlike the feeling on a crowded subway car, he held his breath as they traveled up. For their part, the couple seemed nonplussed, and he assumed they were Greek or from some other European country, which he knew from experience had similarly tiny elevators.

The elevator arrived at his floor first, and he didn't hesitate to exit after mumbling "good night" to his companions. He took the short walk down the slightly shabby corridor to his room at the end of the hall. He noticed it was remarkably quiet. Then again, it was pretty late, and he reasoned that most of the people staying in the hotel had early morning business meetings. This hotel was not the choice of a party reveler. With few exceptions like the young couple he rode the elevator with, most of the people he encountered in the hotel appeared to be middle-aged European business travelers. He used the key card to open his room and stepped in.

Turning the light on, he noticed that the bed had been made and that the cleaning woman had apparently completed her customary stop. On a few occasions, when he'd returned to his room immediately after work before heading out for dinner and sightseeing, he had to wait briefly in the hallway until she was finished straightening up his room. It always struck him as rather late in the day to be cleaning his room, but because he rarely returned to his room immediately after work or during the midday, it did not present a problem for him. At this time of night, nearly an hour after midnight, he was happy to see that she had long since completed her cleaning ritual.

He took his shoes off, walked across the small room to the desk, and picked up the laptop case. Somewhat reinvigorated from his walk back to the hotel, he decided to catch up on a few emails he knew were waiting for him. He grabbed a bottle of water, opened it, and took a deep sip. He was thirsty. As he took the computer to the only real lounging chair in the small room, he felt for a moment that something in the room seemed out of place or in some way different. There was an intangible feeling in the air. He looked around, sniffing the air like a bloodhound on a hunt, and was glad to be alone because he felt silly doing so. He dismissed the idea that anything was awry and sat down heavily in the large comfortable chair.

As he put his feet up onto the small coffee table in front of the chair and unzipped the bag, he was immediately alarmed. In its off position, the laptop was curiously warm. Indeed, it was hot, indicating a very recent usage. But, how could that be? It wasn't plugged in to the wall outlet, and he hadn't used it since he'd left the room early that morning at about 9:00 a.m. It was now 1:09 a.m. the following day! How on earth could the laptop still be warm? His mind raced in vain for an answer. Was it the cleaning lady? Had she just left his room after using his laptop? She never really seemed to make eye contact with him apart from the cursory greeting. He was bewildered and extremely unsettled.

Kyle got up from the chair and began looking around the room for other signs that someone had intruded upon his space and taken liberties with his possessions. He looked in the closet, ruffling through the clothes that were hanging and saw nothing that he could discern was out of place. The two suitcases appeared untouched, and he turned his attention to the drawers. The two bottom ones he had filled with clothes and the top drawer contained various papers, some books, and a few of the smaller pieces of equipment for work he used from time to time. Because of the usual state of disorder, it was hard to tell whether anything was out of order, so instead he tried to figure out whether there was anything missing. He could not tell. His passport was where he expected it to be, sandwiched between two large files containing both personal and professional documents. He could think of nothing that was missing.

But someone had been in the room, and they had either taken the laptop and returned it or they had used it while sitting in his room. *How bold and downright alarming*, he thought. He felt violated and wondered if the person had actually managed to access the laptop. It felt hot as if someone had just finished using it. He hadn't suspected anything was wrong until he picked the laptop up so he hadn't really paid any attention to its placement on the desk. Had it been in the same position he'd left it on the desk this morning? Kyle couldn't remember.

The laptop was secure (or so he thought), and in addition to a password, it required a secure token in order to open any of its files or to access the internet. The security software token was part of the claims identity system that the Smithsonian implemented nearly ten years ago. Reflexively, he felt his pants pocket for his wallet. Inside it was a small loop that held his token attachment. It was there, and he was relieved. But how then could anyone have been using his laptop? Was he going mad? Was he imagining things? No, the laptop was hot. It was clear.

His initial plan to catch up on work and send several emails had folded. He didn't know what to think. He sat down and thought about what had happened that day. He replayed what he could remember. He had gotten up at the regular time, showered, shaved, and dressed. He'd left the hotel room at his regular time. Stopping downstairs for the black coffee and rolls he consumed each morning, he waved goodbye to the front desk attendant before stepping out into the morning's sunshine.

The day had proceeded unremarkably except when shortly before noon, Galena had invited him to join the group after work for dinner and drinks. She was not someone he spoke to often apart from the communal nature of the work-related tasks. He wondered now about how it was that she, of all the people on the team, had approached him. He hadn't thought it particularly unusual at the time, but now when he considered the other members of the team and the fact that there were several others with whom he had a rapport, it seemed a little odd that she would be the one to invite him.

He had been so pleased to have been asked that it never occurred to him that there was anything unusual about the invitation. As he replayed the day's events in his mind, he realized that although the invitation had come from her, all of the team's members seemed to have had a stake in his decision to accept the invitation. He remembered now that they were all observing his conversation with Galena, and he now realized that they were fully aware of it; aware that she was inviting him to join the group later that evening. It was more than just being aware of it, it seemed that they'd hung onto his conversation with Galena like a cowboy hangs on to an angry steer at a rodeo. It was critical. Although the invitation had come from her mouth, he now understood that the invitation was really from the group.

What did it mean that the first and only time when he'd been invited to socialize with his coworkers from the museum an intruder had broken into his room and used his laptop? Was it possible that the two events were related? Kyle shook his head. He recognized paranoia when he experienced it. No, it had to be a coincidence! Why would it matter to them that he was away from his room? Why would any one of them want his computer?

The next thought struck him hard. The significance of it bowled him over and stopped him from being able to consider any other possible alternatives. It was a huge and cascading idea, which changed everything that followed. Had one of the members of his team broken into his room in order to access his laptop? Was this about the contested artifact? He knew that everyone on the team was aware of the argument he'd had with Agata, even those who were not in the lab at the time that it had occurred. He also knew that in the cash-strapped economy that was Greece these days, national loyalties could very well trump scientific accuracy and integrity. Did all the other members of the team feel the same as Agata? Did they disapprove of him and regret having welcomed him?

Was it possible that everyone had been feigning friendship with him? Were all the pleasantries of that evening a farce? He thought back to the round of toasts they'd offered when everyone was seated. There were so many jokes and laughter that it was hard for him to reconcile the sinister thoughts he had now about the intruder in his room with what he had experienced with the team members earlier that evening. He had genuinely enjoyed himself, and it had been fun, but now he began to understand that there was a more nefarious aspect to the gathering. It seemed that someone had orchestrated the event, including the invitation to him, in order to make certain that he would be away from his hotel room. Whoever had done this had gone to great lengths to ensure that they had ample time to gain access to his room and to his laptop.

He had never imagined the cunningness or duplicitous charm of which the team members were apparently capable. He had worked closely with each of them and had come to feel relatively close to them in the short time that he had been working at the National Museum.

Yet, they had thoroughly fooled him, and he was humiliated by their deception. As terrible as the breech in security was—they had broken into his room and compromised his laptop—what was most devastating for him was the loss of face that came with knowing that he had been the target of such dark plans. He felt bad for himself, and he felt bad that his team members had willingly sunk so low.

As painful as it was, he forced himself to see himself through their eyes as they saw him. He considered himself through the eyes of those who had drawn him in and disarmed him in much the same way as a lure baits its prey. What he saw was a man in a foreign country who hungered for social connections. A man who relished an opportunity to engage professionally and socially with others. How could so common and basic a need as wanting the company of others to affirm one's humanity be used so incongruously against him? He was not some sort of weirdo, nor was he looking for love. He had merely wanted a social connection that included some sort of mutual exchange that took place on a plain of conversation with good food and friends.

Did he reek of desperation? Had they sensed a weakness in him from the beginning or had that become evident only after they had gotten to know him? He didn't usually think of himself as desperate in the way that the less fortunate crave human engagement. Indeed, his past belied that image of him. He had friends, lovers, and acquaintances. He was generally sought-after in his regular life at home in the States, so coming here where he seemed to lack a comparable amount of social capital had been somewhat distressing. He'd managed it by donning the garb of the tourist most evenings and every weekend. But they had seen through it and sensed his need.

Of course, there was the matter of his analysis, which was at odds with what the archaeological team of the National Museum had hoped for. Kyle knew that he mustn't obsess over the affront to his personal esteem. There was more at stake here. When all but Agata on the team seemed to have accepted his findings, it was as if a truce had been drawn without the negotiation that typically accompanied detante. Yet, unbeknownst to him, something that resembled a tumor began to grow silently and had settled in their midst. Their relations became increasingly insincere.

When he first arrived, they had all received him warmly. While it was true that they did not know one another well, they would gradually come to know each other. In those early moments, there was an openness and willingness to cross the bridge of unfamiliarity and enter the terrain of friendship. But that had apparently fallen away.

Only as he sat there holding his laptop did he begin to fully understand his Greek colleagues; the breech in the relationship he had had with Agata wasn't just limited to Agata. Instead, it had infected his relations with all the other members of the team, probably even Theo. How simpleminded of him not to have made that connection previously! How typically American of him to see one event—he had quarreled with Agata over the provenience of an important item with a disputed value of at least one million dollars—as unconnected to how each of the other members on the team would perceive him and treat him. It was no wonder that he spent every moment away from the museum's lab alone and that the only social interactions he had while there in Athens resulted solely from his solitary outings at restaurants and tourist-packed cultural sites.

As difficult as it was, and in a matter of moments, he eventually came to the conclusion that the reason his room was broken into and his laptop used was because of the unpopular conclusion he'd drawn regarding the matter of provenience for the item tagged by Agata. He had explicitly and willfully contradicted her assessment and what was probably most damning was the implication of his assessment. The museum would not be able to boast of its identification and possession of that particular item from that period of antiquity. Not only had he slighted Agata, a single person, but he had also dealt a blow to the team's collective ambition. He wondered where Theo stood on the matter and whether he was aware of what had happened.

It looked like his plane had finally received permission to land. He heard and felt what seemed like the engines kicking into gear. He looked out of the small window and imagined that process to be similar to a manual transmission in automobiles. The pilots had shifted from neutral to drive and had nosed the plane downward ever so slightly. Out of the window, he could no longer see the other jets competing for permission to land. Now it was just clouds that looked like white powder and cotton. How misleading they appeared, thought Kyle, who knew the true substance of clouds to feel more like skinny wetness. They were almost as misleading as his Greek colleagues.

That night had signaled the beginning of the end of his adventure in Greece. He remembered that once he had become convinced of the transgression as well as the conspiracy that had given rise to it, he set to the task of figuring out what if anything had been compromised on his laptop. He logged in using his secure token and went immediately to the files he had created documenting the analyses as well as those containing the raw data. At first glance, it looked just as it had when he had opened it last. But he couldn't be absolutely certain that everything was as he left it. The analyses he'd run had taken several hours, and he knew that he was in no shape to rerun them, at least not at that moment. Instead, he decided to contact headquarters and his boss. That would be the first order of business.

He looked at the clock. It was now shortly after 2:00 a.m. That meant that it was just after 7:00 p.m., and the workday had recently ended back home in Washington DC. He would send an email to his boss asking for a time to call and forewarning him of the need to discuss a highly sensitive matter. He opened the laptop, logged in, and wrote the email. Given his personality and typically worry-free manner, he knew that his boss would immediately sense something wrong. He thought about all the times during the course of their working relationship that he had gone to great lengths to assure him that everything was okay. That would not be the case this time. There would be no consolation to follow this revelation. His boss had good reason to worry; particularly in light of his friendship with Theo.

That call had taken place less than three days ago. Everything had happened so quickly after that. Within hours, he found himself sitting across from Theo who tried in vain to convince him that he was wrong in his suspicions. When it became clear that Kyle could not be convinced, Theo did his best to assure him of his own innocence. He never actually came out and admitted that the team had orchestrated the break-in and laptop intrusion (that was how Kyle came to think of it), but by insisting that he himself had had nothing to do with it, he succeeded in throwing shade upon them.

It was agreed that Kyle would not return to the museum's lab to work, and when he left Theo's office, he went to the lockers to retrieve the few personal items he kept there. He'd brought a small tote to carry the work slippers and smock, extra notebook, and gloves. After packing up, he walked up the flight of stairs for one last look around the lab. Most of the team members had arrived by then, and for their part, they seemed unaware that he now knew of their collective transgression. It was obvious that Theo had not had a chance to tell them anything as yet.

Kyle turned quickly in order not to act on the momentary urge he had to tear into the lab and confront them. Because he didn't know what he would actually say, turning and heading out quickly was the best he could do.

On Tuesday, he would be back in his office at the Smithsonian. He leaned back and closed his eyes. He knew from previous landings that although the plane was in its descent to the runway, it would be at least twenty to thirty minutes before it was time to actually deplane. He decided to sleep if only for a few moments. It would be good to be home.

THE SOJOURN
IN PARIS

Josie Wellings had decided on France. Paris to be precise. She had made up her mind on a whim three days after the money came through. She had thought of France as one does any faraway place that one has never visited before. She fantasized about visiting the city known for romance, wine, and the Eiffel tower. Her visions of the country were crisp inviting palettes of adventure that expanded each time she learned a little more about the country. She suspected that when she finally got there, it would inevitably feel a little like the fall she experienced as a child on Christmas morning. The anticipation of it managed to chip away at the joy of the moment's actual arrival.

After deciding to travel there, she jumped head-first into the business of making it happen. For someone who had never left the country before, that first meant getting a passport. She'd heard it took forever, and based on her interactions with other government agencies, she was inclined to believe the rumors, so it was with some surprise that she learned she could "fast-track" processing of the passport if she paid an additional fee. She did so gladly, and in less than three weeks, she was in receipt of the crisp blue book-like document bearing her likeness and identity that would allow her to leave and reenter the United States.

She also learned that she was required to apply for and obtain a visa because she was intending to stay for nearly six months. Had she instead planned to stay for half that time, less than ninety days, she could forgo the extra step of getting the visa. But as the idea to visit France took hold, so too did the plan for an extended break. A break from what was familiar. Before even leaving the US, she had already begun fantasizing about starting anew when she returned home. She was convinced that the trip to France would forever change her. She'd read that travel expanded a person's mind, and she fully expected to return with more dimensions to her personality, greater depth within her perspective, and a newfound enthusiasm for living.

By the time her uncle finally got around to calling and asking about her plans, any uncertainties she might have had were long gone. She had said, "I'm going to Paris!" with enough defiance that it seemed she dared him to protest. He hadn't, but he had asked her a bunch of questions like, "What did she plan to do there?" and "Why was she planning to stay so long?" She closed her eyes as she spoke to him on the phone and imagined the expression he had on his face looking slightly askance with his eyebrows raised. She heard the skepticism in his tone. She knew him well enough to know he had doubts about her plans even before he expressed them. She also knew that he bore more than a passing interest in the money that would finance her trip.

After taxes, it was close to a million dollars that she'd received. The attorneys had taken another portion, so she walked away with a little over $700,000. She was smart enough to know that at her young age, she could not expect to live comfortably on that forever or even for an especially long time. But she recognized a "sojourn" when she saw one, and this was it. She'd go to France, look around, see what was what, and figure out her next moves.

She would have to figure out the proper strategy for investing what remained of her funds after the trip. She'd leave a substantial amount of the money in a regular checking account that she could access regularly. But she would have to invest the remaining money in a variety of investment vehicles, and because they would probably be linked to stock market growth, she'd need someone she trusted to hold her hand along the way. That would wait until after the trip, until after Paris.

She had always imagined traveling abroad. But until now, it had never really reached the level of possibility and was little more than a fleeting thought; not something she had ever truly believed she would experience. How could she have believed it? She'd barely left California. The one time she had, it was for the road trip she had taken several years ago with friends to Las Vegas. As she thought about that trip, that seemed so long ago because of the nearly five years that had passed and because she was no longer in touch with any of the friends with whom she had traveled.

Getting on a plane would be an entirely new experience for her, and she marveled over the fact that this form of transportation would carry her through the clouds over water and over land for nearly ten hours. What would she do for all of that time? She knew that she would be able to watch movies and eat meals and use the bathroom, but because she couldn't remember ever sitting in any one place for that length of time, it was pretty hard to imagine.

So much of what the next few months would hold for her would be new. She felt a little like a bird discovering its wings and flight for the first time, except instead of being put out of the nest by the mother bird, she had opted to leap on her own. It was exciting; from the smallest, mundane activity like buying a traveling suitcase to the exceptional, like deciding on which long-term hotels she would stay in for the six months she would reside in France. In the end, she had bought a large two-piece set of luggage with spinner wheels on sale from Macy's, and she'd rented a small studio for half of the stay in an "aparthotel" in Paris not far from "Île de la Cité." She had needed help in accomplishing the latter and so she had contracted the services of a small store-front travel agency in a strip mall two blocks east of Crenshaw Boulevard and 162nd Street.

The travel agency had seen better days, and it looked little more than a hole in the wall. It stood at the end of a space whose main attractions were fast-food restaurants including *In-N-Out Burger* and *El Pollo Loco*. The strip mall had been there for ages, and it had witnessed the social and economic changes affecting the neighborhood that underwent the first of its significant transformations in the era following World War II. At that time, a multiethnic milieu of middle-class Blacks and Japanese Americans called that area and the many others that bordered Crenshaw Boulevard home.

Despite the ups and downs of economic shifts and demographic social changes that had occurred, the neighborhood in which the travel agency was located retained its vibrancy. And although any resident or regular to the hood might be hard-pressed to attribute its vitality to the travel agency, it was because of the travel agency that the strip mall was more than just another fast-food haven.

Josie had walked past it every day never imagining that one day she would actually have a need for their services, or even more amazing, that she would be planning a trip to France! This had been nothing more than a fleeting thought, and now it was all very real. She had to drop by the travel agency one last time before her departure the following day.

Josie knew that at some point during her stay, she would want to venture out of Paris to see other parts of France. Ms. Johnson, the agency's proprietor and sole employee, had prepared a last-minute packet of materials that while not essential would provide her with additional options for sites worth seeing outside Paris and throughout some other areas of France like the southern region's Cote d'Azur city of Nice. Having this additional information was like icing on the cake.

Josie sensed that there was something about this trip and the adventure that had people she knew (though not her uncle) rooting for her. Ms. Johnson was especially excited for her. Most people who knew Josie attributed her quiet and mostly subdued disposition to the cards she had been dealt in life. She hadn't been particularly lucky so far. That coupled with the fact that she happened to have been born with a personality that more often saw the glass half-empty led her to be less buoyant, less free-spirited, and less upbeat. Although Josie was pleasant enough, she did not exude the kind of energy to which most people were drawn.

When the people who made up her small social sphere of friends and acquaintances learned of her plans to travel and spend a prolonged period of time in France, they applauded her decision. Most of them genuinely hoped that her decision to go to France signaled something of a metamorphosis in personality for Josie.

Of course, there was the bittersweet aspect to the whole trip that she chose not to dwell on. What financed the trip was the money she had received as compensation in the lawsuit that had been filed on her behalf nearly fifteen years ago. It was shortly after that time when her father had died from complications associated with the lung disease he'd acquired on the job. It had been a wrongful death suit and for more than a decade, the company where he worked had denied any responsibility in his death. In the end, a mixed jury had decided otherwise, determining that the company had failed to adequately ventilate the warehouse where he had regularly used a combination of brute strength and technology to shepherd the contents of freight containers from around the world onto loading docks.

She remembered only a few things about her dad and missed him as much as it was possible to miss a loved one lost at age eight. When she thought of him, she thought of comfort, warmth, and love. Until he died, he had been the one constant she had in her life. It was because of his presence and stability that she was able to be a child without the worries she'd be forced to bear in his absence. How comfortable her life had been when he was alive. He had been so much more than a protector. She considered her most distinct memory of him. It was a memory of him picking her up and holding her to his chest where she felt the steady rhythm of his heartbeat.

It was her dad together with a combination of other people close to him, who had set about the business of raising her. They had managed, and it was only after he was gone and she had bounced around in search of a permanent home that she realized what she missed most was hearing his heartbeat.

She had cried for days when he died. When the tears finally stopped, she remained angry and adrift. The fact that he had been her primary guardian and had now been taken from her made her mad. She was mad like any lover whose only real antagonist was fate. His death also signaled the end of stability for Josie. As she was moved from one home placement to another, she never fully recovered the sense of permanency that characterized her life before her father's death.

Now as she packed her suitcases, she thought about the path she'd traveled. Life was full of surprises, some good some bad. Certainly, her father had never expected to be raising his daughter alone. He had married and lost a woman he loved, and although college was never in the stars for him, his wife had been college educated. She had died of an asthma attack unexpectedly and suddenly when her daughter was only three years old. Like Josie, her dad had managed his own rage at that particular twist of fate.

Because Josie was so young when her mother died, she had few real memories of her. There were glimpses she had of fleeting images that lacked any real coherence, and it was hard to know whether they reflected things that had really happened or not. She was visited by the images only rarely, and sometimes, in the space between sleep and wakefulness, she experienced a sighting of her mother. At other times, it happened when she was sick or feeling ill with a migraine, stomach flu, or cold. Then it seemed that when she most wanted the comfort of her mother's hand, she willed her presence and there she was. She always felt better at these times, even if it was only some dreamlike version of her mother who comforted her.

Josie sighed and sat down on the bed in the small set of rooms she called home. She looked around taking stock of everything in plain sight. These were the things she had acquired and had come to value at some point. They were small things and not likely to be considered particularly valuable by anyone else, but she had purchased them on her own, and she took some measure of pride in her resourcefulness. She would divvy out to friends and family members the things that she cared about but no longer wanted to have around. Things like the chair she'd purchased and spent countless hours sitting in while staring outside the small window. It was a cloth-covered chair with bright print, and although it was still in great shape, she felt about it the way that those who were unlucky came to feel about their long-time marriage; by and by, tired of it.

Only now as she prepared for the trip was it possible for her to see how much her life seemed to be lived within a state of suspended animation. She went to work each day and came home, and then repeated the routine. It was an endless cycle of just getting by and counting off days that were interrupted by things that mattered little to her. The few friends she had seemed to hold onto her as much out of habit as their own status as outcasts. Josie valued them, but she could think of no one whose absence she would actually miss deeply.

It had been that way for the last few years. Her move out of her uncle's small apartment coincided with completion of the course of study she'd pursued at Los Angeles City College. While working full time as a receptionist at an insurance agency, it had taken her nearly four years to earn the associates degree she now possessed. She'd celebrated with the friends she had at the time and then celebrated again when she moved into the place she now called home. At the time, for her, it signaled a certain degree of maturity and readiness to begin her life. But as she looked back at the time that had passed since then, she realized that there was little about her life that actually reflected the excitement and enthusiasm for life that she had hoped for and expected.

Now as she made final preparations for the trip to Paris, she felt vindicated if slightly behind schedule. It had taken more time than she had planned, but now it seemed that at last she would be stepping into the path of where her life could actually begin. She was still young enough to believe that there was a formal point at which a life lived in fullness actually began. She took comfort in knowing that she was finally headed in the direction she believed signaled progress. For her, this belief seemed to lessen her anxieties about wasting time.

She glanced at the clock and realized that she needed to get moving if she was going to make it in time to pick up the folder of vouchers that Ms.

Johnson had waiting for her. She had reserved space on several tours during her first few weeks in Paris, and each tour seemed to come with its own separate voucher entitling its bearer to a special perk or pleasure withheld from the masses. Ms. Johnson had explained that like gravy, some of the perks were unnecessary excess, but every so often, one of them turned out to be just right. Josie hurried out to the travel agency and a final goodbye to Ms. Johnson.

The following day, quite unexpectedly, her flight was canceled. The airline, an American carrier, had provided little in the way of an explanation and what was even more upsetting, the representative she spoke with had intimated that she was lucky that they'd rescheduled her on another alternate flight for the following day. The airline's attempt to satisfy by rescheduling fell short in a number of respects; not the least of which was that she would now have to fly on two separate flights in order to get to Paris. She would no longer be flying on a nonstop flight.

Ms. Johnson, who had worked the hardest so far to make sure that this trip went well, was especially upset about the delay and change in schedule. She spent much of her Saturday morning communicating with the airline's representatives and confirming Josie's travel on the substitute flights. The new reservation required her to change planes in Miami, which seemed oddly off course for an itinerary that began in Los Angeles and ended in France.

Josie was mildly concerned about the prospect of flying and wrestled with feelings of fear. The whole

idea of being so far up in the air without the bene-
fit of actually having sprouted wings was unsettling.
That coupled with the heightened security for flights
resulting from the US 9/11 catastrophe made her
uneasy. She hoped that once on board, she would
relax and no longer feel worried.

On the day of departure, everything proceeded smoothly, and the departure for Miami left
on time. Although the airlines required a one-hour
check-in before boarding for domestic flights (her
first flight was to Miami), she'd bested them at their
own requirement and got there nearly three hours
early. She'd arrived at what she thought was only an
hour earlier, but because her first flight was actually a domestic one ending in Miami (though they'd
checked her luggage straight through to Paris), she
really only needed to be there one hour in advance of
takeoff. At LAX, she realized her mistake and spent
time scrolling Facebook, wandering the airport's bou-
tiques, and reading magazines. Hours later, following
the two-hour layover at Miami International Airport,
she finally boarded the jet headed to France.

Although the flight was only the second longest
flight she had ever taken, she felt like an experienced
traveler. She had managed to contain her fears about
flying, and with the exception of a few moments of
turbulence, the previous flight from Los Angeles was
smooth. It was only slightly shorter in length than
this final flight that would take her to Paris would be.
The fact that the original itinerary, which included a
straight flight from Los Angeles to Paris had changed

and was now separated into two flights, provided her with the opportunity to graduate somewhat quickly out of the class of novice flyer. She now knew what to expect, boarded the plane like someone in the know, and headed for her window seat. She definitely preferred being able to look out of the window, though she recognized the value of being in the aisle seat where one could get up and exit the row without having to climb over and apologize to one's seatmate. That had happened twice on the previous flight.

As she put her carry-on bag in the overhead compartment, she wondered who her seatmate would be on this flight. On the flight from Los Angeles, she sat next to an older woman who seemed pleasant enough but had slept for most of the flight. In heavily accented English as the plane began its descent, she began talking excitedly about the visit she would have with three small grandchildren who lived in Miami. Apparently, this was a visit that she tried to make at least once every two to three years, but she had not actually been back there for four. Indeed, she had not even met the newest addition to the family. Josie felt like sharing some of her own story with the woman—about preparing to embark on her own personal journey abroad and about getting ready to cross the Atlantic after their flight together ended. But it was not to be. Josie recognized the woman's nervous energy for what it was, and so she was reluctant to interrupt.

When the plane had touched down at Miami's International Airport, she was glad that the flight to

Paris was scheduled to depart in less than two hours. She muscled her way into the aisle as some of the flight's passengers seated well behind her row rushed forward to deplane. She wondered about their rush and rudeness. After retrieving her carry-on, she said goodbye to the happy grandmother and headed for the gate from which her connecting flight was scheduled to embark.

The plane arrived in Paris at eight forty-five the following morning. Josie was bleary-eyed and exhausted. She had not slept. A combination of the effects of anxious excitement, too much wine, and too much movie viewing had kept her awake. After exiting the plane, she followed the signs (there were enough in English) through Charles de Gaulle Airport in order to pick up her luggage and pass through customs. Ms. Johnson had explained each of the things she'd need upon arrival. Even though she was tired, Josie was eager and excited to have finally arrived in Paris.

After she got her luggage and navigated customs to immigration, she found the "I" for the RER public commuter train to central Paris. She walked for another fifteen or twenty minutes through the airport with crowds of people down a straight, wide, and extremely long corridor. Eventually, she arrived at the area where there were elevators to the tracks of the commuter rail. There was a large crowd of people. *What was this about?* Josie wondered. Within minutes, she realized that the line was not moving and that the entrance to the elevator was barred by several paramilitary personnel bearing AK-47 rifles. Something was amiss.

Had there been some threat or disturbance? Her mind immediately went to the possibility of there being yet another act of terrorism. It had happened the previous year. Paris was not immune to the current fanatical terrorism and state-sponsored aggression on Western nations, citizens, and peace of mind. What was going on? Had she had the misfortune to have flown directly into another Paris disaster? Although one of the soldiers guarding the passage seemed to understand English well enough, he would not answer her questions, and she could not tell what the problem was. She stood and waited with the other uneasy travelers.

It was hard to keep track of time given her fatigue, and she had not looked at her watch since she arrived because she was somewhat overwhelmed by the fact of the time difference. Eventually, after waiting for another thirty minutes, she learned from some English-speaking tourists that there was a problem with what appeared to be a suspicious looking package. Josie waited with the crowd and even more time passed. It all seemed a little surreal.

After another thirty minutes, the soldiers stepped aside and waved the now teeming crowd through but prevented them from taking the elevator. The crowd surged down two flights of stairs. Josie offered silent thanks at that point for having decided not to travel with an additional bag despite her temptation. She would have found it difficult, indeed impossible, to manage the extensive walking required down the long corridors of the airport's international corridor, and up and down the escalators and stairs required to board the train.

Eventually, she figured out how to purchase an RER ticket and headed to the platform to board the train. She had watched how others used their credit cards to purchase the ticket, and with a mixture of pantomime and good intentions, she managed to discern what the French-speaking though good-natured ticket agent had advised. Finally, with ticket in hand, she followed the signs and made it down the stairs to the platform for the train headed to central Paris. There were two trains available that seemed to both be heading in the same direction, and she decided to board the train that had the most people already aboard because she figured it would be departing sooner. Her excitement ticked up a notch, she was headed to Paris!

On board, she took a window seat and kept her bags next to her. The train was not terribly crowded so she didn't feel pressured to put them above her seat. She breathed an audible sigh of relief. The glance from a passenger seated next to her across the aisle signaled that she had sighed louder than she intended. As the train got on its way, the countryside she passed was more industrial and dreary than she imagined it would be. Finding less of an interest with the outside images than with the other passengers inside the train, she turned her attention to them. They were a diverse lot and included at least half, who like her, had just arrived from the airport. Their oversized bags gave them away.

As the train got closer to Paris, it passed a number of brown, drab, multi-tenement high-rise apartment buildings. At each stop that the train made at these buildings, the passengers who entrained were of shades of brown, tan, and cocoa. It seemed that there were few if any White people in these parts. She vaguely recalled an article she'd come across in the weeks before her departure, which described the racial and ethnic divide that characterized modern Paris and its suburbs. She wished that she had paid more attention to it.

When the train entered central Paris, its route went underground. Twenty minutes later, they pulled into the St. Michel-Notre Dame underground stop. This was it! She gathered her bags and prepared to exit. After getting off the train, in order to exit to the street level, she had to make her way up two flights of fairly steep stairs. There was no elevator. How did those in wheelchairs or families with strollers manage this? Out of breath and more fatigued than she thought possible, she was blinded by the sunlight as she exited the underground subway and came above ground.

It was hot, really hot. She wiped the sweat from her brow, and with her two large suitcases in tow, she stood looking at all the activity around her. Making a full circle, she surveyed her surroundings and then stopped. She was standing in front of a huge cathedral with twin towers. This was the famed Notre

Dame, which she had heard about. Ms. Johnson had suggested she exit the train system there to take a taxi to the place where she would stay, which was not far. Notre Dame was located on the Île de la Cité, an island located in the center of Paris. This warranted a special visit of its own, and Josie had definite plans to return there another time during her stay. *It was a good omen*, she thought. She was pleased to have glimpsed the famed attraction upon her arrival.

At first, Josie felt a little odd, sensing that she stood out because she had her luggage with her at the site of one of Paris's most famed monuments, but when she looked carefully, she noticed that there were quite a few other people like herself who were also traveling with luggage in tow. After getting over whatever self-consciousness she might have been feeling, she turned her attention to the actual task of navigating the crowded street and its cobblestones. She discovered that modern luggage, which came with wheels that made 360-degree circles to facilitate moving the bag, actually interfered with transporting it on streets composed of cobblestones.

Through throngs of tourists and other pedestrians, she made her way and succeeded some fifteen minutes later in securing a taxi. The driver of the small black taxi opened the trunk from his seat, never moving to help her with her luggage. She was left to heave the heft of the bags into the trunk alone. She managed it, slammed the trunk close, and quickly settled into the taxi's back seat. She handed the driver a small piece of paper with the name and address of the aparthotel where she would be staying. He nodded without saying anything and immediately started the vehicle.

Josie looked out of the taxi's window, noticing everything that was possible in each of the fleeting moments that the car whisked her along. At one point, she saw a man—he looked to be middle age— and a teenage girl, and she thought once again about her uncle. She was twelve when she came to live with him. She wound up there after a series of less than desirable stops that included friends of her parents, as well as her father's mother and her paternal grandmother. The sixty-eight-year-old woman continued to support her surviving eldest son, a man in his late forties, who was Josie's uncle. She believed her son needed her care and support because he was ill. Yet she refused to see that he was ill in the way that most addicts are who routinely feed their addictions.

Josie knew only what she saw, though even as a child, she sensed the debilitating aspects of her uncle's condition. There was something terribly wrong for a man of forty-five years of age needing to be taken care of by his mother when he should have been personally responsible for his basic needs like eating and having a roof over his head. His mother took care of his most basic needs and more for him.

The taxi sped along passing buildings, shops, and boulevards. Josie was clueless about where they were or how far they'd traveled. It wasn't supposed to be that great of a distance from where she had started, and just when she began to wonder whether the taxi driver had decided to take advantage of her ignorance by taking a more scenic route, they pulled up to a small unremarkable doorway on a tiny one-way side street. There with letters appearing prominently on the window to the left of the door that said *Apartement-Hotel Les Jardins Eiffel.* She recognized the words "apartement" and "hotel" and the name "Eiffel" so she knew it was where she was supposed to stay.

After getting her bags from the trunk, again the driver chose not to move from his seat, Josie headed through the narrow doorway in to the aparthotel. As she entered, she surveyed the dim interior that made up the reception area of the hotel. After giving her name to the clerk at the front desk who checked her in, she received the disappointing news that they would not provide her with a refund for the previous night. Though they seemed apologetic, they were not willing to refund the money for the cost of the previous night's lodging even though she was not there.

Josie understood this, of course, but felt obligated to at least request a refund for the money she had paid for the room that was not used. Of course, because she had booked it (and had every intention of using it), the hotel proprietor was not able to rent it out to anyone else. *So be it*, she thought. At least she could now check in to the room hours before the designated check-in time because it had been waiting for her arrival since yesterday. She chose to look at the bright side. It was easier that way in part because she was exhausted and desperately wanted to shower and rest.

The studio itself was small, very small. But Ms. Johnson had prepared her and so what she reminded herself in surveying her surroundings was that she had a window, a refrigerator, and her own private bathroom. Ms. Johnson had warned her that they were small luxuries in many of the aparthotels in Paris like the one in which she was staying. The room didn't feel terribly luxurious, but she took pleasure in knowing that there was sunlight in daytime as well as the privacy that came with a personal toilet and bath, and refrigerator.

After putting her bags down, she breathed a sigh of relief, kicked off her shoes, and like a child of seven, jumped with abandon onto the studio's full bed. She had made it, she was in Paris—a place she had only read and dreamed about. And though she had been in the country for the last three hours or so, it was only now that the full realization of where she was sunk in. A year ago, she had never imagined the possibility of actually being here in Paris, France.

She unpacked her bags, and because she would call this small space home for the next few weeks, she hung her things in the narrow wardrobe and used the small chest of drawers in the room to store her remaining clothes. She stopped abruptly, realizing just how uncomfortably hot it was in the small room. She walked to the window and examined the small air-conditioning unit. Within seconds, she had a cool blast of air purring from the unit. She stood in front of it for at least a minute, feeling the film of sweat on her face and neck dry. She turned away and resumed the task of unpacking, feeling the stickiness that comes from dried sweat and the urgency of a shower.

After showering and dressing, Josie put on a short skirt that she would have opted to wear only on the hottest days of summer in Los Angeles. Even with the small unit blowing at high speed in the tiny room, she felt the outside heat's effects and wondered how long it would be before she began sweating again. She was tired, but the sun still shone on the city of light. That coupled with the excitement of being there was energizing. It was nearly 2:00 p.m., and she realized that she was hungry. She decided to head out to find something to eat, and with a small map of the surrounding neighborhood she'd taken from among the offerings for guests at the front desk in the lobby, she walked out of the aparthotel onto the small side street. The heat was severe, and though it came close to dampening her enthusiasm for walking about, she was not deterred.

Two blocks later, Josie wondered which café, among the many which lined the boulevard she now found herself on, she would enter for a bite to eat. They all looked similar so she decided she would opt for one where the sidewalk seating was actually enclosed and where she would find the cooler air comforting. She entered the next café she came to whose diners looked comfortably at ease under the air-conditioning.

She was greeted promptly by a slim waitress who brusquely seated her at a tiny table sandwiched in between two equally tiny tables. The menu was in French, but there were pictures, and she used the iTranslate app she'd familiarized herself with before coming to France. She understood enough on the menu to get by and ordered the Saumon au pastis avec un légume et des pommes de terres sautées. Some kind of salmon with vegetables and potatoes. When her dish arrived, she was pleased to see that it was as she had anticipated—salmon (although she did not recognize the sauce in which it was prepared) with green beans and sautéed potatoes. She was pleased with herself and ate heartily, enjoying the food because it tasted good, and she was hungry and because she had ordered correctly.

When the check came, she stifled a gasp. The total amount she owed appeared in euros, which made since because she was in France which was a part of the European Union. She had been so focused on translating the words to understand what was being offered on the menu that she had neglected to consider the prices. It was a good meal so she hardly felt as if the nearly fifty euros were wasted. And given her newfound wealth, she could very well afford any one of the dishes on the menu, but she knew that she could not continue to be so cavalier with respect to prices. She silently reprimanded herself and then took out the requisite euros.

As she waited for the change, she noticed there was a young man staring at her. He was seated two tables over and looked to be in his late twenties or early thirties. When he was confident that he had caught her eye, he smiled and nodded at her. Reflexively, she smiled before quickly turning away. When the waitress returned with her change, she retrieved the paper bills and left the small coins as a gesture, knowing that a standard tip was not required because like most in Paris, the restaurant had already included a service charge. As she was preparing to leave the restaurant, the young man hastened over to her and sat down with great flourish.

"Allo, mon chere," he said in that breezy way she would come to associate with all things fun and light in Paris. He had taken her by surprise, and she responded with a smile and a far more reserved "hello." As if to confirm his suspicions, the young man said, "So, you are American, I can tell." She smiled at that and nodded. He introduced himself in heavily accented English. He was "Pierre."

Of course, he was, thought Josie. She found this amusing because it seemed so quintessentially French. She even said, "Of course, you are," when he'd said it. She told him her name and that she'd just arrived that morning, and with that, her sojourn began.

For his part, Pierre was not immune to the sparkle of her eyes, which shone brightly reflecting the combination of sleeplessness and delight at being in Paris. The two chatted briefly, until the waitress returned. Without saying anything, the woman made it clear that they would have to leave the restaurant or order something. Pierre waved her aside, but the waitress who directed her remarks primarily at him insisted. The two communicated in French, and Josie figured Pierre had outstayed his welcome before Josie had even arrived. It was clear that the waitress was none too fond of him.

Josie gathered her purse and got up to leave the café. She hoped that she would not be regarded as persona nongratis, though she knew that with its prices, regardless of its proximity to her hotel, she would be unlikely to frequent the café. Pierre followed her out.

"If you will grant me the pleasure to walk with you, Mademoiselle Josie?" he asked.

"Yes, uh, I mean, oui, that's fine," she said, noticing for the first time that he was quite tall. Indeed, in order to make eye contact while speaking with him, she had to look up. Josie also noticed that he was slim and wore fashionable slacks and a light blue Ralph Lauren polo shirt. He also carried a small handbag, which would have been sorely out of place in South Central Los Angeles. And as for Pierre himself, he would have stood out like a sore thumb in Josie's neighborhood bordering Crenshaw Boulevard.

Yet, here he was. A Frenchman. He was interested in her, it was clear, and at that point, she hadn't a clue as to whether she felt similarly. He managed to violate all of her assumptions and expectations about the laws of mutual attraction. Having had only one other significant relationship before, she knew herself to be a novice. That relationship had ended abruptly when she realized that monogamy was far too difficult a goal for the man she had dated for two and a half years. She also realized that the monotony of being with him had drowned any pleasure associated with the relationship.

Pierre was White and Josie was Black, or African American or whatever it was that people in France called people from the US who looked like her. More than anything for her, it was this fact of difference that threatened any possibility of them getting together. It would require not only that she let down her guard, but also because she'd grown up in a world where her most frequent and meaningful interactions tended to take place with people who did not resemble Pierre. It would require getting past the fact that she was most comfortable with people who mostly resembled herself. They tended to be wrapped in shades of beige, yellow, chocolate, and cocoa brown.

The few White people whom she knew she interacted with through financial transactions across municipal and government counters by way of requests for refunds or in conversations through phone calls for doctors' and service appointments.

As they walked along the street together, Josie thought about these things. She thought about the way that someone like herself was automatically encumbered by skin color in America but far less so in France. She had read something about this in online posts and websites, so she was somewhat prepared for it. Nevertheless, Pierre's attention took her somewhat by surprise. Although she had learned that ordinary Black women in France were regarded as attractive in a way that they were not in the US and that Frenchmen pursued them, she hadn't ever really expected to be on the receiving end of that attention.

In France, it was as if Black women were seen as more human and less restricted by the perceptual constraints of race that operated in the States. At home, she knew that when White men and women looked at her they typically failed to fully see her. They saw her only in ways that the limited portrayal of images of Black women in America permitted. She did not possess many, if any of the American standards of beauty for women of color. Her hair was neither straight nor long, and her eyes were well placed in a visage whose color most resembled a cup of warm coffee with just a dollop of cream. She had curves though not particularly remarkable ones like some African American and infamous White celebrities boasted. Nor did she carry herself in any real way that stood out. As such, when she was home and White people saw her, she was often dismissed and passed over.

She remembered the time she visited the private gym in Torrance during the two-week free trial period that the gym hosted to boost membership. She had showered and dressed after a workout, and she had taken a place at one of the small mirrored vanities in the women's dressing room to comb her hair and apply light makeup. How surprised she'd been when a recently showered White woman had come up to her and said, "Excuse me." She then proceeded to nudge her way in front of the mirror. She needed to use the outlet to plug in her hair dryer. Josie was as surprised by the interruption as she was by the woman's intention to push her way into the space of a vanity that was meant to accommodate one person. As she turned to look at the woman, she'd noticed that the larger vanity located a few feet away at the back of the locker room was completely unoccupied. She pointed the woman to it and suggested politely that she avail herself of it. The woman clearly hadn't noticed it and thanked her for pointing it out.

That situation resolved itself but had there not been another space free, Josie doubted that it would have. What bothered her the most was the woman's decision to inconvenience her rather than any of the other women who occupied the single-person vanities at that time. All of them were White, and Josie couldn't help attributing the woman's disregard for her to her status as a Black woman and all of what that meant in America. It had taken her some time to reach this conclusion.

It was not an automatic conclusion. She reached it only after she replayed the event in her mind and while gathering her things to leave. Once she latched on to it, she was sure that the woman's decision about who to interrupt would have been far more difficult for her to make had Josie been White, like all the other women who occupied vanities in the locker room at that moment. For Josie, this represented a very real example of how she felt less than at home in the States. She hadn't come to France because she expected something else, but to the extent to which she discovered it, she would embrace the experience.

Here in France, not only was her star somehow greater, but there was also a certain shine to it. True, she was the same person who spent the last quarter of a century living in the exact same skin, with the same brain and same gait, and looking like who she was, but all of what that was seemed to amount to someone different here. Josie knew that this was something she could get used to because it felt right.

On the other hand, she knew far less about how she felt about the prospect of dating a White man, French, or otherwise. Almost in much the same way as the thought to travel abroad had gently tapped her but not taken any root until she actually had the means to do so, the prospect of this type of liaison had only barely ever touched her thoughts.

The one significant relationship she had had was with an African American man, and because of how poorly he had treated her and how the relationship had subsequently ended, she had shut down that part of herself. She rarely, if ever, entertained thoughts of romantic love or intimacy. Indeed, by traveling abroad, she had assumed that she'd effectively held those kinds of fantasies or daydreams about admirers at bay. However incorrectly, she assumed that the trip would distract her from thinking about love or intimacy with a man. All in all, the prospect of dating someone in France was pretty far removed from her consciousness, and the idea of dating a man in France who was White was beyond the realm of anything she had ever considered before.

As they walked along the street, he commented on a couple of busy shops they passed. There was the "boulangerie" with the smell of fresh bread wafting out each time a customer opened the door, "la boutique de vêtements pour femmes" that Josie made a mental note to return to another time because the clothes in the window looked super chic, "la boutique de lunettes," and a Starbucks, which surprised her given its distinctively American brand of coffee and essentials.

Pierre invited her to join him for an outing the following day. His invitation came as they rounded the corner and neared the entrance to her small aparthotel.

"So, Mademoiselle Josie, I would like to make an invitation to you. Would you give me the pleasure by accompanying me to les Jardin du Luxembourg tomorrow?"

"What is that? Where is it?" she asked him.

"Ah, it is quite beautiful. It is a wonderful garden in central Paris. It is quite famous. You must see it," he explained.

Josie realized then that she had heard of "Luxembourg gardens," as her English-speaking guidebook referred to it. She had read about the gardens and knew that they were nearly five hundred years old. She planned on finding her way to the section of the city where they were located someplace between the neighborhoods of Saint-Germain-des-

Prés and the Latin Quarter. It was a definite stop on her "to-do" list while there. But here was a new friend, Pierre, who was offering to take her there tomorrow.

Should she accept his invitation and see the gardens with him? It was sort of like opening the front door and stepping out into a foggy outdoor space. A place and experience that would hold surprises because it lacked familiarity. She didn't know what he expected of her or what she should expect of him. And she realized that in all likelihood, she was overreacting but could not help herself. This was completely unchartered terrain. She needed a compass, a barometer, or a magnifying glass at the very least to figure out the course required. Without a sense of the desired end point she should be striving to reach, she couldn't decide whether or not to step out.

As they rounded the corner, she pointed out the entrance to the aparthotel at the other end of the block.

"Do you like the hotel?" he asked. And before she could answer, he asked her whether it was a good choice of place to stay. He was curious about her decision to stay in that particular part of the city and wanted to know why she had chosen that place.

Because Josie had not yet made up her mind about him, she was reluctant to let him know that she planned to stay in Paris for several months. She said only that a friend who was a travel agent suggested the hotel because of its proximity to other attractions in the city, its reputation and price. This was not at all far from the truth she realized, as she explained her reasoning to him.

She also told him that her room with its private bathroom was relatively comfortable if small. As she described its amenities, she thought about his invitation.

Pierre opened the door and held it for her to pass through. Ever so lightly, he touched her lower back as she passed through the doorway, and he followed her into the aparthotel lobby. She was acutely aware of his touch. She glanced back at him, but his eyes did not meet hers. The gesture, it seemed, had been unconscious for him. He was looking attentively at the dimly lit room, which appeared dark given the absence of large windows.

The hotel clerk at the front desk greeted her, and Josie noticed that it was someone other than the person who had checked her in several hours ago. This time, the clerk was an attractive young Black woman, with an inviting smile and friendly disposition. She greeted them in French followed by English, and Josie noticed her strong accent. Although the young woman resembled any number of "sisters" back home in Los Angeles, she was clearly not American. Was she French? Was she African? There were many Africans in France who hailed from countries in West and Central Africa where the French had colonized. The clerk spoke to Josie and Pierre as if they were a couple. She assumed that they were and had no reason to think otherwise. There was nothing unusual about them being together as far as she could tell.

And she knew nothing of Josie's background, or fears or reticence about being with someone who was White.

It was in that moment that Josie understood that it was because it was France and not America that the clerk automatically assumed that they were a couple, and it was with this understanding that she decided to accept his invitation.

"Thank you so much for walking with me. And thanks, too, for inviting me to the gardens tomorrow. I would love to go."

Pierre was pleased. They decided to meet later in the afternoon when it would be cooler, and after agreeing on a time to meet, they parted ways.

He left the hotel, and she made her way up to her small space. As she waited for the small elevator to take her upstairs she knew that tomorrow would be the beginning of something she hadn't really planned. She had made the decision to come to France for a sojourn—the term for a break she'd only recently become familiar with, and she would follow the course as it unfolded.

She would begin the day the next morning with a walk to the Avenue des Champs Elysees, the street that she'd heard so much about. She planned to spend the morning exploring on her own. She would also use one of the vouchers, which her vacation package had provided to take a bus tour in the early afternoon before it was time to meet Pierre. She caught a glimpse of herself smiling in the mirrored wall of the elevator and hardly recognized the young, brown-complexioned woman she saw. She looked attractive and happy. Once in the studio, she undressed quickly and prepared for bed. She read her guidebook for a little while but was quickly overcome with fatigue. Amazingly, she experienced no jet lag. Josie slept soundly.

A TRANSACTION
IN TURKEY

There were 67,000 Syrians who had exiled to Turkey in the last few months. Embrie had read the latest statistics from the comfort of her office in Washington DC. The situation in Turkey continued to devolve, and there were frequent reports of abuse of the Syrian refugees ranging from out-and-out assault on the men to the kind of things against women and children, which no one ever really wanted to witness. It was hard to know how much to believe, but reports of the Turkish border guards' aggression had been confirmed by at least two credible, third-party sources.

The Turkish response to the matter had begun to resemble that of a country wrestling with bipolar-manic dysphoria. There didn't seem to be any rational approach to their madness. While generally embracing its embattled southern neighbors, Turkey periodically succumbed to its baser instincts by kicking the Syrian people down even when they were at their lowest.

Embrie shook her head as if to dislodge the negative images, which colored her thoughts about this latest crisis. To distract herself further, she looked around the small space that made up her office. How many desperate Syrians could fit inside? As far as offices went, it was nothing to write home about. But it was her space, and she had added just the right personal touches to make it comfortable—all seven square feet of it.

Apart from the interior decorations, which included pictures of her family, framed certificates, and important photographs taken with political dignitaries, what mattered most about the space was that it was a reflection of her time in the trenches of the world of foreign aid. She had worked her way around the world to help those in need at the worst time in their lives. Without even realizing it, she'd worked her way into a highly prized and coveted office in the so-called C-suite of the Washington-based global humanitarian agency. In some ways, the ten years she had worked there seemed to have passed quickly. In other ways, when she confronted the brutality of human nature at its worst, the ten years seemed interminable.

It was her most recent promotion, which resulted in her now having the solo space and a small window. There was no real view to speak of given the structure next door, which her building abutted, but the window adequately served as a barometer for weather conditions outside. At times, she looked longingly at the sunlight she missed while hunkered down over reports and at the computer, and at other times, she savored the fact of being indoors during inclement weather and storms.

The crisis in Turkey had reached a critical point. As the media reported on the influx of Syrian refugees and Turkish responses, most people learned something of the disaster and its collateral effects as they evolved. This month and last month, the world was just waking up to what had become the new normal—Turkey closing its own borders. Within the last few weeks, five European countries had instituted quotas, and tens of thousands of Syrians had desperately fled their homes.

For Embrie, however, the crisis arrived much earlier; well before the word *crisis* entered the popular lexicon to describe what was going on in Syria. Because her work required a sensitivity and awareness to nuances as well as changing dynamics in the world's hot spots, she always knew about even the slightest changes before everyone else did. Often, it was the small-scale changes that had the most extensive rippling effects throughout the various diasporas.

She was in the business of helping to reduce fatuous conflict and obviate the need for large-scale state intervention long before the world community and global media decided that something was actually wrong. Sometimes, it wasn't so much that a situation had been characterized as wrong as it was that some regime or national state was determined to be on the other side of right, and "right" was often determined by those in power within the US government.

Embrie Motts-Crawford approached her work with a passion that could only be explained by the role of genetics and her atypical upbringing. As the child of Christian missionaries, she learned early on the importance of compassion for others. By the time she was six, she'd internalized the tenet to love thy neighbor long before she learned that neighbors could be anything but loving. Even at that young age, she yearned to make sure everyone she knew had enough sweets, blankets, and dollies.

She had spent the better part of the first decade of life in the central African nation of Niger. Her parents founded a small Christian church that served as a place of worship for the tiny population of Christians in the southern region of the primarily Muslim country. Although there had been nearly thirty-five intervening years in the time since she'd left Niger, the average life expectancies for today's "Nigerois" man or woman had yet to exceed sixty years of age. Though better than they had been in the midseventies, things remained far from ideal in Niger.

Embrie remembered many things about her childhood spent in the settlement where her best friends were local Nigerois girls. When she turned five, her mother began homeschooling her, and later, after some pleading, she had convinced her mother to allow her closest friend, Samira, to participate in the lessons. She really only needed to promise that the two would behave well given that her mother was happy to include Samira. But that did not matter to Samira's parents who were convinced that girls should not learn how to read or write.

There had been recurring arguments between her mother and Samira's parents. They had exclaimed, "No good will come of Samira's reading and writing! She will not be able to marry. It is bad luck!" In response, at one point, Embrie's mother had shouted, "That is ridiculous. She will be that much more valuable if she can read and write!"

"It is not America, and she is not like your daughter. She should not learn this. It will do her no good."

"You are correct, this is not America. But you are wrong! She should have the right to learn."

They had gone back and forth, and seemingly agreed to disagree.

It was hard to argue with them when the only future prospects for young girls in that part of the world included early marriage and child bearing before the age of sixteen. What good would it do to open a mind and fan an imagination that would in the long run come to regret what it had seen? What would Samira have to look forward to? There was little good that would come of it.

This was the reality in which Embrie's mom pushed and pushed, and although Samira's parents never agreed to allow her to learn to read and write, she learned. She continued to visit and play with Embrie, and each time she did, Embrie's mom was there with the alphabet and notebooks in hand.

Years later, it all seemed as clear as her own mirrored reflection—Samira's life unfolded as her parents had intended. The life they envisioned for the child they bore was the life, at least on the surface, that they had wanted for her. Of course, if one were to look more deeply with little regard to the pain that such looking might bring, it would have been possible to see the fault lines responsible for the change in direction that Samira's life had taken. Certainly, her parents, who never once found it necessary to hit Samira, did not intend to have arranged a wedding for her to a man who regularly beat her.

No one of them could have predicted it back then. There was no way to know this. At that time, one could only step firmly out on faithful ground and trust. In Samira's case, the early homeschooling lessons she'd received from Embrie's mom had encouraged her to peer forward into a future that was not hers to have.

Years after Embrie left that small village in Niger, she learned that Samira had been betrothed at age thirteen to a thirty-three-year-old man. She had had four children before turning twenty. Embrie couldn't really imagine what Samira's life had been like and how she'd managed to live her life in the body of one who'd glimpsed and longed for another entirely different one.

As for herself, Embrie, who had by then lost touch with Samira, had married at the ripe old age of thirty-five. She had two children in rapid succession because she'd been burdened by fears about her biological clock. Looking back at the choices she had made, she chose not to dwell on regrets. Indeed, she very consciously made a point of not looking back when it was impossible to actually go back. On the other hand, looking back when there were positive emotions in the line of sight was just fine because it avoided glimpses of "should haves" and "if onlys."

The heavy-duty decision-making she'd made over the years like marriage, having children, and choosing a career were the kinds of decisions that did not permit revising. Embrie only looked back on what she favored most about those decisions.

Her children were in elementary school. Apart from work, her husband was a homebody. Her career's evolution progressed and continued, although there had been discussion, indeed more than that there had been prayers, about her following in her parents' footsteps.

It was often that way with missionary families. Although it was something that would have pleased her parents greatly, she eventually realized it was not something that was meant for her. That call had not come. Instead, she had come to think of her calling as a mission to ensure that relief and aid were made available to those in crisis around the globe.

She thought of her impending plans to travel to Turkey the following day. Among all the places where the migrants who were fortunate enough to have scattered went, the worst of the situation continued to be in Turkey. She had not been to Turkey before, but as always before she embarked on any mission, she'd spent a fair amount of time reading about the country's history, its culture, and its contemporary challenges. In addition to the continuing issues associated with the Syrian civil war, the conflict was exacerbated by the growth and expansion of the Islamist extremists. She was traveling to a cauldron of violent political instability. That she represented an aid group made her only slightly more tolerable in the eyes of the Islamic extremists than if she were there as a Christian missionary.

When she traveled abroad in her capacity as an aid worker, she was typically away for about two weeks. It was always a challenge at home because her children missed her terribly, and she would miss them as well. Her husband would care for them and see to it that life carried on, but there were the inevitable blips in the normal course of life that would happen unexpectedly. Even when these chance happenings were anything but serious, their impact was magnified if only by her absence.

When she returned home, she'd spend the next two weeks trying to catch up and make amends for her absence.

It was a familiar dance of engagement with her children and husband, and each of them knew the script. She was the penitent mother and wife, and they were the aggrieved though each for different reasons. Her husband bore the greatest burden during her absence as he traipsed the mire of single parenting. Yet, ironically, he tended to be the least resentful, while her daughter and son rivaled one another in their resentment of her. The worst of it had usually passed within two to three days after her return. Although she traveled only four times each year and those trips were evenly spread out so that they never occurred more frequently than every three months or so, it seemed that she had just gotten back into their good graces when she found herself preparing to leave again. It took that much time for them to let her back into their hearts and elevate her once again to the secretly coveted position of "preferred parent."

Although she never said as much and hardly admitted it to herself, she was just grateful that it was even possible to be reinstated to such a lofty status. She was the one the children would ask questions about the universe that only the young could ponder. Any and all the unanswerable and some answerable questions they routed to her. Questions like, "If these weeds look like flowers, why are they called weeds?" She was very much aware that they rarely asked her husband about such matters, and she wondered what happened to their curiosity while she was away. Did it burn with anticipation awaiting her return, or did it tire from weariness and rest until then?

The first time she had left them and they were old enough to notice, she wondered whether she would ever be able to do it again. Although being away was difficult, modern technology with all of its communication media made it possible for her to actually speak with them daily. When she returned home, she was unprepared for how long it seemed to take to get back into the swing of things. Now, after nearly two years of the routine of quarterly travel, she knew the drill, what to expect, and how to make it less painful for everyone.

She rummaged through her log and pulled up her calendar online. Based on the reports she'd just read, she was glad she'd made plans to travel to Istanbul tomorrow. Time was of essence. Given the latest turn of events, the ranks of those in urgent need of food and medical supplies would grow quickly. She needed to be clear about what the various aid entities had achieved so far and what they were planning over the next few days. In addition to the four UN agencies, which included the United Nations Development Program, the United Nations Refugee Agency, the United Nations Children's Fund, and the World Food Program, there were a number of other international organizations such as the kind she worked for that delivered relief assistance on a smaller scale. Her agency was part of a network of midsize relief agencies that worked together.

After several phone calls, a bunch of emails, and conversations with staff in her office, she packed up her bag, shut down her computer, and left the office. As she made her way to the parking structure where her car was located, for the first time that day, she noticed the light rain that moistened the US capital's sidewalks. They glistened in the pre-dusk light of the day. *It must have just begun raining*, she thought, as she chided herself for not having brought an umbrella. She hurried along to begin her second most important job. With any luck, she would be in the comfort of her home within the next hour, making dinner preparations as she learned of the day's events that occurred in her children's and husband's lives.

The following day, she arose earlier than usual and immediately set about the daily routine of getting the three other people in her home up and going for the day. In addition, there was a host of other tasks she took care of that had become fairly routine with each overseas trip she took. She wrote several notes and placed them strategically about the small frame house. Some of them were functional as in the ones she left to advise her husband of foods she had prepared and frozen for dinner for several of the nights she would be away. Other notes she left to make its recipient's heart smile in her absence like the smiley face and "I love you" note she left in the bottom of her son's left sneaker, which he wouldn't wear until the following day when he had PE.

By the time everyone had said their goodbyes and they had each headed out of the door, she had an hour to finish packing before heading to the office for the last day of meetings and planning needed for the two weeks she anticipated spending in Turkey. She was scheduled to depart that evening for the ten-hour Turkish Airlines flight to Istanbul.

Later that day, she dashed out of the office and took a taxi to Washington Dulles International Airport. The airport was technically in Virginia, though it boasted the name of the nation's capital.

The lines were long at check-in, and after having dropped off her checked luggage, she made her way through the long line at the security checkpoint. This was the part of the journey she most disliked. Added to the inconvenience of the more than forty-five minutes spent standing in line, there was also the matter of having to take off one's shoes, as well as unpacking all electronic and mobile devices, and restrictions in carrying on various items. She sighed as she snaked her way through the specific line to which she had been assigned. She reminded herself that she really needed to get the express service now available through TSA.

Embrie preferred navigating this part of the departure process from US soil directly behind business travelers. They were among the more savvy of the international travelers, and they tended to be prepared when it was their turn to proceed without shoes through the full body scanner, and they placed their items on the conveyor belt for scanning. This was not to be the case this time as she found herself following a young family of three including a man, a woman, and a small child, which the woman carried in her arms.

As a parent who had traveled multiple times with her children when they were small, she knew very well how challenging it could be to manage everything and not lose a child, a shoe or a treat. But now that her own children were older, and she happened to be flying solo at this particular time, her patience was in short supply. Nevertheless, she reached out to help the woman who struggled to remove an iPad from a larger tote bag while holding an active toddler who was seated on her hip.

In addition to long stretches of walking, international departures from Dulles Airport also required a brief train ride to the departure terminal. As Embrie walked along the conveyor belt, which made it possible to cover a greater distance faster, she allowed her mind to wander and to consider what flight travel would be like if it were possible to simply drive up and board the plane. How very different that experience would be! Gone would be the long lines for check-in, additional lines for security checks, long stretches of corridors, train rides, long waits, and more. In her fantasy, the experience of flight travel would be greatly simplified. It would no longer be the ordeal it now was.

When she arrived at her departure gate, she noticed that the waiting area was pretty full. She spotted an empty seat somewhat removed from the center area and settled in. She had a little over an hour to wait. For a moment, she looked distractedly at the television monitor. It was a news segment covering the recent air disaster involving a flight from Paris en route to Egypt. She glanced at some of the other passengers to see who was paying attention. Despite air industry assurances that flying remained one of the safest forms of transportation, it was hard sitting there hearing about the details of the cause of the crash of the international flight that had occurred several days ago as she was waiting to board.

Throughout that week, there had been no shortage of stories on the crash. Like others, Embrie found it difficult to ignore the various reports. The plane had gone down somewhere in Egypt's airspace, and all sixty-six passengers on board were presumed dead. Although there was one day during which the plane was officially declared to be missing by Egyptian authorities, by the following day, wreckage of the plane had been spotted some 150 miles south west of the coast of Egypt. The broadcast on the television monitor did not appear to have any new revelations about the cause of the crash, though commentators had begun speculating that the plane had been brought down by insurgents. Embrie consciously turned away and focused on some of the work-related reading material she'd brought along.

When her boarding zone was called, she boarded with the other passengers according to her row assignment. She was flying coach to Turkey, but even now with the trip still ahead of her, she looked forward to the return trip that would be in business class. Her organization would not pay for the upgrade to business class, and she could not regularly afford it, but she had enough frequent flyer miles to cover at least one segment of the trip. She knew that after the intensity and challenges of the work she was heading to do, she would most appreciate the luxury of business class upon her return. She would be exhausted when she arrived because she could never sleep well in coach, but she would sleep once her head hit the pillow in the hotel where she would stay.

Her seatmate for the flight was a Muslim woman who wore a traditional headscarf. She was also traveling alone and appeared to be a business traveler. She was engaged in an animated conversation on a cellphone that apparently involved materials, which she displayed on her laptop. Embrie put her own carry-on in the space above her seat and was pleased to find that there was room to do so. So often, this was not the case. As she eventually settled into her aisle seat, Embrie noticed the woman's fragrance and thought it pleasant enough though quite heavy. She spent the next ten hours zoning out on movies, eating whatever was offered to her, and reading her notes. Her seatmate slept throughout most of the flight, so they never actually spoke at length.

The plane touched down in Istanbul at 4:40 a.m., and even after she had retrieved her checked bag, used the bathroom, and gotten some of the local currency from an ATM, there was very little traffic on the roads. Her taxi sped through the streets as if determined to deliver her to the hotel before the sun completed its ascent. With the help of a bellman, she stepped through the doorway of the hotel. The first thing she noticed was the security doorway placed just inside the hotel's entrance that required all entering guests to go through it. She did so with all of her luggage and fully expected it to alarm. When it did not, she wondered whether it was even turned on. Something about its location and the man who stood beside it, he was well dressed in a business suit, caused her to question its authenticity.

As she checked in, she took a place on line directly behind a very well-dressed African couple who were apparently also checking in. The man wore a conservative Western style suit, and the elegant woman accompanying him wore traditional African clothing, though Embrie did not know which country they were from. No matter how important or powerful her husband may have been, it was clear that the woman hijacked the attention of everyone the two encountered. She was beautiful.

Embrie eavesdropped because she was captivated by the woman and because she was curious about the country they came from. They spoke English like the English did, but given the magnitude of colonization that had occurred in Africa, she could not readily determine where on the continent was home for them. Eventually, they completed the check-in process, and it was Embrie's turn.

The front desk clerk was polite and exceptionally formal. He wore a name tag that said, "Tariq," and he made a point of looking her directly in the eye as he inquired as to whether she needed an additional key for her husband. She held his gaze and explained that her husband would not be joining her. Because he hesitated for a just a moment that someone less sensitive might have missed, she was left to wonder whether there was an unspoken admonition or rule she had overlooked about unaccompanied female guests staying in the hotel.

It was a Muslim country after all, and she was well aware of the less than equitable way that many

Muslim countries treated its female citizens relative to males. Although there was nothing suggesting this in the limited reviews she'd read about the hotel when she made the decision to stay there, she considered whether she should make alternative last-minute arrangements. The hotel was part of the large international chain of ANA InterContinental hotels, so she was somewhat surprised by this possibility. She suspected that her status as a woman traveling alone made her vulnerable in some way to certain assumptions about her worth, her intentions, or right to be there.

She finished the check-in process and declined the clerk's offer to provide assistance for transporting her bags to her room. She made her way up to the seventh floor, found her room, and entered. The room was welcoming, containing comforting small luxuries (there was a box of expensive European chocolates on the table by the bedside table) as well aesthetic design features worthy of a five-star rating. She quickly got over the apprehension she'd experienced in checking in and concluded that whatever the clerk's motives, she was pleased with her choice to stay there.

Because of geographic providence, Turkey and, in particular, the city of Istanbul where she now found herself as she prepared to travel to the refugee outposts enjoyed the reach of its neighbors to the east and west. Long considered the gateway to Asia, the city of Istanbul boasted the efficiencies of modernity as well as the centuries old pleasures that existed only because of its geographic proximity and historical role in the past. As such, her hotel room contained the finer comforts that were possible only in a city that had its feet firmly positioned in the east; at the same time that its arms embraced the efficiencies it loved most about the west.

As she came physically closer to the people she had come to help, her sensitivity to these kinds of amenities was heightened. She was acutely aware that because she was lucky enough to be borne in the US, she had an excess of things that none of the people she was headed to meet had or could possibly ever imagine having. She thought of this often and wondered how the fates conspired to ensure that she, unlike the poor souls she helped around the world, had a life in which hunger never took root. She remembered the scriptures of her father who in his missionary zeal was fond of saying, "From everyone who has been given much, much will be demanded; and from the one who has been entrusted with much, much more will be asked." It was a tenet that she'd internalized and one that had stuck with her.

A knock on the door interrupted her thoughts. She headed to it and without thinking to ask who it might be, she quickly pulled the door open. A woman whom she had never seen before of an indeterminate age stood there, and for several seconds, neither she nor Embrie said anything. The woman eventually broke the silence by turning her gaze from her and looking down at the small child who held her hand and shook her arm. It was as if upon sensing that she'd been forgotten, the child sought to remind the woman of her presence and the reason for their intrusion. She shook the woman's arm and spoke passionately in Arabic to her.

Embrie took in the woman's headscarf, as well as the hesitation that seemed to explain her delay in saying anything. She decidedly spoke first and offered a tentative questioning, "Yes?" The woman immediately looked back at her, smiled with her mouth and her eyes, and said, "Excuse me, madam." In heavily accented English, she explained that she and the child were in trouble and that she needed (she'd said wanted) to leave the child with her.

"Please, please, help us, madam. We have trouble, and I cannot make care for the little girl. She is my daughter, and I give her to you. Please take the care of her. Please, madam."

It was hard to understand everything that she said and even harder for Embrie to fathom her request.

The woman clasped her hands to her breast the entire time she spoke and pushed the little girl forward into the room.

Was she really asking her to take her child? She mentioned something about being separated and fearful about "the darkness" that awaited them.

At first glance, the child looked to be about four or five, but Embrie knew that because of a constellation of stressors that typically impacted life for those in this part of the world, it was very likely that the small girl was a good deal older. As if to confirm her suspicions, the little girl seemed to be encouraging the woman, her mother apparently, to say more. *Yes*, Embrie thought, *the child was probably closer to seven or eight years old.* The woman was anywhere from twenty something to forty something. It was impossible to tell.

She spoke in hushed tones, making eye contact with Embrie and began by explaining that following the recent death of her husband, she was left alone with four children. She told Embrie.

"My children, they are boys except this one, the little girl. I want the good for all of them, and I can help my boys to be okay, but I cannot make right for my little girl."

At this point, she paused, and in order to speak even more quietly, she whispered, "You can take care of her for me. I know you will be kind for my daughter."

Embrie listened in the way that people do when they hear what they don't wish to believe but know in their hearts to be true. More often than not, it is for bad news that arrives unexpectedly, but it sometimes happens in the face of unexpected good news. Although Embrie firmly believed that children were a blessing, she was also well aware of the challenges it took to grow them into healthy and well-adjusted adults. In a region of the world plagued by war and bloodshed, the challenge was exacerbated by factors over which any mother had very little control.

Wait a minute! Did this woman really think that Embrie could simply take the child as her own and raise her back in the US? What were the logistics of accomplishing this? She would need a passport as well as a visa to exit the country. Would the US Embassy be willing to provide this? Wait, was she seriously contemplating the woman's plea? What of her own family back home? What would her husband say?

At that moment, her cell phone rang, and she knew it was likely to be her contact with detailed instructions about visiting the "Temporary Protection Center" or refugee camp. She was scheduled to meet her later that day at the camp called Akçakale located in the Urfa province of southeastern Turkey.

With the second ring of the phone, Embrie quickly said, "Excuse me," to the woman, turned, and ran over to the desk where she quickly rummaged through her purse to get to her phone. As expected, it was her Turkish colleague. She briefly exchanged pleasantries with her before getting to the reason for her call, to provide Embrie with the time and directions to the meeting place near the camp.

There was a small writing pad from the hotel on the desk along with a pen bearing the hotel's name. Embrie quickly wrote down the information. In order to make sure she had understood and copied the information correctly, she read it back to her.

Travel to the camp would require a train followed by a nearly five-hour-long car ride. It would be a long journey. The call ended with an agreed upon date and time to communicate again.

With that done, Embrie was immediately reminded of the pressing matter of the Syrian woman and child at the doorway. As she turned back to them, she was surprised to see that they were no longer standing there. Had they left? Had the woman feared that she would deny her request to take her daughter? Embrie walked quickly to the doorway and looked out into the corridor. It was quiet, and there was no one there. Where had they gone? She turned back into the room and shut the door behind her.

She gasped, clearly startled. Directly in front of her was the little girl sitting on the small beige sofa to the left of the door. It was one of two sofas in the room, and so each one was quite small. Nevertheless, because of the little girl's small frame, it dwarfed her.

Embrie realized that the woman's unusual request could not have been choreographed better. The Syrian woman, the child's mother, had apparently left while Embrie was speaking to her colleague on the phone. The little girl looked elfin and desperate.

It was clear that Embrie would have to do something. Because the women had left, the situation was now at a point where she was well past simply being able to say, "I am sorry, but I cannot help you." Would it be something as heroic as taking the child from Turkey and bringing her to the US to the safety and comfort of her own home? Or would she choose an easier, perhaps more practical course of action, and bring the child with her to the refugee camp?

There would be resources however slim to care for abandoned children there.

Although this would be Embrie's first time visiting this particular camp, she had a pretty good idea of what conditions would greet her at the camp. There would be no running water, families would be crowded into limited spaces, and food would be distributed at two times during the day when the camp's inhabitants would stand in line for extended periods. Sleeping would be on cots and blankets, and one would need to protect oneself with a vigilance they'd likely never needed before. Because the little girl was alone, she would be at the greatest risk, representing prey for human traffickers and other unsavory characters that populated the places where people were most vulnerable and in greatest need.

For a moment, time seemed to stand still as Embrie and the little girl stared at one another. She could tell nothing from the little girl's countenance about how she was feeling and what she understood to have just transpired. Her mother had just left her. She was now sitting alone in a hotel room with a woman who was a stranger, and she had nothing but the clothes on her back. No doll, no toy, or blanket. What struck Embrie most as she studied the little girl was her apparent composure. She appeared to be at ease despite the unfamiliarity of the present situation. Was her normal life so chaotic that this situation failed to faze her?

What was her name? Embrie started there. For a moment, she worried that she did not speak

English, and her heart leaped when after asking her, she responded, "Aisha." Her voice though soft rang clear. *Aisha, that was a pretty name*, Embrie thought. She knew it to be popular among Muslims because of its association with the child bride of the prophet Muhammad.

Embrie decided that she would remember that name easily, and after saying it aloud, she smiled broadly at her. Aisha did not smile back but instead seemed to be carefully taking in her surroundings. Her eyes stopped at a fixture on the desk across the room. There on the desk was a bowl of fruit. It was a courtesy of the hotel, and Embric wondered if the little girl was hungry. She offered the bowl to her and Aisha took it, inspected the fruit, and selected a large orange. Embrie offered to peel it for her, but she declined her offer and skillfully unpeeled the orange herself. Within minutes, she had unpeeled it and consumed it, dripping some of its juice on her well-worn dress.

What would she do with Aisha? She was scheduled to head to the temporary refugee site first thing in the morning. Should she bring her along? If she didn't, what would she do with her? And beyond that, what would happen to Aisha in the long run? It wasn't as if the little girl's mother had left a forwarding address. Embrie was not convinced that leaving the girl at the refugee camp would be the best option. She had not spent any time with Aisha at this point, and yet already she knew that the harshness of the camp would discourage her from leaving her there.

Embrie decided that she would take this new situation one step at a time. It might mean just feeling her way through rather than as she was most accustomed—strategizing, plotting, and planning. It was in much the same way that a blind man thrust into unfamiliar terrain would make his way. Arms outstretched, feelers attuned, and anticipating something. She'd proceed in that way and hopefully figure out what to do.

For now, a bath was in order for Aisha who had smudges of dirt on her face and arms. "Would you like to take a nice bath and watch some television?" Embrie asked. Aisha nodded enthusiastically. Embrie turned the television on, and within minutes, the familiar voices of the animated figures her own children watched at home filled the hotel room. It was the Cartoon Network. She left Aisha in the sitting area and went to the bathroom to begin running the bath. How about a bubble bath? A treat to anyone, it was sure to be a hit with the little girl who probably never had a bath before. Embrie used the hotel's complimentary bath gel and poured half of the little bottle under the warm water spout.

"What about clothes?"

"What would she put on?"

It hadn't occurred to her to see if Aisha's mother had left any behind. With the tub still running, she ducked out of the bathroom. The little girl was fixated on the television. Embrie stood in front of the television and asked, "Aisha, do you have any other clothes with you? Did your mommy leave a bag or anything for you?"

Apparently, "no" was expressed similarly in Turkey. Although Aisha said nothing, she shook her head vigorously from left to right. Embrie sighed. Aisha's mother had not left anything for her to wear. She looked more closely at what she had on. Well, the clothes did not seem too dirty. Her little dress was more frayed than soiled. She would just have to put them back on, at least until Embrie could find something else for her.

She'd seen a shop downstairs in the hotel lobby. Perhaps they might have something for a little girl to wear. *It would probably cost a lot more than it was worth, but at least the child would have a clean change of clothes*, she thought.

Embrie returned to the bathroom. The tub was now filled, and she turned off the water. At that very moment, the hotel phone rang. She hurried out of the bathroom to answer it, glancing at Aisha who remained transfixed by the television. She answered the phone quickly, realizing just as she said, "hello," that apart from the hotel manager who had checked her in there was no one else who would know to reach her by this number. She had checked in with her husband and her work contact using her cell phone. Who could possibly be calling her on the hotel phone?

There was a piercing sound that rang in her ear, and just when she thought that a fax machine had been accidentally connected to her line, it stopped, and a male voice came on the line. Heavily accented, the man addressed her by name and accused her of kidnapping Aisha. Except according to the man, the little girl was not Aisha. He said the little girl's name was Pinar, and that it was because her mother was disturbed that she'd taken the small child away from her home. He accused Embrie of conspiring with the child's mother to kidnap her, and he warned her that justice would be swift and harsh. Only then did he pause and give her a chance to speak.

Embrie was alarmed at the accusations and the man's tone. "Look, whoever you are, I have not had anything to do with kidnapping anyone. Someone, yes, it was a woman, came to me and said that her daughter, Aisha, was in grave danger, and she needed my help. I never got the chance to agree or disagree with her request because the woman left the child when I turned around. I never saw that woman before in my life."

Even as she spoke, she knew that her words sounded less than convincing, so it was not surprising when the man began shouting at her through the phone again.

"You are a thief! You are an American kidnapper. I will send someone there now who will get the child shortly, and I will report you to the authorities! You will be in trouble! Do you understand? Do want that kind of trouble?"

"Look, I don't want any trouble. But who are you? How do I know that you are someone that Aisha should be with. Her mother said that her husband was dead. So how is it that you say that she took her from you? Who are you anyway and what do you want? I am not just going to turn Aisha over to a stranger."

The caller had something else in mind. He said, "In this country, we don't talk nicely to people who kidnap children. The police don't either. You have been warned."

With that, the caller hung up the phone. Embrie slowly replaced the phone to its headset. The sound the phone made hitting its headset was a click. A click that resembled the sound of the snap of a hypnotist's fingers. In that moment, Embrie knew that she had no real way of confirming the caller's story, and she also knew that she couldn't turn Aisha over to someone who sounded like that on the phone. How could she possibly even know whether he was telling the truth or not?

The woman who had left Aisha or Pinar or whatever her name was might have actually done so to protect her rather than as she had said because she could no longer afford to feed and clothe her. In a heavily paternalistic society like Turkey where behaviors were dictated by principles of Islam, she knew that men almost always had the upper hand and the last say.

Embrie realized what she must do. She would have to find out the truth about the little girl's situation before she agreed to hand her over. How much time did she have before they would be coming for her? Embrie glanced at her watch. The call had come in less than ten minutes ago, and the caller said that someone would be there soon. Did he mean within minutes? Within the hour? There was no time to waste.

She ran across the room and quickly sorted through her carry-on bag and purse. She decided to bring the carry-on because she did not have the time to cipher through its contents, and it was far bigger than the purse, which she threw in the bag. She confirmed that she had all of her papers, along with her passport and laptop.

Embrie next turned the television off, which elicited a sound of protest from Aisha. Gravely, she told the little girl that they would have to leave at once. She took her hand, grabbed her bag and the key card, and carefully opened the door, aware of the possibility that the man on the phone or whoever it was he'd sent was already there.

It was silent outside her room. With Aisha's hand in hers, the two hurried down the well-lit hallway to the elevator. But then she thought again about the likelihood that the little girl's captors (she'd begun to think of them in this way) might be getting off the elevator just as they were getting on to it, so instead she guided Aisha to the door-marked stairs. They hurried down the stairs.

Once in the lobby, Embrie looked around. At that moment, not knowing whether anyone in the lobby intended to harm her or the little girl, everyone she saw looked suspicious. It occurred to her that a human aid camp where Syrian refugees were currently milling about might actually prove to be the safest place for her to go with Aisha. Yes, she was certain of it. As long as there was no one in the hotel at the moment who intended to follow them, the crowd at a nearby camp would provide a degree of cover. She would find one and travel there immediately until she could figure out what to do about Aisha's predicament.

With this figured out, she was comforted. Even as she continued to exist in this very moment, where the very same predicament she faced just moments before still loomed, she felt relieved to now have a plan. It would be easy, she would just have to find a nearby settlement camp. The one she was scheduled to travel to tomorrow would be too far away and too difficult a journey to make with Aisha.

Embrie grabbed Aisha's hand and hurried to the hotel's entrance where several taxis were queued. They were multicolored and varied in their make, model, and year. It wasn't clear which one she should use. At home taxies at a hotel tended to line up in the order of their arrival, and the one at the front of the line absconded with the first passenger to arrive. That was not the case here. None of the taxis pulled up to her or the entrance, and she found herself having to approach each one.

Was it that they sensed her plight and the potential danger that waited to greet them? Or were they suspicious of the odd couple she made with Aisha? A clearly Western woman traveling with a little girl who appeared to be Syrian.

Embrie could not be sure, but she was grateful to the taxi driver (it was the fourth one she approached) who consented to taking them. The first two were not interested and had locked their doors when she approached, a third simply drove off as she neared. When the fourth taxi driver she turned to did not move or lock his car, she wasted no time and gently pushed the little girl in and quickly followed. Had the driver felt sorry for them or was he desperate for a fare? Embrie didn't care, and within moments, she and Aisha were safely tucked into the back seat of the small taxi, which barreled along the busy boulevard.

The driver spoke in halting English and asked her where she wanted to go. With a combination of pantomime, English, and the little Arabic she knew, she explained her desire to go to the nearest settlement camp. The driver looked quizzically at her in the rearview mirror. Although he understood her, he seemed to be waiting for her to change her mind, to correct herself, and ask to be taken to another destination. Embrie met his gaze and repeated her request, refusing to veer from her plan.

He sighed, saying something under his breath and gestured. He continued driving, and she hoped that he was taking her to one of the many large areas in Istanbul that served as a settlement for Syrian refugees. Embrie felt helpless, not knowing precisely where they were heading as she looked out of the car window. Suddenly, she remembered Aisha and looked at her to see whether the latest segment of her journey had unsettled her. She couldn't tell, the little girl simply stared out the window.

The driver drove with intention and was clearly headed somewhere. As he peered at her in the mirror, Embrie sensed his thoughts. She knew that he was not happy about bringing her and Aisha to the camp. Apart from the occasional glimpses of her in the mirror, it was only the back of his head that she saw clearly. And yet his head and the part of his neck that was visible below seemed to pulsate disapproval.

They drove through traffic and through different areas for nearly thirty minutes. Embrie silenced her phone during the ride but managed to send a text message to her colleague in Istanbul. Someone who knew her needed to know where she was and where she was currently headed.

The car stopped at a busy intersection, and then within moments, they arrived at an alley. It was a wide-open space bordered by walls that made up the back ends of buildings and a storefront that looked out on a street that was heavily trafficked by pedestrians. Embrie saw a heavy crowd of pedestrians through the openings on the sides of the buildings as the car moved slowly along the street. The driver said nothing and pointed to the alley.

"Thirty lira," he said.

"Shukraan," Embrie responded with a thank you in Arabic. She promptly handed him fifty lira, which included the cost of the taxi along with healthy tip of twenty additional lira. The driver avoided eye contact with her and simply nodded his head.

As they got out of the taxi, she stared at what she saw some fifty yards ahead. It appeared as a mass of humanity that had simply been put there, moving slowly and slightly. As she looked to its right and left, it occurred to her that calling the muddy, despoiled expanse a camp was an injustice to the word camp and spirit of campers everywhere. This was despair in all of its depths.

She took the little girl's hand and resolutely headed forward. With that first step toward the hundreds of displaced people whose lives had been unimaginably altered, she knew that she would not be leaving Aisha there. No. Though she did not know what steps would be required to change the child's life and open the door for a future with promise, she knew that she would do everything possible to make this happen. For now, it was a matter of ensuring both of their safety.

ABOUT THE AUTHOR

Kellina M. Craig-Henderson is a former professor of psychology who graduated from Wesleyan University in Connecticut before attending the master's program in the Social Sciences at the University of Chicago. Immediately following that, she attended Tulane University in New Orleans, Louisiana, and earned an MS and a PhD in psychology. She has served on the faculty at both public and private institutions including Howard University in Washington DC, where she was promoted to the rank of full professor. Later, while serving as an employee of the federal government, she worked collaboratively with international agencies to address the global challenges of gender inequity among other things. Her travels around the world have inspired her and provide the backdrop for the characters whose lives are brought to life in *Plane Tales*.

CPSIA information can be obtained
at www.ICGtesting.com
Printed in the USA
BVHW081214231121
622338BV00005B/26